SMASH

TROJAN #3

S.M. WEST

Cover Design: RBA Designs
Edited & Proofed: Happily Editing Anns
Cover Photo: Wander Aguiar Photography
Cover Models: Joli Irvine & Sonny Henty

"The beauty of a woman must be seen from in her eyes, because that is the doorway to her heart, the place where love resides." ~
Audrey Hepburn

PLAYLIST

Listen On Spotify

"Pretty Hurts" – Beyoncé
"Summer Dress" – July Talk
"Carnival Town" – Norah Jones
"Ooh Laa" – John Legend
"The Archer" – Taylor Swift
"Magnificent (She Says)" – Elbow
"Tightrope" – Michelle Williams
"Got Me" – St. South
"That Kind of Love" – MAX

1

DAISY

YOUNG AND PRETTY

I grasp and twirl the wand of the flat iron tightly, careful not to get burned. Smoky tendrils waft up and around my fingers, and I wrinkle my nose at the acrid hint of singed hair. Beauty, or in this case beachy waves, comes at a hefty price.

A flash of movement behind me and I release the steamy, blonde curl, spinning in my seat. Henry, arms loaded, plops onto the bedroom carpet, dumping a pile of wooden building blocks between his short, chubby legs. *Thud.*

Messy honey locks crown his head, and he stuffs a sharp, unyielding corner into his mouth, gnawing viciously on the block. At his age, everything goes in his mouth.

"Hey, Lovebug, what are you doing?" I lean forward, lowering my gaze to his level.

"What ya doin', Mommy?" He's just shy of two years old and mimicking most of what he hears.

My fingers thread his soft wisps of baby hair, combing it

into some kind of order, and he gifts me with a blinding sunshine smile and toothy grin.

"I'm getting ready to go out." My phone rings and I half turn to see who's calling, glimpsing my made-up self in the mirror.

Why am I going to all this trouble? Doing my hair, dressing up for a date I never wanted in the first place. Just thinking about Samuel's spontaneous dinner invitation yesterday still jars me. What was I thinking when I agreed to dinner?

Jerome's name lights up the screen and I press talk.

"Hello, my beautiful." His low husky voice does nothing to lessen my dislike of the nickname.

Any term of endearment from Jerome makes me uncomfortable. We're friends, at best, and more through circumstance than anything else. I'm not his anything and I don't think that's what he intends, so I don't get why he can't just knock it off. Despite my objections, he insists on the moniker.

"Hi." I pull the plug on the flat iron, giving up on the curls, and grab the shiny black tube of lipstick, gliding the bright red tip across my mouth. "What's up?"

"I was thinking about the awards dinner and if you need, ah...someone to take you, my tuxedo is ready. We'd make a dashing pair." His raspy laugh only causes me to stiffen further at his ballsy comment.

Is he for real?

We once worked together, in another lifetime. Both transplants from Paris, the fashion mecca of the world, and both alone in LA, it was natural that we gravitated to each other.

He knows better. If I'm taking anyone to accept the emerging photographer of the year award, it's Gray. I hope he'll come with me. And if he doesn't want to go, I do have other options. I'd certainly take Pansy, my sister, before Jerome. What is he thinking?

Avoiding any awkwardness, I chicken out and lie. "I haven't decided if I'm going yet."

"What? You'd be crazy not to go. I understand if you take Gray, but thought I'd put it out there in case you wanted to have a good time." He chuckles again, not bothering to hide his disdain in the way he says my closest friend's name or the insult.

"Not funny." My exasperation is clear in my voice.

Jerome and Gray don't get along, and it's a shame because I don't have a lot of friends. They tolerate each other for my sake, but at times, it's annoying. And I wonder if it would be easier to ditch Jerome than suffer through their mutual potshots.

"Don't be so touchy. Just sayin'." He releases a scornful huff and irritation bubbles inside of me.

I rake the brush harshly through my waves, and Henry comes to stand at my side, watching with keen blue eyes. He's like magic, and my frustration all but vanishes as the corners of my mouth rise at the slobber tracking down one side of his mouth. My beautiful boy.

"Well, if I do go, Gray is my first choice." I find my backbone, no longer tolerating his games.

He'd love nothing more than to attend the photography awards dinner, and while I'd like a way to help him out, being my date isn't it.

For nearly half a century, Europe was his playground where he was in high demand, turning down more work than he could possibly take on in one lifetime. Surprisingly, when he moved to the US, the city of Angels was far less enamored of him, and while he's been here for almost a year, he has had to hustle for decent gigs.

A chance to network at the dinner with those in the US fashion industry could change all that. Although I don't fully understand how he went from being a god behind the lens in Paris, London, and Milan to a nobody in LA.

"Mommy, look." Henry's sticky fingers pat my arm and I gasp.

My boy has Erotic Dreams, the very expensive lipstick I put on my mouth, smeared across his own. He grins from ear to ear, looking like the Joker with his teeth covered in a scary crimson goo.

"Ah, Jerome, I've got to go. Henry's...my makeup...ack, it's a disaster." I smile at my baby as he admires himself in the vanity.

Giggling, the budding makeup artist covers his painted mouth with a hand, and like a contagion, I giggle too, more nervous than amused. This stuff needs to come off now, before it gets on everything.

Jerome huffs. The man has no patience for children. "All right, my beautiful. If you change your mind..."

"Bye." I hit end and shove the phone into my purse, returning to the task at hand—Operation Erotic Nightmare.

"Oh, Lovebug, this color just isn't you." I wipe at his mouth with a wet cloth, trying to keep his hand—the one that just moments ago was on his mouth—from my dress.

If I get this sure-to-stain red on my outfit, I won't have time to change. I already took way too long to settle on what I'm wearing, and if I have to go back into my closet, I might as well wave the white flag and accept defeat.

He sputters and spits. "Mommy, it's yucky."

"Yes, it is. We don't put lipstick in our mouths." I gingerly rub at his precious baby skin. Of course, the stuff is a bitch to come off, and I had to buy the long-lasting lip wear.

Ten minutes and a full packet of makeup remover wipes later, he's cleaned up, save for a smudge on his shirt and a lingering redness on the lower half of his face.

"Let's change your shirt before Amy gets here."

Great, there isn't much time left, and I still have to feed Henry. Maybe this is an omen and I should just cancel dinner.

"Mommy, go?" Big eyes stare at my reflection in the mirror, watching me run fingers through my hair, loosening the curls.

"Yup. Let's go, bug." With Henry's hand in mine, we exit the room and the doorbell rings.

It's official, I've run out of time. I'll have to ask the sitter to change him.

"Hi, Amy." I step back from the door to let her in, and my son clings to my leg. "Things are a bit chaotic. We just had a little incident with my lipstick."

My head sways toward Henry and his rosy chin, the remaining remnant of his first foray with makeup. "I'd wanted to have dinner done before you arrived but—"

"No worries." She smiles, bending. "Hey, little man, do you remember me? I'm Amy."

Now on her haunches in black shorts, a tank top, and brown hair in a ponytail, she waves at him. He steps cautiously from behind me, his smile unsure but growing stronger by the second.

"Say hi to Amy," I coax, taking his hand and walking toward the kitchen. "You remember her, don't you? She's Aunt Pansy's friend. She took you swimming in the ocean."

Both my sister and Amy are studying marine biology. I'd first asked Pansy to babysit, and since she couldn't because the ask had been last minute, she suggested her friend. I'd met Amy only a handful of times, but Pansy trusted her, raved about how Amy spent a lot of time taking care of her nieces and nephews.

Suddenly guilt pricks at my chest. Gray is a better choice to watch Henry, and normally, he's my first choice. He's the closest thing to a father for Henry. But if I'd asked him, then I'd have had to tell him about my date.

Opening the fridge, I take out the small bowl of pasta and pop it into the microwave, then pour milk into a sippy cup. Henry's warmed up to Amy, showing off his arts and crafts table in the corner, littered with crayons, coloring books, alphabet blocks, and more.

"His shirt has some lipstick on it." I point to the red slash near his collar. "Could you change him after dinner? His sleeper is on the changing table."

"Sure." She peers at me from one of the tiny, plastic chairs. "Where's Grayson?"

"Gray?" I pause at wiping down the counter and stare at her, a strange prickle at the back of my neck. "Why would he be here?"

"Oh, I thought you were going out with him. Aren't you two, uh..." Her cheeks flush tomato red, and the seconds tick by in silence. Finally, she clears her throat and boldly asks, "You're not dating?"

Her question and the way she asks jab at my chest uncomfortably. Her bright eyes gleam as if she's only now realized something. What? That Gray and I aren't a couple? That he's single?

Instantly, she's perkier, if that's possible, like a wilting hydrangea springing to life after being immersed in water. The thought of Gray and I not together gives her life, renewed hope.

"Gray isn't here." I avoid the question, and her expression flattens.

The microwave dings, and Amy grabs the bowl and straps Henry into his highchair. A sinking sensation engulfs me. She isn't much younger than I am, although I'd bet she's closer to Gray's twenty-seven than my thirty.

Young and pretty. Why does that suddenly bother me?

Come to think of it, her awe of Trojan, a world-famous—and now retired—rock band, isn't a secret and maybe I got it all wrong. Maybe she isn't a huge fan of the band but my best friend, Grayson Bennett, the drummer.

It's been about a year and a half since they stepped away from the stage with a farewell world tour. But the Trojan name and their music is still alive and strong. And now I'm seeing things in a different light.

Unlike most groupies, where the lead singer is catnip, Amy is nuts for Gray. And the thought makes me sick, and beads of sweat break out under my arms and on my back.

"Daisy?" Amy's tone is pressing, like this isn't the first time she's called my name. "We're all set if you want to head out."

"Oh, yes." Discombobulated, I grab my clutch and go to the table. "Henry, you be good for Amy, and I'll be home soon." His fresh, baby scent brings a glow to my insides, erasing any residual queasiness, and I kiss the top of his head. "I love you."

"Love you too, Mommy." The words mix with a mouthful of buttery penne.

"You've got my cell number, call me in case of anything."

"Of course. Have a good time."

"Thanks." In the doorway, I grin at my pasta-eating monster, his cheeks now covered in a greasy sheen. "I'll grab my shoes in the bedroom and then I'm gone."

Amy nods, her attention fixed on Henry, and I go to my room, second-guessing this evening once more. Maybe I should arrange for a fake emergency phone call to get me out of tonight's date?

But who? Pansy would refuse to do something like that, and I can't ask Amy. Gray is a definite no. Sasha would do it but she's in Paris. Isn't there an app for this?

Damn, why the hell did I say yes? I'd been caught off guard when Samuel cornered me on the final day of the shoot with an invitation to dinner. *It's only dinner.*

And it has been years since I've put myself out there. I haven't kissed a man, held hands—well, that isn't true, sometimes Gray and I hold hands... No sex. God, I miss sex.

But there would be no sex tonight. Most probably never

with Samuel. Tonight is just dinner, that's all I want. Just to dip my toe into the dating pool. Dinner doesn't mean sex.

Sex. Wow, it's been nearly three years since I last slept with a man. Holy...three years. And ironically, the opposite sex all but disappeared from my life after I found out I was having a baby.

The doorbell rings, and I slip both feet into my nude slingback heels and rush from the room. "I'll get it."

Amy's taking Henry out of the highchair when I pass the kitchen doorway, and I grab my keys off the entryway table before opening the front door.

My heart stops beating. No, this can't be happening. Gray stands before me, a brown paper takeout bag in one hand while the other rakes through his strawberry blond locks flopping onto his forehead.

"Daze..." Eyes as deep as the bluest ocean fix on me, languid and greedy. He roams the length of me from my black licorice toenails, over my bare legs and dress, up to my blonde beachy waves. "You look amazing."

"Ah...thanks. Um, w-w-what are you doing here?" No sooner has the question left my mouth than I wish to eat every one of those insensitive words.

Gray's always at my house. This is practically *his* house. I want him here, to feel like my place is his, and Henry does too.

"Oh." A disturbed expression crosses his face. "I just came from seeing the studio space and thought I'd fill you in." Judging from the sparkle in his eyes, things went well, and I want to hear every detail. I just can't right now.

He holds up the bag, flashing the logo of our favorite

Mexican restaurant. "I brought dinner. Got my man, Henry, those quesadillas he loves." At the mention of my son, his smile grows tenfold, and my heart melts into a puddle.

"Come in." My hand sweeps into the house, and I'm at a loss for words.

How do I explain to him that I'm on my way out? I don't keep secrets from my best friend and fully intend on telling him about my date—but after the fact. I wanted to tell him once it was said and done, and we could laugh about it. Laugh at how it was a complete disaster.

With me still in the doorway, his arm brushes my stomach as he steps into the house, and his touch elicits a strange fluttering deep inside me. I've been getting them more and more lately and I flush, suddenly hot, and it has nothing to do with the warm October evening air.

"Are you going somewhere?" He now looks at me in a different light, realizing there's more going on.

"Um, I—" My throat's dry, and the words are lifeless on my tongue as Amy bounds into the front entrance.

"Grayson." Her spellbound tone saves me from saying any more.

When I turn to face her, my knees buckle at her adoring expression. The nausea is back, and I furiously swallow.

"How are you?" She wedges in between us, wrapping her arms around him like they're long-lost friends.

Has she always done this and I'm only noticing now? My mouth hangs open, troubled by what's unfolding, and for the first time ever, feeling out of place...in my own home.

He stares sheepishly, his arms loose around the fangirl, and Henry waddles into the room at a fairly fast clip, crashing into their legs. The collision causes Amy to release her vise-grip. *Good boy, Henry.*

"Gaga." The little boy holds out his arms, and Gray lifts him up like a feather.

Gray pushes at my son's shirt, planting raspberries on his baby belly, and Henry squeals. Squirming, his tiny fingers curl into Gray's hair, pulling for dear life. *Ouch.*

That must hurt, but the man doesn't even so much as flinch nor let up until Henry is utterly delighted. Each second that passes is misery and joy. I love seeing these two together, and I'm also dreading the inevitable—when I have to leave.

Gray slides Henry down his chest, and my little man clings to his neck, resting his head on the man's broad shoulder.

"Where are you going?" Gray didn't forget where we'd been interrupted, and his expression sobers.

I struggle to form the words, but they logjam into a lump in my throat. It's only a date, and Gray is my best friend. Next to Pansy, he's the only other person I trust with my son's life. I can tell him anything yet for some reason, not this. Well, not now.

"She's going on a date." Big mouth Amy beats me to the punch, and my fingers ball at my sides, resisting the urge to do just that to her.

I flounder with my tangled tongue, and he stiffens, lips turning down at the corners. Why do I feel like I've betrayed him?

2

GRAY
RAGING INSIDE

"What's in the bag?" The cheery brunette is oblivious to the missile she launched my way.

A date? What the fuck? Daisy's going on a date. Since when? And why didn't she tell me?

"Oh, I love that restaurant." She points at the food, and every word out of her mouth buzzes in my ear like an annoying and potentially vicious bee. "Mexican is one of my faves. I'm starving."

"A date?" I tighten my grip on Henry, leaning my cheek on the top of his head. The heat of his soft, tiny body next to mine and the pure scent of him helps to calm the raging inside of me.

Countless questions fly at me like arrows intending to harm. Did I totally fuck things up? Did I wait too long to tell her how I feel? Give her too much space?

"Ah...yes." Daisy shifts from one foot to the other, gaze darting around the room to the floor. "Um, I was—"

"Daisy, is it okay if Gray stays for dinner?" Whoever this woman is, she's clearly out to lunch and unable to read the room. The air is pressure-filled and gravely silent.

"Sorry, I didn't catch your name?" I stare into her flushed, excited face.

"Oh. I'm Amy. We've met before. I'm a friend of Pansy's. I'm babysitting Henry tonight."

I nod, forcing my mouth into what I hope is a polite smile but failing when the taut muscles in my jaw ache.

Why is she taking care of Henry? Why wouldn't Daisy ask me? What the hell is going on? Is this a nightmare? If so, how the fuck do I wake up?

"Hi, Amy." I shift my gaze to Daisy. "I could have taken care of Henry."

At the sound of his name, the little guy lifts his head and grins at me. "Gaga, stay. Take care of me."

"I wasn't sure if you had plans—" She waves her hand in front of her and a cream-colored purse dangles from her wrist.

"Well, that's why you should have asked." I try to keep my tone neutral, stifling hurt and anger. "I'm free tonight."

I'm pretty much free every night, spending most of my spare time with the two of them. She knows this.

"That would be great if you stayed." Amy bounces, clapping her hands, and Henry follows suit. Then, remembering she's here to do a job, she looks to the beautiful blonde I want to talk to privately. "If that's okay with you, Daisy?"

"Sure." She nods, swallowing with difficulty and avoiding my gaze. "I should get going."

"Awesome. Have a great time." Amy takes the bag of food from my hand, swinging around toward the kitchen.

Unable to control myself and clearly a glutton for punishment, I once more drink in Daisy's slinky blue dress, bare silky arms and legs, and the skyscraper high heels.

Who the fuck is she going out with looking like that? Although she could be wearing sweats and she'd still be gorgeous.

"You look beautiful." My voice is a low rasp, fighting past the growing stone in my throat. "Have a good time."

I mean it even if it's like sucking on a lemon. If this is what she wants, what will make her happy...fuck...I want to make her happy, give her what she wants and needs.

With Henry in my arms, we stroll away from the entrance, and only once the front door shuts do I release the breath I've been holding.

Dinner with Amy gives me a headache.

She's a nice woman and all, but boy can she talk. And while I'm not one to pay much attention to my stardom, she won't let me forget who I once was. The drummer for Trojan, a world-famous rock band. And there's no two ways about it, she's into drummers or maybe just me.

Once our meal is done, I get rid of her. Maybe it's a little harsh, but she's giving me huge clinger vibes, and to lessen any guilt, I pay her generously for the couple of hours.

No surprise, she's reluctant to leave, even pouting as Henry and I wave goodbye from the front door. I can take care of him, and as much as I'd rather not hear about Daisy's date, I want to be here when she gets home.

Daisy's date with some guy, someone who could become more in both their lives, brings on an overbearing sensation as if I'm losing something, and no matter how hard I try to grasp it, it's just out of my reach.

This agonizing impression is so heavy on my chest that it flattens my lungs and compresses my heart. The muscle's unable to fully beat.

While Henry should be in bed, I can't resist the impulse to spend more time with him, and I decide to take him out for a bit. I've got a key to Daisy's home—we traded keys early in our friendship when I quickly became a staple in both their lives.

We go to his most favorite place in the world. The beach. We don't stay long, since it is late for him, but the time we have together is spent collecting shells and getting our feet wet.

Once back at his home, I give him a bath and read him a bedtime story. He's like a shooting star when it comes to getting him to settle. At first, he burns bright, a million questions coming at me as he echoes every word I utter from the book. Then, just as quickly, he passes out midsentence, his light falling silent and fast asleep.

I tuck the blanket around him in his big boy bed, as he calls it, and crack the door to his room on my way out. Not too long ago, he was still in a crib.

Luckily, I'd been here the night the little guy sauntered into the kitchen as if we hadn't just put him to bed. We were shocked and speechless. He'd climbed out of the crib, and since then, there was no going back.

My phone vibrates, and before dropping onto the sofa, I fish it out of my back pocket. It's a text from Eli, my closest bandmate and friend. When I joined Trojan, we bonded almost overnight.

While most of us have gone our separate ways career wise since Trojan, we remain close, figuratively speaking. Eli's thousands of miles away in New York City and has been there now for ten months pursuing an acting career, but we still talk about once a week.

Eli: How'd the studio visit go?

Instead of typing out a reply, I call him, smiling as his familiar, friendly voice booms over the line. "The studio was that good, you had to call?"

"Hey. The studio was great. Perfect." I lift my feet onto the coffee table, settling in. "There's more than enough space for offices, a couple of sound booths..."

"Cool, but it sounds like there's a but."

"Yeah, I need Silas on board." I blow out a frustrated breath.

Silas Palmer is the lead singer of Trojan and the "S" in our company—SG Productions. We went into business together a little over a year ago now, producing records for up-and-coming musicians. We're doing well, so much so, we need our own recording studio.

"Sure, but he'll understand if you lay it all out." Eli believes people have the best intentions, which for the most part is true when it comes to Silas.

"Yeah, but he's too close to this." I rake a hand through my hair, resting my head against the top of the couch.

Being the youngest in the band and the last to join, I fell into the unenviable position of the de facto last vote. Unfortunately, this sentiment has continued even with the retirement of Trojan.

When Silas and I joined forces, I made it clear to him that I had as much say as he did and if he couldn't live with that, then SG Productions wasn't happening.

He agreed, but it's hard to deny your nature. Silas is outspoken and used to getting his way. The hunt for a studio proves that, and it's beginning to feel a lot like old times. My partner wants to build our own studio—which isn't a bad idea, but just not now.

"Look, his studio's too small. He's even said so himself, and building something right now would take too long and stall business. It sounds like you've found the perfect spot." Eli echoes all the points I made weeks ago to Silas when we realized renting studio time wasn't a solid long-term plan.

"Yeah, but he isn't listening." I kick off my combat boots. "He's looking at real estate and talking to construction companies."

"Seriously? And you've told him you don't want to go that route, right?"

Rather than answer, I allow the silence to speak for me. Eli's known Silas longer than I have, so he'll figure it out.

"Damn, Gray, you need to talk to him before this goes too far."

"Tell me something I don't know. He won't even check out

places with me. Anyway, enough about me. How's it going with the show?" I bring the beer bottle to my mouth and take a swig of the now lukewarm liquid. Tastes like piss. Yuck. "Your balls fall off yet?"

The cooler weather in Manhattan is a running joke. When he got a major part in a New York-based drama series, I was both happy for him and bummed for me.

LA isn't the same without him, and I can't resist joking with him about freezing his balls off and missing the sunny California weather.

"The fall is awesome in New York." He chuckles. "And the show's good. Critics like it and we're building a fan base. I'm still getting used to things. I worked late tonight so I'm wired."

"That last episode was epic. If I didn't know you, I'd have believed you are a cold-hearted bastard."

He laughs again, the smile carrying in his tone. "Thanks. It's crazy how the fans love you, or the character, even if you do despicable things."

I snort, imagining fans swarming him. He's used to it and it's nothing new from our rock star days. "Ah, well, you're used to that. Enough about you, how's Crystal?"

"My girl's amazing. She misses you, everyone, like crazy and she's so excited to be in LA for Christmas."

"We miss her too. And we're looking forward to seeing both of you in a few months. Give her a kiss and hug for me."

"I will. And how are Daze and Henry?" His question picks at the fresh wound left by her date, and I release a harsh grunt. "What did I miss?"

I groan, scrubbing a hand down my face. "Would you believe she's out on a fucking date?"

"What? Daisy?" Relief should wash over me at his skeptical tone. At least I'm not the only one having a hard time wrapping my head around this, but I'm still annoyed.

"Yeah. I came over with dinner tonight only to find her on her way out." I grimace and the barbacoa burrito bowl suddenly leaves a nasty taste in my mouth. "She had a babysitter and all."

"Damn, that hurts. Who's the guy?"

"No fucking clue. She could barely look me in the eye much less answer my questions. I told the sitter to go, and I'm here with Henry."

"Are you going to tell her?" He's referring to my more-than-platonic feelings toward Daisy.

He was the first to call me on it nearly three years ago when Daisy showed up on her sister's doorstep pregnant and alone. She's gorgeous—just one look and you're a goner—but that isn't what captured my heart and grabbed me by the balls.

No, it's her vulnerability and kind heart that she keeps buried under her armour of beauty. I glimpsed the real woman fairly early on in our friendship, and since then, I've been hers.

"Yeah, I need to talk to her." I get to my feet at a noise coming from the bedrooms and flick on the hallway light. "For the longest time, she didn't seem interested in dating."

"No, dumbass, she was raising a baby." His sarcastic tone grates on my nerves even if he means no harm. She put her life on hold for Henry, with no regrets. She's the best mother I know.

Eli's gruff tone cuts through my endless thoughts of Daisy. "And trust me, it takes a lot out of you, raising a child on your own. Making time for the opposite sex just isn't a priority."

"I'm aware of that, jackass." I lower my voice and head toward Henry's room at a faint sound, maybe the call of my name, coming from that way.

"Seriously, Gray, she cares about you. No matter what happens, you won't lose her or Henry."

Like a punch to the throat, air is trapped in my lungs at how easily he's read my thoughts. I choke out a "yeah."

Now at Henry's room, I lean on the doorjamb, catching my breath, and swing the door open. The little guy lifts his head from his pillow and rubs at his sleepy eyes. "I can't sleep."

I chuckle, marveling at how insomnia, dehydration, or both, hit most children around the same time each day—bedtime.

"Hey, Eli, I gotta go." I step into the dark room. "Henry's up."

"All right. Give him a hug for me and talk soon." He yawns, reminding me it's nearly one thirty in the morning on the east coast. "And, G, try not to overthink this. Daisy and Henry are your family."

"K." I force the one letter past the rock lodged in my throat and end the call, resting the phone on the small night-stand. "What woke you up?"

"Dunno." He plops his head onto the pillow. "Gaga, you sleep with me?"

I stifle another laugh. Daisy will kill me, but she isn't here and I can't leave him like this.

"Okay, just until you fall asleep." I scoot onto my side, bringing his tiny body against my chest with my arm around his middle.

He rests his head on my bicep. "Night, Gaga."

"Night, Henry." I kiss the top of his head and close my eyes at his sweet smell.

The glow from the hallway light streams into the room, stopping just before the foot of the twin bed. Thoughts of Henry and Daisy swim in my mind. The memory of Daisy pregnant, her belly like a basketball under her shirt, puts a smile on my face.

Usually, a woman like her—beautiful beyond words—can be intimidating, and in some ways, she used that to keep people at a distance. But not me. When we first met, we fell into an easy friendship. And damn, that's where I've been ever since. Her friend.

Best friends for sure, but I'm stuck in the friend zone. Some of it's my doing as I didn't want to pressure her. Alone and scared, she was pregnant and definitely not looking for a man in her life.

I consciously parked my feelings for her, content to be what she needed. A friend. And I more than willingly filled the position. I had always wanted more and intended on doing something about it. But as more time passed, Daisy and Henry became family.

Family.

Eli hadn't been wrong when he voiced my deepest fear. I'd had a family before, not once but twice, only to lose them both times. Losing Daisy and Henry is unthinkable.

Things are now at a point between us where I won't ruin our relationship, or lose them, because I'm a greedy bastard. But I'll be damned if I let some guy make a move on the woman I love.

3

DAISY

STEAL YOUR HEART

*A*ll is quiet when I get in, a stark contrast to the blood roaring in my ears. Amy's text earlier in the evening about Gray watching Henry put a smile on my face, but it was brief.

I desperately wanted to talk to Gray, and I couldn't shake my need to apologize. Instead, I was at a fancy restaurant, sitting across from a man I barely knew. In that moment, I contemplated using the text as an excuse to bail. But I didn't. I had said yes to dinner, so I sucked it up and tried to make the most of it.

Just inside the front door, I remove my heels and wristlet, carrying them in my hands as I stroll through my place, expecting to find Gray. In the kitchen, printouts of the specs on the few beach homes for sale I contemplated seeing—or more like *wished* I could buy—are spread out on the counter. Was Gray looking at them?

I put them into a neat pile and turn off the light. Most of

the lights are still on, and I'm a tangled mess as I move from room to room, only to find it empty. Where is he?

I flick the lights off and make my way to the bedrooms. The hallway is lit, and Henry's door is ajar. Gray better be in there. But what if he isn't? Why would I even think that? There's no way he'd ever leave Henry alone.

Concern rushes in like a rising tide, ebbing and flowing up my throat, and the need to lay eyes on my son—and Gray —is something fierce. I'm quick on my feet, and at the doorway to the room, my heart swells and settles comfortably in my chest all at once.

Gray and Henry are fast asleep.

Instead of my usual annoyance at him sleeping with Henry—it's happened before—a small girlish giggle pushes past my lips. I'm going to pay for this, but right now I can't bring myself to care.

Despite sleeping in a big boy bed, Henry isn't one to pass up a chance to sleep with Gray, me, or just about anyone. He isn't too picky.

And Gray is the first to cave, much like tonight, I'm sure. This will mean battling with my son for the better part of the next week to get him to sleep in his bed. Alone.

Kids. You give them an inch and they'll crack your chest wide open and steal your heart. Both Gray and I are victims to Henry's adoring smiles, big sky-blue eyes, and just about anything else he does.

Grinning, I stare down at the two of them. So peaceful and so perfect together. Henry's a cute little ball cuddled into Gray's chest with Jellycat, his stuffed octopus and most beloved toy, nestled in his arms.

And Gray... His large, inked hand curls safely and securely around my son. The sight causes a fleeting pitter-patter low in my core, and I want to cuddle with them. Hold them close to me.

Strands of gingery-blond and tawny-brown hair spill across the pillow and flop onto Gray's forehead. His long eyelashes, so light it's as if they are dipped in gold, fan across the sharp ridge of his cheekbone, and his perpetual scruff dusts the hard line of his jaw. Slightly parted and relaxed, his lips expel soft puffs of air that sail over Henry's head.

I leave them for my own bed but end up tossing and turning throughout the night. Gray crawls into my mind, keeping me awake when I should be sleeping. Maybe it's because he's down the hall even if that isn't new. He's slept over before, usually on the couch.

Or maybe it's because I have to explain and apologize tomorrow. Not about the date, even if I should, but more so why I didn't ask him to watch Henry. It's got to sting, my thoughtless and foolish snub, and I never want to do anything to hurt Gray.

He's always there for me. The one person I can tell anything. I don't want things to change between us if I were to start dating and find someone. That's if I want to find someone. Could I lose him? Or worse, what if he finds someone?

Neither of us have dated anyone since meeting each other. And it isn't lost on me that our friends, the guys from Trojan and my sister, treat us like we're a couple.

It doesn't bother me, though sometimes it makes me yearn for more. But the hint of fear always stops me cold.

What if we get together and screw things up? Or worse, what if I tell him how I feel, and he only sees me as his best friend?

Yet something is happening and has been for some time now. Tonight is proof of that. On my date and now in bed, Gray is front and center.

The very thought of a woman in his life grips me with panic.

No, Gray wouldn't keep something like that from me. Would he? Shit, I kept my date from him.

Oh, I have to stop this. My head hurts and my mind is overactive, going places it shouldn't venture in the dead of night.

Eventually, I fall asleep, and when I wake in the morning, nearly an hour later than usual, happy voices from the kitchen tell me all I need to know. Henry didn't wake me up because he has Gray.

I slip on my bathing suit, then shorts and an oversized T-shirt, collecting my brittle blonde locks, thanks to the flat iron, into a messy bun. We're going to my sister's for a day at the beach and lunch.

I've been saving for a house close to the water. I want nothing more than to give my son the sand and the sea all the time. Come on, we live in LA, why not?

And while my photography business is taking off, I can't afford a home on the beach. We're talking well over a few million if not more for something nice, but I'm saving every penny I can spare to make that dream come true.

Gray and Henry are at the kitchen table, talking and laughing, when I enter the room.

"Morning." I smile, holding open my arms for Henry.

"Hey, Lovebug." I wrap him in a hug and lift his little body off his chair, kissing the side of his head. "Did you sleep okay?"

"Mommy, we made breakfast. Look. Bacon." He points to a plate, half full of the greasy deliciousness.

"I can see that. And it looks like you've had your share." I tickle his tummy and rest his feet down on the tile.

"Morning." Gray's warm voice and easy smile calm the little that's left of my nerves as he hands me a coffee.

"Thank you." I inhale the rich aroma before bringing the mug to my lips.

"What'll you have for breakfast?" His hand glides along the countertop, littered with a bevy of choices. "There's yogurt and granola, eggs, toast, and cereal."

I laugh, shaking my head, so very grateful Gray is his usual self. Warm eyes, sparkling smile, and his quiet—some might think reserved—demeanor that's both reassuring and at times unnerving because of his intensity.

When he looks at me, it's as if I'm the only woman in the world. Shit, I'm doing it again. Romanticizing our friendship.

"Wow. I'll have yogurt with granola, thanks." I head to the cupboard, but he holds up his hand, motioning for me to sit.

"Yay!" Henry jumps around. "Gaga says you want that. Booberry or stwahberry?" He points to the freshly washed and cut fruit in a bowl on the table.

Gaga is my son's name for Gray. He still hasn't figured out the Rs yet and sometimes, if he says it too fast, it sounds like Dada. Oh man, I've got it bad.

"A little of both, please." I grin and my son pops a big strawberry into his mouth.

Vibrant red juice instantly squirts from the corner of his

mouth and dribbles down his chin. Gray puts my breakfast together while I clean Henry's mouth.

The little guy then rests his hand on my legs, looking at me solemnly. "Mommy, don't be mad."

"What? I'm not mad." I cock my head to one side, looking down at him. "Why?"

"Gaga sleep with me last night." His expression is a mixture of worry and determination. "Don't be mad."

"Yes, I know. You're a lucky boy." I ruffle his downy soft hair. "I'm not mad. It was a special treat but no sleeping with anyone tonight." I waggle a pointed finger at him while giving myself a stern internal pep talk about staying strong when the tears start tonight when he wants to sleep with me. "Remember, we all have our own beds to sleep in. Alone."

"Aww wight, Mommy." He nods, but his reluctance to fully commit is clear in the wrinkle of his light brow.

"Here you go." Gray sets the bowl in front of me, and Henry scampers from the room to play. "How was your date?"

And there it is, the inevitable question I'd been dreading. But it's for the best to just get it out in the open and over with despite the flurry of nerves his question unleashes.

Now several feet away, he leans his backside against the counter and folds his defined arms across his lean chest.

"It was meh." I shrug, trying not to play it off as insignificant but also needing him to understand it wasn't great.

Samuel is a nice guy but not for me. No sparks. No flutters. And the conversation, outside of the photoshoot, was forced and flat.

"Who's the guy?" His stare is intense.

"Ah, he was a client." A blast of heat rushes up my neck and into my cheeks, sure to make me look like a strawberry. "He asked me out after the job was done, so there was no conflict of interest."

He nods, pressing his lips together as if to keep what he's really thinking from breaching the confines of his mouth.

"Gray, I'm sorry. I should have asked you to take care of Henry. Thank you for staying last night. I'm sure he had a blast. You're his favorite person in the world."

And mine.

"No, you're his favorite as it should be, but I'll gladly take second spot." His gaze is now warm and sincere. "And yes, you should have called. I shouldn't have to say that. You going to see him again, this client of yours?"

My smile is tight, glad he's moving past my goof but not glad that we're still talking about the date. "He's no longer a client, and no, I won't be seeing him again."

"And if someone else asks you on a date, would you say yes?"

The question is a little unnerving and causes a whole lot of fluttering in my stomach.

"Maybe. I mean, I didn't realize I was ready to date until someone asked me, and that's why I said yes. I think I just wanted to do it." I pause to study him, and his expression is unreadable while his gaze never strays from me. "But I don't want to go out with just anyone."

"I see. So you're ready to date?"

The strange flutter happens again. What is he asking exactly? Is he asking for himself? And if he did, what would I say? Seriously, that's a stupid question. I'd say yes.

He's still staring and I'm quick to respond. "I think so. I mean I'm not downloading a dating app or anything, but I'm ready to put myself out there." I let out a nervous laugh.

I'm not sure where this is coming from. Three days ago, dating never crossed my mind. I was too busy juggling motherhood, photography, a nanny search, and daydreaming of a beach house to think about much else.

"And who are you looking to date?"

I nearly swallow my tongue at his question. *You.* I want to scream his name but I dare not.

"I don't know." Heat creeps into my cheeks and I glance down at the table, but movement from him brings my head up.

He presses his lips together, and I'd pay a lot of money to be inside his head right now, to know what he's thinking. I want him to say something. No, I want him to ask me out.

And with that outrageously wild notion, I'm unbalanced, weak-kneed, and...and suddenly, I'm questioning everything.

"Are you still coming with us to Silas and Pansy's this morning?" Normally, I wouldn't ask since we've already made these plans, but things no longer feel solid and sure. "And you can still watch Henry? I have to leave at one."

Until recently, my days were spent with Henry, and Gray or Pansy pitched in where needed. But since the award and subsequent online article about the model-turned-photographer, my career has exploded.

"Yeah, I said I could. I'm free today and looking forward to it." He takes my empty bowl and puts it in the dishwasher. "Any news on a nanny?"

"No. I haven't had a chance to book any more appointments."

I was reluctant to find someone to take care of my son, especially since the first round of interviews were horrible, but now, as I book my clients and really need the money to live and for the beach house, I have no choice.

Henry could go to daycare, but he's still so young and I try to spend as much time with him as possible. It's one reason I didn't go back to modeling. A nanny will provide flexibility.

"I could do some of the interviews." He grips the back of a chair, leaning in my direction.

"No, I can't ask you to do that. You're busy, too, running your own company. I appreciate all that you do already."

"I don't mind. I like taking care of Henry...and you. He's like a son to me." His admission isn't new. I've heard it before, but each time, I melt a little more.

Regret could wreak havoc on me, wondering if I did the right thing in not fighting Costa, Henry's father, to be a bigger part in his life. But why? Henry may be young but he's no dummy.

It would take two seconds for him to figure out his father is a narcissistic, self-serving asshole, and would Henry be better off? No.

And when Gray says things like this, so easily and so genuine, there's no question. I did the right thing. My son is better off with Gray in his life and no bio-dad in the picture.

"And you're a father to him." I squeeze his arm as Henry wobbles into the room, off-balance.

He's sheepish and serious at the same time. "Stinky." He wrinkles his nose, and I laugh.

"Did someone do a number two?" I hold up my fingers and he scrunches his nose, not really sure about this number thing when it comes to his diaper. "Let's change you and get ready for the beach."

He lifts one small foot and then the other in an awkward giddy-up motion, a green crayon in one hand and a wooden block in the other. "Yay."

"I'll finish up here and get changed too." Gray pulls at the hem of his plain black T-shirt, and the fabric rides up his taut stomach. I nod, averting my gaze but unable to move my feet.

He keeps a small duffel in the front closet with a spare change of clothes, after learning the hard way that with babies, anything can happen. There's been more than one nasty incident where a fresh shirt or a full-on shower was required.

Shirtless, dirty T-shirt in hand, he strides past me, and my tongue sticks to the roof of my mouth. He isn't overly muscled but lean and defined. Hard planes, tight muscles, and tattoos everywhere.

Every inch of his torso tells a story through script, images of people, objects, and dates inked along his carved muscles. There's so much cut perfection to look at, and I stifle a groan of satisfaction, forcing myself from the room.

4

GRAY

PUNCH THIS ASSHAT

*T*he cars are packed for Silas and Pansy's. We're taking separate cars since Daisy has to work this afternoon. I packed up her photography equipment in her car, and I've got what I need to take care of Henry.

Daisy locks the front door, and Henry bounds across the small patch of grass to my car. I scoop him up into my arms, staring at Daisy strolling toward us with a beach bag, doubling as a diaper bag, in one hand, her oversized T-shirt hanging off her silky shoulder, sandals and shades on.

"Henry, you coming with me or Gray?" A soft smile plays on her pouty lips, already anticipating her son's response.

"Gaga." He gnaws on a carrot stick, and I laugh, shaking my head. "All right. But you have to finish that before I put you in the car."

With his feet firmly on the grass, I take the bag from Daisy as an orange Corvette Stingray roars up to the curb in front of her house. Shit.

"What's he doing here?" I fail to hide my disdain, tension building at the corner of my eyes as I wish we'd left earlier.

She turns to watch the older man slide out of the car. "I don't know."

"Good morning, my beautiful." Jerome ignores both Henry and me, ambling past us on his way to the gorgeous blonde.

He places his hands possessively on her shoulders and plants his wrinkled lips on her cheek. I strangle the order to get his hands and mouth off her before it even leaves my throat.

I'm not a jealous person but Jerome Pascal—said with a French accent which is total bullshit because the guy has no more French in him than I do. He was born in middle America and I'm willing to bet his surname is something like Smith or Jones—this guy rubs me the wrong way. He's arrogant and acts like he owns Daisy. Bastard.

"What are you doing here?" She tilts her head to one side and moves back. "We're on our way out. Five more minutes and you'd have missed us."

"Ah, well, I guess I'm lucky then." He takes one of her hands and smiles. "We still haven't picked a date for the shoot."

"The shoot?" She tugs on her hand, stepping back some more so he has to let go. "What are you talking about?"

I inwardly groan and wonder why Daisy ever agreed to his stupid photo shoot in the first place. At the time, she said she felt bad for him, but things have changed. Her business is booming with only an upside in sight.

"My portfolio. Don't you remember? I'm updating it, and you agreed to be my model."

"Jerome, you've got world-famous models in your portfolio—no offense, Daze." She's still the best in my mind, but she has also been out of the business for some time now. "You could find someone else."

She isn't the least bit troubled by my comment, nodding and smiling at me, grateful for the backup. She no longer wants to do this, and Jerome is deliberately ignoring the signs.

"Not that I need to explain myself to you, Grayson, but I want something current, something from LA."

"Then use one of the jobs you've already done." I'm matter-of-fact and unyielding in my stare.

He sniffs, lifting his chin a little higher. "Daisy is perfect for what I have in mind. In no time at all, everyone in the LA fashion scene will know her name." He says it in a way that suggests he isn't looking forward to that day.

"So basically you're looking to cash in on Daisy's good name."

"Gray." Daisy arches one perfectly shaped brow, disappointment coloring her expression.

"Daisy, let's make this work." Jerome angles himself in a way that he can no longer see me.

"It might be tricky. With the award, I've been getting a lot more business, and finding time for the shoot will be difficult." She twirls a long blonde strand around her finger, uncomfortable. "Why don't I see if I can get a few models for you, and that way you can have variety."

"I want you." His sharp tone straightens my spine, and her eyes widen.

"Hey, she said she can't do it." I step in between them, forcing him to take several steps back. "Find someone else."

His steely grey eyes turn frosty, and he twists his leather lips into a tight frown. He's more than annoyed that I'm here and most probably thinking what I'm thinking—I want to punch this asshat.

With a blink, the hint of anger or annoyance is gone, and he turns away from me, once more signaling my insignificance to him. That's more than fine with me.

"I'll work around your schedule, but for what I have in mind, no one else will do. You'll be spectacular."

Henry darts in and out of the three of us, making car engine noises like we're an obstacle course. Jerome casts a dark look down at the child.

"Um...ah...well, I can't give you a date right now."

My head snaps to her, eyes widening and imploring. This is her chance to walk away. I gave her the perfect opening, and I'm here to back her up.

She nibbles on her lip, a painful smile ghosting over her mouth. "The next two weeks are insane. Maybe after that. Can we talk some more about this? I want to help, and I can get some great names for your shoot, but it's going to be difficult for me."

"Because of the award and your career taking off?" The question is harmless, but his tone carries a jab, maybe even a hint of jealousy.

"Can I pencil you in?" She mashes her lips together, wearing a distressed expression.

"Parfait, my beautiful." He beams, puffing out his chest and casting me a smug, satisfied look as if he's won.

I want to rip his tongue out whenever he calls her that. This isn't over, and if Daisy needs me to tell him to get lost, I'll gladly do it.

Henry bumps into Jerome's leg on another sweep around us, and the old man scowls, closing the distance to Daisy. But the little boy doesn't get the hint and barrels between their legs once more, nearly knocking down Jerome.

"Dammit." His face twists, eyes narrowing on Henry.

"Jerome," Daisy admonishes, and at the same time, I glare and command, "Knock it off."

"I better go." He presses a quick kiss to her cheek and jogs back to his car.

We stand side by side watching him leave as the *vrooms* and *roars* from Henry fill the silence.

"Why didn't you just say no?" I run a hand through my hair, shaking my head.

"I tried...he just doesn't know how to take no for an answer."

"He's a selfish jerk." I lower my voice, careful not to let Henry overhear the less than nice word.

"He's not all that bad. He can be an okay guy. It's just sometimes he infuriates me."

"I don't get it. The man is in his early sixties and had a lucrative photography career, one most would die for from what you've told me. But now, because he's hit a rough patch, it's your job to help him out of it?"

My pointed question causes her to flinch, and she tries to cover it with a shrug, looking away from me. I follow her line of sight to Henry, on the grass, taking off both his shoes like a man on a mission.

"Daze, would you even be friends if not for his fall from grace, or whatever it is that happened?"

When Jerome first made his appearance in Daisy's life, I'd tried to be open-minded even if he gave me jackass vibes. But the more I learned and the more I saw of him, the less I liked him. Fortunately, I don't have to see him a lot, but from what Daisy tells me, he's trying to ride her coattails.

"Well, I mean, we worked together in Paris. Not all the time, but once in a while."

"And now he clings to you as if you're his saviour. I don't like him."

"Not this again." She rests her hands on her hips, staring at me sternly.

We've had this conversation many times. I don't understand why she just doesn't keep her dealings with him civil but from a distance.

"C'mon, Daze. The guy insists on making his comeback your problem. That isn't a friend."

5

DAISY

A SILLY FLIP-FLOP

*W*hy does talking to Jerome make me feel shitty about receiving one of the most prestigious photography awards in the city?

In the car on the way to Pansy's, I mull over the conversation with Jerome and the award I still can't believe will be mine. It's life changing, and less than a month ago, like so many other photographers, I was a small fish in a big pond.

The fashion industry is dominated by a small group of photographers. They get all the shoots, all the campaigns, all the covers and ironically, this group is mainly male photogs. Yes, mostly men land the most coveted gigs. All. The. Time.

This award changes that for me. Since the announcement, I have the likes of Vogue, Elle, and a few Fashion Houses calling, wanting to book me. I'd been getting noticed before the award, finding it easier to snag those plum jobs, and the calls were increasing. But my breakout piece changed all of that and virtually overnight.

It was a feature on indie, underground LA designers, and it didn't hurt that I had the likes of some high-caliber names modeling. My photos were featured in several trendy online magazines, and things snowballed from there.

It's all surreal; I hadn't planned on straying from modeling but Henry changed everything. Between breast-feeding and diapers came this fierce—and surprising—pull to be on the other side of the photo lens.

Gray standing at the rear passenger door of his car, unbuckling Henry, brings me out of my musings. I park the car, and with my baby on his hip, he waits on the curb for me.

"Ready?" He quirks a blond brow. I nod and we start to walk.

The sun blazes above us, and arrows of honeycomb yellow splash onto the black, weathered pavement.

"Hey, Gray?" Nibbling on my bottom lip, I pause midstep, and he does the same, peering at me. "Would you go with me to the awards dinner next week?"

"I'd love to." The hint of a smile flirts with the edges of his mouth.

"Great." I inhale the salty sea air and release any residual nerves.

Did I just ask him on a date? No, it isn't a date. This is Gray. My best friend.

"I'll send you the details." I fidget with the hem of my baggy shirt, overthinking this.

"Cool. You nervous?" He snatches my hand, threading our fingers and pulling me alongside him.

For the briefest moment, sparks zoom through my veins,

straight for my chest, causing my heart to do a silly flip-flop. *Get a hold of yourself, Daisy.*

"A little." With a shaky voice and legs, I force my focus on putting one foot in front of the other and not on how his strong, callused hand curls around mine. "I mean, it's so surreal. I can't believe I got the award, that this is happening to me."

"Why?" He stops at the crosswalk, directly across from Silas and Pansy's home. "You're amazing."

Resting his forehead against mine, his fingers cup the back of my neck in a gentle, reassuring way, and he's everywhere. His breath warms my lips and the fresh citrus scent of him showers my senses.

Henry pats his chubby, sweaty palm on my cheek. "Mommy amazing."

I snort, he giggles, and Gray's lighthearted laughter wraps around me. "Thank you. It's just I never dreamed of getting to this level in my career."

"This level?"

"Yeah, where W and Vogue are calling me." I'm the first to break the connection as his gaze is too intense and mind-altering.

His lips never looked so kissable.

"You're crazy. Your work is fantastic."

"And you're biased but thank you. I am proud of my work."

"Good, because you should be. We're all proud of you, aren't we?" He tickles Henry's belly and my son squeals, tearing his eyes from the rolling, foamy cobalt waves.

"Proud of Mommy." Henry returns to admiring the

ocean, likely overeager to sink his fingers and toes in the damp sand.

Gray hooks an arm around my shoulder, the diaper bag hitting my butt, and Henry giggles again at how close the three of us are. He's on one side of Gray and I'm on the other.

My arm slides naturally around Gray's trim, defined waist, and he leads us across the street. Contentment floats through me in the same way warm water quiets and soothes one lounging in a deep bathtub.

For the first time in the past twenty-four hours, things feel normal again and not fleeting. No, more than normal. Better than normal.

"Hey, guys." In the doorway, Pansy waves, beaming at the sight of Henry and his stuffed octopus clutched to his chest.

As a marine biologist, Pansy's first gift to my son was Jellycat, his stuffed octopus that he is insufferable without. Henry takes the thing everywhere and can't sleep without it. My sister doesn't gloat, but she's beyond tickled pink that my son's most beloved toy was given by her.

We're no sooner in front of her than she snatches Henry from Gray, peppering his cherub cheeks with kisses.

"Hiya, Henry." Kiss. Kiss. "Did you have breakfast?" Kiss. Kiss. "Do you want something to eat, big guy?"

Both of us forgotten, she prances into the house, absorbed in the babe in her arms. My sister is still in school, and in her mind, any baby-making plans are on hold, but Silas wants nothing more than to knock her up—his words. She'll make a great mom.

"No, we ate, thanks." Gray's playfully sarcastic since we're both used to being invisible when my sister is in the vicinity of a child, especially Henry or Crystal, Eli's daughter.

Pansy pauses, glancing over her shoulder with a flush to her alabaster cheeks. "Good. I'll get this little one a snack." She mock-munches on a balled fist, setting off peals of laughter from Henry.

"Where's Silas?" Gray shakes his head.

"Out back with Jared and Eva." Pansy disappears into the kitchen.

Through the doorway to the kitchen, Lucia, their house-keeper and like a second mother to Silas, coos a string of melodic Spanish all for Henry. And while the translation is lost on me, I can't help but sport a gooey grin.

I wave at the three of them as we pass by. "K, we'll see you out there."

Today is a rare day when we're all free and we're able to hang out for a few hours. It doesn't happen often since all of us have busy lives.

Since coming to LA, pregnant and lost, who knows where I'd be right now without my sister and her friends. Silas and his bandmates, especially Gray, have become family to Henry and me.

And it's moments like this, when the guys are pairing off and settling down, I'm so grateful to be a part of this close-knit group and only hope nothing changes.

The deck's hot on my bare feet, and I drop my sandals, slipping them back on. Jared's arms are wrapped around Eva, his fiancée, like he never wants to let her go. Laughing at something he says, she stares up at him as if no one else exists but him.

Silas turns in our direction. "Good to see you."

Gray and Silas do that thing guys do—where they shake with one hand and with their other, they clap each other's back.

"Hey, Daisy." Eva detaches herself from her man, coming over to hug and kiss me, three times, on alternating cheeks like they do in Europe. "So good to see you."

Until six months ago, Eva had lived in Spain for most of her adult life, but LA was where she was born.

"You too." Behind her, I stretch to hug Jared. "How are you? Are you settled in?"

"Daisy, looking good." Jared squeezes my side and smiles. "We're almost moved in."

"Almost?" Eva arches a dark brow and wraps an arm around his waist, resting her head on his chest. "We're not even close. Boxes are everywhere, but we love it."

He laughs. "She exaggerates, but yeah, we love it."

They just moved into a small beach home, and Jared sold his Beverly Hills monstrosity. Silas, waiting his turn, moves in for a hug, tanned arms wide.

"Hey, Daze." He looks around, puzzled. "Where's Henry?"

"Where do you think? I'll give you one guess." I cock a hip and purse my lips.

Tipping his head back, he releases a deep, throaty laugh. "Of course. Let me go in and get them. Pansy will hide out with him all day if she has her way."

"Not a chance." Gray lifts a hand behind his head and whips his shirt off in one smooth move. "Henry's here for the beach. If she doesn't bring him out soon, snacks or no snacks, he'll stage a mutiny."

His magnificently inked torso and arms pop in the blinding sunlight, drawing my eyes to the intricate designs, and I lick my lips, suddenly parched. Not willing to tempt myself further and unsure as to what has gotten into me—looking at my best friend like a piece of meat is not something I've ever done before—I edge over to the lounger in the shade.

"I'll be right back." Silas goes inside to rescue my son from his adoring aunt.

My relationship with my soon-to-be brother-in-law is solid, but it wasn't always this way. He didn't particularly like me when I first arrived in LA, and truthfully, at the time, I didn't give him a lot of reason to.

I was wrapped up in myself and didn't go easy on Pansy. Not because she deserved it but more, you know, that old adage of taking things out on the ones we love. And despite our bickering, Silas's protectiveness of my baby sister instantly endeared me to him.

"Daze, can you put some on my back?" Gray runs a hand through his tousled hair and holds up a tube of sunscreen.

Nodding, I straighten my oversized shirt, looking anywhere but at the firm, stacked muscles of his stomach and the light trail of hair dipping below his swim trunks.

He hands me the tube, and I'm faced with the smooth expanse of his back. A dollop of cool lotion splats onto my palm, and I rub my hands together, trying to warm it up. Still, he hisses when my palms first rest on his heated skin.

"Sorry," I half chuckle, half grimace, gliding my now tingling hands over his tight, angular shoulder blades.

My fingers brush against the sides of his torso, working

their way down his back, and I relish how he quivers at my touch. Desire curls low in my core, and I press my knees together to lessen the ache. What is happening to me?

One date and my eyes are suddenly open to the opposite sex, or more specifically, my very hot and very single best friend. It isn't like I was unaware of his hotness. Hell no.

The guy is handsome and a sweetheart. And I love him...I love him like a friend. That's it. Isn't it?

I steady my gaze toward the glass doorway, conjuring something boring and not as mind-bending as loving my best friend in more than friendly ways. Like the two weeks' worth of laundry, spit-up, stains, and other unmentionables waiting for me or the hours of photo editing I have to do at some point soon.

Pansy and Silas come outside with Henry leading the way, and I pat Gray's shoulder, signaling I'm done.

"Thanks." He drops to his haunches and picks up Henry before turning to me. "We're going down to the water. I'll put sunscreen on him. Where's his hat?"

"He's already got some on." Pansy sidles up to me as I unzip the diaper bag to fish out his sun hat.

I watch Gray and Henry descend the deck stairs to the beach, and once out of sight, my sister steps in closer, untying her cover.

"So how'd your date go?" She twirls her long red locks into a loose knot on top of her head and dabs sunscreen onto the tips of both shoulders.

"Ugh, don't ask." I shimmy out of my shorts and get rid of my shirt.

"That bad, huh?" Working lotion into her thigh, she rests her foot on the edge of a lounger.

"Not really bad...but it wasn't great either." I dip onto a cushion, rummaging through the bag for my hair tie. "I mean, it felt like I was having dinner with a client."

"Ah, that sucks." She picks at a loose strand of hair clinging to her neck. "I was excited for you."

"I guess." I shrug, no emotion at the thoughts of the dinner.

"I mean, it's been a while since you put yourself out there...too long, if you ask me."

"No one asked you," I mutter under my breath.

She rolls her eyes and squirts lotion on my back. "Whatever. I'd always hoped you and Gray—"

"Stop right there." My heart rate spikes and I scan the deck, breathing easier with Jared, Eva, and Silas fully engrossed in a conversation several feet away. They aren't listening or even interested in our conversation. "We're not talking about this again."

"Hey, easy." A slow, laidback grin slides across her face. "You can't blame me for hoping. You know instead of waiting for Gray to make the move—"

"Who said I was waiting for him?"

6

DAISY

CAN'T KEEP HER HANDS TO HERSELF

*A*m I waiting for Gray to show interest? Is that what's been going on? And only now, after a less than stellar date experience, I'm rearranging things in my head? Feasting on my best friend at every chance I get?

Once more, I look to our friends, busy chatting at the balcony as they take in the ocean view and most probably, Gray and Henry messing around in the sand below.

"Fine. Fine." She drops the subject a little too easily or so I think, but I'm proven wrong a blink later. "Is everything okay with the two of you?"

"Why wouldn't it be?"

"I don't know. There was some kind of weird tension between the two of you when you got here."

She noticed? Great, did Gray pick up on my weirdness too? What is my problem?

"No, we're good." I tuck the beach bag under my chair,

not willing to go into my misstep with not telling him about the date.

"Is it the date?" She stares, unrelenting. Why does she always pick up on what's *not* been said?

"What?" I act confused or disinterested...or at least, that's what I'm going for.

"Did you tell him about your date?"

I nod, removing my sunglasses to clean them. There's not a speck on the lenses, but my sister has this uncanny ability to read my mind, especially when it's none of her business.

Argh, she can be so annoying.

"And?"

"And what? You know, I came here to hang out with you guys. Swim and relax before I go to work. This,"—I flick my hand back and forth between us—"feels a lot like grilling."

"Okay. You don't have to be so touchy. I'll leave you alone." She plants a quick kiss on my cheek. "I'm taking Boy for a walk. Want to come?"

Boy is Pansy's dog, and my son adores her. Yes, Boy is a *her*. Don't ask.

"I'm good. I just want to chill, but where is Boy anyway?"

"Sleeping in our room. Once I bring her down to the beach, Henry will go wild." Her eyes glitter, unable to contain her excitement and I nod, laughing.

"Great." I lie back on the chair, securing the straps of my bikini, and close my eyes, soaking in the crashing of the waves, the briny salt in the air, and the radiant heat.

Not long after, someone steps in front of the hot rays, casting dark shade along my body. Blinking, I stare at shards of shining honey tracing the solid lines of a broad, shadowy figure. The sunbeams fracture, glittering and spiking outward all around him. Gray.

"Do you want something to drink?" His eyes are on mine, piercing ocean blue, not once straying below my neck to peruse the rest of me. "Henry's gone for a walk with Pansy and Boy."

A little saddened by his refusal or disinterest in my bikini-clad body, I shift uncomfortably. This strange and budding attraction may be one-sided. Am I wishing for something that isn't there?

"I'd love a water, please."

He pauses, eyes now dipping lower to linger over my breasts, nipples erect and hard at his attention, then down my flat stomach to the scrap of fabric between my thighs.

He sinks his teeth into his bottom lip, gaze smoldering. "Do you need me to put on any sunscreen? I wouldn't want you to burn."

I swallow. Hard. And ignore the impulse to scream yes from the rooftops. "I'm good, thanks."

He nods and saunters to the cooler only a few feet away and then he's back in no time, wordlessly handing me a bottle.

"Thank you." I'm unable to stop myself from tracking his casual, assured moves across the deck.

He leans against the railing, arms crossed over his chest while striking up a conversation with Eva. Like always, my eye is drawn to the curve of his hard bicep and the sleeve of black ink, curling and twisting along his arm.

The man is a contradiction in so many ways. Quiet—some

confuse it with shyness—and compared to the other guys in the band, he often gets overlooked. Yet by all accounts, he doesn't pine for the attention and prefers to fade into the background, drinking in his surroundings. He's observant and thoughtful, catching a lot more than others give him credit for.

A rock star in his own right, at the young age of twenty he scored one of the most coveted gigs in the music industry at the time. Gray, competing against several other wildly talented musicians, landed the part of drummer for Trojan when the original one stepped away from that life to get clean.

"Hey, guys." India Holt, the rock world's newest sensation, dances onto the terrace, twirling her arms in the air.

A bottle of vodka is in one hand and tequila in the other. The barely twenty-something singer and songwriter demands all eyes on her and deservedly so.

She's stunning. Long midnight tresses flow down her back, bangs beautifully framing her deep soulful eyes, and as if that wasn't enough, her racer-red thong bikini leaves little to the imagination.

Tiny triangles of fabric just cover the nipples of her generous chest and her firm butt cheeks bounce, cellulite-free, with every one of her whirls and spins. Look out, Beyoncé and Jennifer Lopez, India is in the running for best booty.

When our gazes meet, I give her the obligatory wave and smile before lying back onto the lounger, pretending to shut my eyes. Thank goodness for sunglasses.

"Oh my God, Gray." Like a baby chimpanzee clinging to

its mother, her arms and legs wrap around him as she plants kisses on his face. "It's been too long."

The poor guy tries to keep his hands away from her body but eventually grasps her hips to keep them both upright.

He mentioned SG productions had just signed her on as a client for her latest album. Silas had secured the contract. *Bastard.*

She has never hidden her lady boner for Grayson Bennett. Normally, you'd think a lead singer like India would want someone of equal stature, say Silas or even Jared—the most sought-after members of Trojan. But not so for Ms. Holt.

And I suppose, if you really think about it, Gray makes sense. She isn't one to share the spotlight, loving the glory for herself. Both Silas and Jared eat that shit up, or at least they used to before settling down.

Uh-huh. There'd be too much competition.

And it isn't as if I don't understand her attraction to Gray. Unfortunately, I understand all too well. It's just...until now, it had never bothered me.

And truth be told, India had only been around once or twice before. Both times, I was either huge and pregnant, or sleep-deprived and breastfeeding. Even if I was interested in Gray at the time, which I wasn't, I was no threat to her.

Rather than sulk about the intrusion, I force my eyes shut and try to relax. It's short-lived and useless. She can't keep her hands to herself, and while Gray isn't encouraging, he also hasn't backed away.

Every flirty comment or innuendo from her mouth hits

me in the chest like a bag of oranges. Hard and painful, but careful not to leave any bruises.

Ugh, why am I doing this to myself?

Twenty minutes later and I've had enough. It's time to leave and get a jump on setting up or maybe even editing some shots from my last shoot. I slip on my sandals and shorts and peer over the railing to spy Pansy and Henry playing fetch with Boy.

I make quick work of going down to say goodbye to them, hugging and kissing my son and successfully dodging my sister's quizzical comments about my early departure.

They follow me back up to the deck where I head straight for the house, hoping to make it inside without being noticed. But no such luck.

"You're leaving?" Gray saunters toward me, arching his blond eyebrows.

"Yeah, I brought a change of clothes, but I want a shower."

"Why don't you have one here? And what about lunch? You have to eat before work." While not unusual, his tender concern sends my heart free-falling.

"I'm okay." My stomach knots, not hungry but uncertain if I should leave earlier than planned or stake my claim.

Am I ready for that? I'm in limbo, unsure if I want things the way they were yesterday or ready for a new tomorrow.

Watching India hog the limelight doesn't appeal to me. And while I wouldn't say I dislike her, we aren't friends—and I hate to stereotype but I'm going to. I've met too many people like her.

Underneath her party-girl, 'I love everybody' persona,

she isn't nice to those she deems as competition. Working for years in the fashion industry, you quickly adopt a fake, everyone's my best friend image. But behind closed doors, many wish the demise of anyone even remotely prettier or more successful than they are. Sadly, I used to be one of those people.

"Okay. We'll most likely have lunch and then head to your place for Henry's nap. I might take one too." His smile is cute and childlike.

Henry would love napping with Gray. So would I.

Like a stealth bomber, India sneaks up on us, draping her body over him, boobs pressing into his arm, and leaning in as if we invited her into our conversation.

"A nap? Sign me up. I would love a nap with you." Her green eyes fix on him in a naughty, flirty way and I want to gag.

"Well, you guys have fun." Not looking at either of them, I hustle to the sliding glass door, pausing to peer at him over my shoulder. "And call me if anything comes up with Henry."

Attentive eyes stare at my mouth, lingering as if he's thinking about kissing me. My tongue licks at my lips imagining the taste of him, the thrust of his tongue and bite of his teeth.

Would his kiss be soft and sweet like he is with my son? Or hard and demanding like how he beats on the drums?

7

GRAY

DEMANDING A PIECE OF YOU

*I*ndia hangs off my arm and I push away, motioning for Pansy to watch Henry while I follow Daisy inside.

"Hey, Daze, wait up."

She's out of sight and I jog to the hallway, and my insides are out of whack for fear she's already gone. But she can't be.

Daisy stands with her back to the front door, facing me, and I suck in a breath. Her hair is swept up, tendrils spilling from the messy knot on top of her head. Wisps of vanilla gold frame her sun-flushed face.

The sight of her sweetheart face, little nose, lush mouth, and her perfect tits in the white bikini top torment me.

So much tight, bronze flesh to feast on and I can't help myself. My hungry gaze trails the tantalizing valley of her breasts down her smooth stomach to her shorts, riding low on her slender waist.

She's gorgeous.

Beautiful perfection.

When I first met Daisy, it wasn't her beauty that drew me to her but what she hides beneath. She's used to people gawking at her, wanting her, wanting to *be* her. Because of her looks, not for who she is.

And in those early days of our friendship, she expected me to be like all the others. Blinded by her sun-kissed skin, long hair spun like gold, the dips and curves of perfection.

But that isn't what I saw, not what I see at all. She was lost, alone, and pregnant. Motherhood was something she equally revered and feared, and she was on edge.

She'd snap at everyone, even when people tried to help, convinced she had to do it on her own. Pushed them away. Daisy believed they'd reject her once they got past the outside.

Beauty was a weapon she wielded to entice and also shut people out because she expected them to get tired of the simpering Barbie doll and be woefully disappointed in what they found deep down.

What a waste of time.

What a mistake.

She's kind, caring—a loving person. A little insecure but who isn't, even with the way she looks.

And even now, as I drink in her stunning body—the silky skin, the long, toned legs, and her luscious breasts—her physical beauty is made more alluring because of who she is.

That's what I see and what I crave.

Her mind, and heart, and body.

"Is something wrong?" She bites her lower lip, and it's tough to remember why I chased after her.

We stare at each other, and I could easily dive into her brilliant blue eyes, lose myself all day in her sweet, feminine splendor.

"Ah, yeah. I mean, no, nothing's wrong." Stepping closer, I take her hand, interlacing our fingers like we've done so many times before. "You want to go to dinner one night soon?"

Her lips part but nothing comes out, and her eyes slowly round as what I asked sinks in. "Um, you mean like a date?" Her words are barely a whisper, and she tries to pull from my hold. *Uh-uh, she isn't going anywhere.*

"Forget I said that." She's tripping over her words. "Of course it isn't, it's dinner."

"Hey." I tug her by the hand toward me, and her cute awkwardness is like an electric current jolting my already buzzing nerves. "Date. Dinner. You call it whatever you want. I just want to spend some time together."

Her brow furrows, and the little lines at the bridge of her nose appear. Something about this unsettles her. I'm not happy with that, and the drive to calm things down kicks into high gear.

"It's been a while since we've had dinner." My fingers squeeze around hers and I shrug, playing down the invite.

What the hell am I doing? I want this to be a date.

"I'd love dinner." She nods, her expression more relaxed.

"Cool. I know we're busy but let me know when." I lean in and kiss her cheek.

"Okay." Her eyes bore into mine, and I see it as it happens. How she struggles to slide from this new, maybe a little scary, and definitely exciting place we've dipped our toes into, back to us.

Daisy straightens her spine and sharpens her focus. "Please make sure Henry gets his nap. It's important. He's a wreck without one and so am I."

She's serious. No tip-up at the side of her mouth or sparkle to her eye. She's grabbing the reins of how things usually are between us. Friends.

I open my mouth to respond but she keeps going. "I mean a nap. Alone."

"Ah, yeah." I scratch at the back of my neck, hanging my head remorsefully at the memory of breaking her rule about sleeping with Henry.

I could defend myself, my actions. I was afraid of being kicked to the curb...of losing them, my family, if Daisy found some other guy. Sleeping in Henry's bed was my most basic way of not being left out, of clinging onto the thing I cherished the most.

Nah, I couldn't tell her all that. Not now.

She purses her lips, studying me when I finally get the balls to face her. "Bye, Gray."

"Bye, Daze." Grudgingly, I let go of her hand and walk away, mentally kicking myself for screwing that up.

Maybe I should just tell her how I feel. She probably thinks it's dinner like any of the other times we've eaten together. I'm an idiot.

I'm going to have to be more direct. This dinner will be a date.

Once outside, Daisy still on my mind, I amble down to the beach where Henry's sitting on the sandy beach floor.

Eva and Jared are with him, and India bounds from the shoreline to stop at my side.

"I miss you. Want to swim?" She grabs at my arm.

"I need to get him changed and ready for lunch." I glance down to the sand where Henry plays while Jared watches our exchange with keen interest.

"Okay." She's cheery and light, shadowing me like a second skin.

"Give me some space." I keep my voice flat, needing her to take a hint.

"Sure. I can help." She goes for the toddler who is happily amassing clumps of sand into his small hands, only to lift them above his head and uncurl his fingers like the claws of the cranes in a junkyard.

The gritty blinding-agent disperses into the air. Jared slides an arm around Eva and turns her away while Henry squints and grins in triumphant glory. I swiftly sidestep her, bending and ducking my head from the sand floating in the air.

"Nah, it's cool." I scoop him into my arms. "You ready for some lunch, little man?"

"I'm hungry." He shoves a sand covered finger into his mouth and puckers his lips.

Yuck. As anticipated, India's on my heels, across the beach and up the stairs onto Silas's deck. I grimace and share a quick, knowing look with Jared—yeah, she's going to be hard to shake.

Clearly, she isn't giving up or leaving me alone, and I relent, frustrated at her and the damp sand Henry's so affably rubbing into the scruff along my jawline.

"Can you grab that, please?" I drop my chin to the beach bag that's peeking out from under a chair.

Quick to oblige yet not one to take the cue—or maybe she's intent on getting her own way—India follows me into the house. Fortunately, Pansy asks her for help, and I'm finally alone to wash the sand off Henry.

We eat lunch on the deck under the large umbrella protecting us from the relentless rays. Once done, Henry sits near my feet, half under the table, playing with the dog while India dominates the conversation.

"That was amazing. Thanks, Pansy and Si." She folds her napkin and smiles at our hosts. "Hey, Gray, I know you're busy with SG Productions, but I wanted to ask you a favor." She pauses, making sure she has the attention of everyone at the table.

It works. All talking ceases, eyes on the two of us. "Would you play the drums on my upcoming album?"

"What?" I place my fork on the plate, turning to my left to face her.

"Yeah. Sarah bailed on me yesterday, some bullshit—"

"Language," I grit out, pointing beneath us to the child.

"Oopsie, sorry." She giggles as her hand loosely covers her mouth for a nanosecond. "Anyway, I'm down a drummer, and you're the best there is. As you know, we start recording next week and I'd love to have you. With you on drums, you'll make the album even more epic."

"Um." I'm torn with what to say. "I-ah..."

The chance to play would be awesome, and the songs for her new album are great, but I'm part owner of a business. Juggling both responsibilities is doable, but that doesn't take into account my commitment to Henry and Daisy. Not to mention, it wouldn't leave time for much else.

"That's an awesome idea." Silas's carefree smile fixes on his face, and it's plain to see he already knew about India's little drummer dilemma.

He may have even known she had plans to ask me. So much for loyalty. A heads-up would have been nice. The two of us still have things to hash out, like the recording studio garbage, and this crap doesn't help.

The churning sensation in my stomach, causing my lunch to revolt, leaves me anxious and annoyed. Silas would love nothing better than to keep me busy with India's record so he could run SG without me.

"Gray, you'd be great." Pansy stands to grab the plates and smiles encouragingly at me.

I've never expressed my desire to play again to Pansy, but Daisy has likely told her. It would explain why I'm getting a strong *do it* vibe from everyone at the table. Well, except Eva, who's studying me with her knowing glances and sage silence.

"You should do it." Jared lightly bumps shoulders with me, sitting on my other side, and he dips his voice lower. "This way it's short-term and you get to play. It's the best of both worlds."

Like Eli and Silas, I've shared with Jared the urge I sometimes get. The loud and incessant calling to make music and play again. Without having to say much else, we're all on the same page.

The four of us have had jam sessions, few and far between and even more so now that Eli's on the other side of the country. And while it's great, it doesn't compare to performing live or recording an album.

"So, you'll do it." India should be asking a question, but it comes out like a declaration, and her hand wraps around my forearm as she leans in to plant a kiss on my cheek.

Pansy and I share a loaded stare, my unease mirrored in her gaze. She's the first to turn away, taking the plates inside with Eva at her back.

"I don't know." I rake a hand through my wind-swept hair. "I'd have to think about it. There's SG and—"

"Hey, don't worry about that." Silas waves away my responsibility to our company like it's nothing. "I've got that covered."

I huff and bite back the disparaging *I bet you do* ready to jump from my mouth. My frustration at Silas's lack of regard for my role in the company won't help the situation, and Henry's here. If things get heated, I don't want him anywhere near that.

"I said I'll have to think about it." My tone is sharp and unapologetic as I step from the table. "India, I'm flattered you've asked, but give me a day or two. I'll let you know as soon as possible. I won't leave you hanging, and if I don't do it, I'll help find someone to play drums."

"Okay, sure." For the first time today, she's at a loss for words.

Not willing to take on her disappointment and let the guilt eat at me, I squat down to Henry. "Want to go for a walk with Boy?"

"Yay." He jumps to his feet, nearly hitting his head on the

underside of the table if not for my hand sliding in between the two to buffer the blow. *Ouch.*

"Just a short one. You need a nap." I take his hand in mine and pat at my thigh for Boy to follow us.

"I'm not tired." His yawn chips away at his protest. Chuckling, I lift him into my arms and take the stairs down to the beach.

"Hey, want some company?" Jared's behind me, coming to my side when he hits the sand. "You okay?"

"Fine." I shrug and turn to look out at the ocean.

"This is none of my business..." He hesitates and I turn back to him.

"What are you talking about?"

"You and Silas." Just the mention of my partner causes my back to stiffen, but I try to hide it and listen to Jared. "I've asked before how things are going between you two and SG Productions. I know you've said they're good and Silas says the same—"

"You're right." I cut in and readjust Henry on my hip. "This isn't your business." My tone is harsher than I intend, but Jared is no different than Silas.

They aren't alike in personality, but they are close, and with the band, those two got their way most of the time. Jared wouldn't understand my challenges with the former lead singer of Trojan—the man used to the top spot and final say.

"Look, you're going to need to be more forceful with Silas."

"What?" I cock my head to one side, confused.

"I know we never talked about this, but it didn't go unnoticed how you kept quiet on a lot of things where Trojan was concerned. You just seemed to go with the majority. And that's cool, but this is your company too. Shit, I'd say it's more yours than his; it was your idea."

There's an uncomfortable tangle in my belly. I don't want to lord anything over Silas. I want a partnership. That's all.

"Hey, it was my idea, but we're fifty-fifty."

"Good. Remind him of that. Show him by not holding your tongue." He quirks one of his brows, giving me a pointed look. "Silas respects you. Values your opinion but he's also happy to have things go his way if you let him." Jared lifts up his arms. "Let me take him."

He swings Henry from my arms, bringing him to sit on his shoulders. The boy squeals, fingers threading into Jared's longish, dark locks.

My friend hisses and I laugh, shaking my head. "He'll make you bald if he stays up there too long."

"Yeah, I can tell." He winces and says to Henry, "One quick horsey ride and then I'll put you down."

Nodding and shrieking, Henry hangs onto Jared's hair for dear life as the man jogs toward the shoreline with his hand wrapped around the little guy's waist. Boy barks, maybe a bit concerned and also playful, chasing after them.

With a moment alone, Jared's words bolster my conviction to hold my ground with Silas on our latest debate—a recording studio. Then India's request plays through my mind. As tempting as it is—and it would be easy, in some ways, to give in to the indulgence—there's a lot more to consider.

In the world of Trojan and India Holt, the music is not only a joy but also a burden as it comes with obnoxious record executives, fame, and everyone demanding a piece of you. All of which I'd rather do without.

And above all else, there's Daisy and Henry. What would recording an album mean for spending time with them? Daisy still hasn't found a nanny, and Pansy's schedule doesn't allow for her to take care of Henry whenever Daisy can't.

The three of us have been juggling care of Henry, and I want to be part of it. There's no way I let a day go by without seeing him...and Daisy if I can help it, but working on India's album would change that.

Some days could be long, starting at sunup and going until well after the sun is down, depending on what we're working on and how on or far off schedule we are.

When Daisy left, hours ago, my first inclination was to grab Henry and leave with her. Although that wouldn't have been fair to Henry since his mother was only going to work and he loves the beach.

My desire to leave wasn't only because Daisy was going but also to get away from the handsy songstress. What would working with her on an album look like?

Can I handle her incessant flirting and who knows what else? I'm not worried about starting something with her, I'm not interested. I want Daisy. But more...I wonder what Daisy would think.

I sensed the shift in her mood once India arrived, and no matter what she said, the singer was part of the reason she left early. And now, I have to face the human barnacle again.

8

GRAY

RETIRED TROJAN ROCK GODS

My head pounds like the hard thrumming of drums, and while that's my beat, right now it's irritatingly painful. Squeezing my eyes shut, I push my skull into the sofa cushion and try to block out everything.

It isn't working.

The last of India's cheery voice and lilting giggles somehow bulldozes my deep breathing and attempts at silencing my mind. She's finally leaving, and Silas graciously offered to walk her out.

It's difficult not to feel like an ungrateful jerk because signing India Holt is huge for SG Productions. Her next album will be good, and it will sell millions, I've no doubt. The woman is on fire. You can't scroll through social media or any of the streaming music channels without seeing her. And the lyrics for her new album—I'd been fortunate to see some of the songs—are pure gold.

But I'm no closer to determining if I'll take her up on

playing drums for her album or not. Silas should have talked to me before hammering out a deal with her.

We're partners in this together, and we're both supposed to have equal say in every decision. And Jared's comments on the beach come back to me.

Does Silas even know what it means to be in a partnership? Shit, that isn't fair.

When Trojan was a thing, from time to time there would be tension among the four of us. I mean, it's to be expected, and usually, it stemmed from one of Silas's arbitrary decisions where he didn't consult the band. Kind of like when he walked away from Trojan without even a warning.

That isn't a great example. Truth be told, both Eli and I were also thinking about getting out. I could have gone on for much longer, being younger than the rest and also with no ties or demons—or at least that's what it looks like on the surface.

Yet it became clear we weren't going to ride the wave of success forever. Not because of the quality of our songs or performances. No, Trojan was as strong as ever.

But because Silas was showing signs of wear, his anger management had become a problem. Eli's lifestyle made it difficult for the guy to give his daughter any kind of normalcy, and Jared was one high away from an overdose.

And me? Well, I'd never really given the fame any thought when I auditioned for Trojan. I just wanted to make music. What a cliché, but true. I still want to make music and miss playing the drums every day.

I also wanted to make money. Lots of it, more out of

necessity than any master plan to be filthy rich. That kind of stuff didn't matter to me. I only want to live comfortably.

But money is important. My parents weren't poor. We were middle-class, but that lifestyle vanished almost overnight.

Dad died in a freak accident when high winds sent a traffic sign flying and it took off his head. To this day, I still get chills if I think about it too much. Then less than three years later, Mom was diagnosed with early-onset Alzheimer's at forty-five.

By that time, the rapidly advancing brain disease had robbed me of my mother, taking any of her memories of a son. She needed around the clock care.

Yeah, money is critical. Dad's life insurance was dwindling fast as her medical bills piled up. Trojan was a stroke of luck, but the fame was daunting.

So Silas's announcement that he was leaving the band couldn't all be on him. I was mulling over my next move, how to use the name I'd built for myself with Trojan to launch a different but just as lucrative career without the limelight.

When I hatched the idea to produce records, it wasn't playing or making music but close enough. I went to Silas, looking for an investor, not a partner. I could have plunked all my money into the company, but I'd have been left with not much else, and there were still Mom's medical bills and ongoing care to consider.

Rather than take on all the risk, I explored options. Eli expressed interest, but he had Crystal to think of and he was venturing into a new career. At the time, Jared was in no position to consider backing me, let alone figure out his own future.

A bank loan was an option, but I didn't want to owe or pay interest, so I approached Silas. To my surprise, he wanted more than to just invest. He wanted in. All in. A full partner.

"You okay?" He stands in the doorway, a hand in the front pocket of his jeans. "You want a water, beer, or something?"

It's just us. Jared and Eva left, and Pansy is putting Henry down for a nap. I really could use one too.

Henry's 'big boy' bed isn't so big for a grown man, and last night, I slept precariously on the edge, literally. I was fully prepared to wind up on the floor, on my back at any moment. So let's just say, I didn't sleep well.

A nap would be great, but nope. No nap for me. Silas and I need to talk about a recording studio. I can't put it off any longer.

"No. I'm good. Let's talk." I point my chin to the living room, encouraging him to have a seat.

He saunters over and drops into the seat beside me, tapping his fingers on the leather arm of the chair. "Sure. What's up?"

"I could be pissed at you for signing India without talking to me, but it's good for business. But don't do it again. We're partners."

Silas raises his brows in shock. Admiration? Guilt? It's hard to say but he's speechless, and encouraged by his silence, I continue.

"And that's not all. We need to talk about the studio." I

lean forward, resting my forearms on my knees and clasping my fingers together in front of me.

Through it all, I maintain eye contact. He needs to understand I'm serious.

"Go on." Some of the earlier stupor wears off, and it's replaced with caution.

"We have to shelve building a studio right now. You and I both know financially it's not the right time for us. We've got a lot of good momentum going and great clients lined up. If we start building a studio, we're going to lose some of that. We need to keep moving forward, and later, we can shift gears and focus on a studio."

"Building our own recording studio is progress and does keep us moving." He scratches at his ear. "We're wasting money renting studio time and scrambling for locations every time we have a recording session. We're at the mercy of other people's schedules."

"True. It can be a pain and it doesn't help that we don't have admin staff, so we're the goofballs who put us behind the eight ball." We share a wry grin.

Neither of us are particularly skilled at planning and organizing, and we should probably hire an assistant. Add that to the many things we haven't gotten around to doing.

Usually, we'd ask our previous band manager to take care of something like that, but Bianca Ramirez is no longer in our lives.

So, in the absence of someone organizing our business lives, we make things work and get through by the skin of our teeth.

"But we can get ahead of that by signing a one-year lease

at an existing recording studio," I say, further pushing my preference. "It'll save us time and money."

"And while we lease, that's money we could be putting into our own pockets."

"Not necessarily. You and I both know that building a studio is going to take time and money. And in the interim, we'll still need to find a recording studio...for every album."

"Fuck," he mutters under his breath, avoiding my gaze.

He's a smart guy and he can do the math. I've got him even if he won't easily admit it. What I'm saying is the right thing to do right now.

"Come on, Silas." I nudge his foot with mine. "We'll build a studio eventually. I'm with you. We could even set a date to get that ball rolling—"

"You mean like a plan and shit?" Now he's smirking, and the flash of mischief in his gaze tells me he's coming around to the idea.

"Yeah, a plan. Crazy." It's a wonder how successful our company is, and has been from the onset, since we're terrible at keeping track of everything.

And deep down, we both recognize being retired Trojan rock gods has a lot to do with our success. For the most part, we aren't seeking out musicians to work with us. It's the other way around.

"I just really want our own studio." He runs a hand through his blond hair.

"In time. Recording with India starts in a little over a week." Which thankfully, I've already secured studio space for. "And then right after that, Candyland, then Irwin. We've got a packed schedule for the next couple of months. We can't—"

"Yeah, yeah, I hear you." His jaw tightens. "Before we make any final decisions, come talk to the real estate agent with me. She found a great location."

Shit, he isn't giving up that easily. "Fine, but you also have to check out the studio I found for lease."

"Gray, it's a fucking great location." He's sitting up straighter, eyes bright and animated. "And we could have everything in one place. Our offices—"

"I'll take a look, but when the time is right to build, we'll find an awesome location." I inject as much confidence in my voice as possible.

There's no way I can be certain we'll find a great spot when we're ready to build our own studio, but I have to believe we will. If I give so much as an inch with Silas, he'll blow an opening as wide as a football field and push his preference all the way to a touchdown. And before I know it, we'll be building our own recording studio.

"I want you to meet the agent soon." He points at me. "And I'll go see this studio. But just so we're clear. I'm not agreeing to anything until we've explored both options."

"Fair enough." I bow my head, grateful for this small concession.

I hang around for another hour or so, and Silas and I work, making a few phone calls and attempting to get more organized. Once Henry's up, we head back to Daisy's, and I send her a text letting her know I've got dinner covered.

She doesn't respond right away, which isn't unusual when she's on a shoot. It could be hours before I hear from her, and as expected, a few hours later, she lets me know she's on her way home.

Dinner is on the table when she strolls in a little after seven in the evening. She looks both exhilarated and exhausted. Blonde curls gather on the top of her head in a chaotic bun, and she's wearing jeans and a blue T-shirt.

A big smile breaks across her face at the sight of her son busy creating a masterpiece at his table in the corner of the kitchen. He casts her a sideways "I'm busy at the moment" glance and doesn't stop what he's doing.

"Is that all I get?" Dropping her bags on the floor, she crouches to his height and opens her arms.

Henry pauses, studying his mother and then the colorful array of crayon scribbles on the piece of paper, before racing toward her for a hug.

We eat and clean the kitchen, bathe Henry, and put him to bed while chatting about various things like the visit to the beach today and her photo shoot. She doesn't bring up our upcoming dinner.

Once it's just the two of us, I pull her outside to the backyard. It's a small patch of grass, fenced in and private. There's a square of patio stones no bigger than the average size drum kit and it's usually quiet, even if sometimes muggy when the air is stagnant.

Tonight, there's a cool breeze—maybe too cold to stay out for too long. We sit in the two Adirondack chairs, dropping our phones onto the table between us when hers buzzes.

She glances at it, the movement slow and almost too much for her weary muscles, then she releases an aggravated sigh. "I wish he'd just knock it off."

"Who is it?" I could peer down at the screen, but it isn't my business.

"Jerome." Her eyes close, long blonde lashes fanning across her high cheekbones.

"Not again?" My exasperation with that guy slips past my control and blankets my tone.

While I can't put my finger on it, something about him bugs me more than it should. And maybe it all stems from the fact he has a huge crush on Daisy.

There, I said it. The asshole is old enough to be her father, or her grandfather for that matter. Yet he flirts with her shamelessly like he's fucking George Clooney or some other aging celebrity women of many ages still swoon over.

This time, Daisy doesn't indulge him and ignores the text, flipping the phone screen down.

"You don't have to do it. You know this, right?"

"Gray, not this again. I can't leave him stranded." She leans toward me, her blue gaze filled with sincerity.

"And you won't. You told him you'd find someone else to model for him."

"He won't take no for an answer, but I'm busy and likely going to be swamped soon." She rubs her hands over her arms, shivering. "Don't get me wrong, this is the kind of problem I want...but Jerome isn't listening."

I grab her hand and pull her to standing. "Let's go inside, you're cold."

She nods, letting out a tiny *brrr* and follows me into the house. "Yes, it's nice out but chilly."

Shutting the door behind me, I lean into it and watch her walk to the middle of the room where she turns to face me.

"Can we forget about Jerome?"

"Yes, I should get going." I step closer, sliding a finger under her chin to tilt her head up and capture her gaze. "But know that I'm here for you, if you need me to talk to him."

"I don't but thank you. Before you go, I want to talk about you. Did you get a chance to talk to Silas about the studio?"

"Yeah. He wants me to check out some property for sale, and he agreed to seeing the studio for lease."

"Is that a good thing? Sounds like he might be open to waiting."

"Yeah. I think he'll come around. I only hope it's quick so we can sign the lease before someone else snaps it up."

"It's going to work out, I know it." She pauses and stares at me. "So how'd it go with India? Did she stick around and nap?" Her cynical tone contradicts the blank expression she's trying to keep in place.

A warmth spreads through my chest at the change in subject. India must have been on her mind, and a deep rumble of laughter bubbles up my throat. "Are you jealous?"

"What? No." She steps back and spins on her heel, giving me her back. "I was just asking. Why would I be jealous of India Holt?"

Her hand reaches back to me, and I take it as she tugs me toward the front of the house. Damn, I did say I was leaving.

"Exactly. You've nothing to be jealous about." I stop and yank on her hand gently, causing her to stop.

Patiently, I wait for her to face me. She's rigid and still for a few beats, but eventually, we're face to face.

"India is a client, and I suppose, a friend. But that's it." I'm now in her space with only a few inches between us. Once more, my hand glides under her chin to bring her gaze to mine.

"She's a lot more than that." Her voice is a hesitant whisper. "She's talented and beautiful, and she likes you a lot. And—"

"She may be all those things." I take her hands in mine, lifting one to my mouth and planting a soft kiss on the palm of her hand. The heat of her and the gratifying scent of vanilla and warm sugar surround me. "You are the only one I see. Always."

9

DAISY

DEEPEST SECRETS AND WILDEST FANTASIES

*M*y neck aches from slanting to one side for the better part of the afternoon while I clicked shot after shot from what was a successful photo shoot. One hand works the tight muscles of my shoulder while the other turns the key in the ignition.

The engine starts and my phone buzzes in the cupholder. My best friend Sasha's name and Paris number lights up the car dashboard. It's early for her, almost five in the morning Paris time, given it's nearly eight in the evening here.

"Hey, girl. Are you starting your day or going to bed?" My droll tone doesn't hide that I don't miss how the lifestyle can do a wicked number on your body's internal clock, among other things.

Her lyrical laughter greets me. "Daze, I've just gotten up. I've got another one of those long days with Jean-Luc, you know how it is."

"Ah, no, not anymore. I haven't worked with him in

years." There's a hint of nostalgia to my tone while I needn't remind her of my absence.

Jean-Luc is a fabulous photographer and just one of many fantastic people in the industry. Sometimes I miss modeling. It was my dream from a young age.

Well, honestly, I miss the people more than anything else, especially Sasha. I'd have gone insane, packed my bags, and headed back to the USA early on in my career without her.

"Don't remind me. Paris just isn't the same without you." I can see her pout in the tone of her voice. "I'm calling because I miss you." She sniffs and my smile is melancholy, feeling the same way.

It's been nearly two years. She came for a few days after Henry was born and that's been it. Despite not seeing her in what feels like forever, we're close and talk at least once a week.

"Aaand, I've booked my flight to LA. I'm coming in two days." She's all squeals and giggles, and despite how tired I am, I find my inner cheerleader.

"That's amazing." My hands drum along the dashboard. "How long are you staying?"

She has promised to visit for months now, but that's easier said than done. Her career is booming, so scheduling has been tricky. This will be the third time she's booked a flight, but the last two times she had to postpone. I only hope this one sticks.

"I'll be there for two, maybe three weeks. Or maybe forever. I haven't decided yet." Her chuckle is forced since she's itching to make a move career wise or life wise but she's undecided. Before I can question her, she barrels on, "I'll text you my flight and hotel details."

She's welcome to stay with me, but I only have two bedrooms. While we've slept in the same bed countless times, she's also accustomed to a certain lifestyle that my modest bungalow can't provide.

"I'm so excited. If you stick around longer, maybe we can go house hunting together?"

"Ooh, you're still looking for a beach house?"

"More like wishing, but yeah. Oh, on the day you arrive, I have the awards ceremony so we'll definitely have to see each other the next day. Okay?"

"Hell yeah. And you can tell me all about the evening."

"For sure. I can't wait to see you."

"Me too, but something is...what's wrong?" Sasha's tone brooks no room for denial, but I'm at a loss.

"What do you mean?"

"I thought you'd be jumping around and screaming."

"Well, for starters, I'm in a car so that would make jumping difficult. And it's the end of a very long workday so my energy is low. But, babe, I am excited."

"Don't lie to me. I can hear something in your voice."

"What am I supposed to do with that? You're being vague and totally off base."

She huffs, not amused. "Daisy, tell me what's going on with you. You sound sad or confused...and before you say it's nothing, it's something. So. Tell. Me."

I blurt the first thing to come to mind. "I went on a date last week."

"A date? With who?" Sasha's voice rises, fully invested.

"He's a client. Well, he was a client. He just asked me out of the blue, catching me totally off guard. We'd just wrapped his shoot and I'd been paid..." I don't know why I feel the need to make it clear he was no longer a client at the time of the date, but it's important to me.

"Whatever, go on." Her predictable impatience brings a small smile to my face. "How was the date?"

"Fine. I mean, he was a nice enough guy, and we had an okay time. Truthfully, I don't think of him as anything more than a client and nice guy. And our dinner didn't change that. And then he texted me today asking me out again."

"And? Did you say no? Or are you going to give it another try?"

"I haven't responded, but it'll be a no."

"Is it the whole working together thing?"

"No, not that. I doubt we'll be working together anytime soon. I just don't want to. I'm not interested in him that way."

"Okay, so why do you sound so...so glum? It feels like you're not telling me everything. What are you leaving out?"

My hands grip the steering wheel, and I stare out into the darkness. Voicing my silly and sometimes illogical opinions out loud can be scary. "I haven't seen anyone since Costa."

"Oh God, please don't tell me this is about that man." Now she's irritated.

"No, not at all. I'm over him. I mean, you know I was never in love with him."

"True, but he's the father of your child. Worthless bastard that he is. Don't even get me started."

I chuckle and shake my head. The truth is Sasha would love nothing more than to rail on Costa. And she could easily kill an hour doing so. To say she doesn't like him would be an understatement.

"No, this has nothing to do with Costa. What I'm trying to say is, having Henry changed my perspective on almost everything, including men. Until this guy asked me out, I hadn't given the opposite sex any thought in years."

I press my lips together, holding the mention of Gray. I'm not being entirely truthful, because he's the only man I've thought about and at times, like more than a friend.

She releases a sharp, abrupt laugh. "I wish I could forget about men, but I love sex too much." We're both silent and I'm stuck in my head when she says, "Go on, darling."

"That's changed now." If I can tell anyone my deepest secrets and wildest fantasies, it's Sasha.

"What's changed?"

"Aren't you paying attention?" My tone is lighthearted even if my insides are growing heavier with each passing second.

All of what I'm sharing, saying out loud, isn't something I've even fully acknowledged to myself. It's a verbal mind-dump and I'm not sure if I'm ready.

"Daze, it's the ass-crack of the morning here, and I'm exhausted but tell it to me straight. I'm listening and I want to help."

"What I'm trying to say is I think I'm ready for more. I might actually...no, not might...I want a relationship with someone. And that's why I said yes to the date even if the guy held no interest. It was more out of exploration. You know, why not?"

"Of course, I get it. You had dinner or drinks and it was

fine, but you don't want to go out again. That's cool. Go out with someone else. It doesn't have to end with this one blah date."

"I know."

"So what's got you in knots? And before you tell me I'm crazy or it's nothing, don't bother."

The words strangle my tongue. I open and close my mouth, but nothing comes out. Why am I so scared to say it? What's the worst that can happen? She laughs at me. Tells me I'm crazy?

"Gray." My throat is near parched and it takes everything in me to say his name, holding my breath for her response.

"Gray! Grayson Bennett...ahhh, how is that fabulous man?"

Air whooshes from me on a laugh, relieved at the sound of her voice, filled with a smile and hearts in her eyes. Sasha met Gray once. Once. And fell immediately in love with him. One look at Henry in his arms and she said, "Snag that man before someone else does."

"He's...great. Amazing as always."

"Of course he is. And you've finally admitted your attraction to him. Hallelujah. I thought I'd be living at an old age home by the time you did." She cackles at my expense. "You have feelings for your best friend. This is what you're saying, right?"

I don't answer her. She's dragging this out like I did, and now I want the conversation to be over.

I haven't even mentioned his dinner invitation, which I still can't figure out if he meant it like dinner between friends —which we've done a million times before—or a date. My stomach is a bundle of nerves, and a strange queasiness teases its way up my throat.

"Daze, what's the problem?"

"I don't think it's new. My feelings. I think it's been growing over the months and I didn't realize it. And it's like things changed or something shifted in me when I was asked out on a date. And then, when I had to tell Gray...argh, I felt awful."

"Uh-huh."

"Now I feel awkward and I'm second-guessing myself when it comes to him. And I don't want that. We haven't talked in days."

"What? You haven't talked? That doesn't sound like him."

"No, we have talked, and we see each other nearly every day. He sees Henry every day."

No matter my schedule or his, he never fails to see my son. For instance, today, Henry was with Pansy at my place and Gray had dinner with them.

"Then what do you mean?"

"It's just...when we do talk, because we're so busy, it's short and to the point, scheduling around Henry, how was your day and stuff like that."

This is where my confusion with dinner comes in. It has been a while since we've had dinner together. And now my life is getting busier than ever, so picking a night for a meal together isn't strange. And could be so unlike a date.

"And...why am I dragging this out of you? Just say it. We'll both feel better once you do."

I snort out a laugh and put on my seat belt, needing to get

home and to have something else to occupy my troubled mind while I spill my guts.

"And I feel...a bit lost because usually our conversations are more than that, and I think I'm the one making it awkward."

Sasha doesn't fill the silence, and it's plain to see her passive-aggressive maneuver is designed to keep me talking. "Something happened last week, and I don't know if it means anything."

Still she says nothing, but I swear I hear her "Oh my God, Daisy, just tell me already" in the silence.

To torture her some more or maybe me, too, I say, "I won't bore you with all the details—"

"No, do because so far I'm only getting half a story and trying desperately not to jump through the phone line and choke you."

She's joking, but I want to throttle me too.

"There's a singer and she likes him—she's always liked him, and he's never shown any interest or anything. But last week, the day after my date, she was there and all over him. I wanted to rip her eyes out, and I've never felt that way before."

The words spill from me like water from a tap even as my brain is screaming "stop talking" and I can't help myself. "And I don't dislike her. She's a nice person, for the most part—"

"Okay, okay. I get it. She's encroaching on your man."

"But that's the thing, he isn't my man. He's my best friend and here I am, getting stupidly jealous, and as if that isn't bad enough, I also let him see that her crawling all over him bothered me. Then he did the strangest thing."

My thighs clench at the memory of his soft, firm lips pressing into the palm of my hand.

"What did he do?" Her tone sharpens, and I envision her eyes narrowing into slits and her mouth tightening as if ready to kill him or rip him a new one if I asked her to.

"Calm down, nothing like that." I hit the blinker to signal a right turn. "He reassured me that he isn't interested in India. In more ways than one."

And maybe that's what the dinner invitation was? A way to put me at ease.

"How'd he reassure you?"

"He asked me out to dinner, and before you get all excited, I don't think he was asking me out on a date. And then he just came out and told me he wasn't interested in her."

And he showed me in not so many words, but the simple, innocent kiss to my hand is for me and me alone. "In fact, he said as much by telling me I'm the only one he sees."

"Daisy! Oh my God! Oh my God! I think my ovaries exploded. He did ask you on a date. He's so into you. See, I told you so."

A strong, weird tugging on my heart causes my hand to press into my chest. "Gray's sweet...and sexy...and you already know that. And I'm not sure what it really means, and we haven't really talked since then."

"You need to fix that. Talk to him. Tonight."

"I can't tonight. I'm on my way home. Pansy's with Henry, waiting for me."

"Well, darling, you need to get in his face and talk to him. You have to find time for dinner and before I get there. I will not stand for you dragging this out like you did this conversation."

"What?" My voice rises at the thought.

"Do you want more with Gray? Or are you fine to continue as good friends?"

My heart spasms. "I-I don't want to lose him."

"You won't lose him, and you may not realize it but I'm pretty sure he's been taking cues from you. And while I don't know Gray as well as you do, I'm also willing to bet everything I own that he's already told you how he feels about you. You've just been blind to it."

I'm ready to protest when the moment in Pansy's hallway and then the night last week rushes at me, his words, his lips on my flesh. Shoot, she's right. Or at least, I hope she's right.

"What if we try this thing and it blows up in our faces?" I park my car outside my house. "He's like a father to Henry, and I don't want to ruin that."

"I understand, and I highly doubt his relationship with Henry is in jeopardy. They have a bond that no matter what, you wouldn't do anything to sever, so don't even go there. But let's play it out if you do nothing. What happens if things stay status quo? Then what? Gray goes out with this India woman. Or someone else. They grow close, move in together, fall in love."

Her game of *what if* throat punches me and I cough, sputtering for the words. "I'd kick myself and then I'd really want to rip her eyes out. I don't know if I could stand seeing them together..."

My mouth clamps shut, not willing to play out any more scenarios as nausea gathers in my stomach.

"And there's your answer. Make your move."

Sasha and I are always brutally honest with each other, and it's one of the things we love most about the other. She isn't saying anything I haven't already whispered to myself in the darkest hours of contemplation.

"I'm sending you my flight details, and I'll see you soon. When we see each other face-to-face, I want to hear all about the mind-bending sex you had with Gray. I love you, Daisy."

A burst of girlish laughter erupts from me, filling the car. "Love you, too, Sash."

10

GRAY
BARING MY SOUL

*T*he heady flavors of garlic and sesame waft through the air and my stomach growls as I walk through the door.

"Hey." Daisy pops her head around the corner, smiling, and it never gets old. Every time I see her, just being near her gets me in the heart. It's both thrilling and calming all at the same time.

"We're going to have that dinner you talked about. I hope you're hungry."

This isn't the dinner I had in mind. A fancy restaurant, candlelight, the two of us—that's more what I envisioned but this is still great. She doesn't get out that often. Neither of us do, and I wanted it to be special.

Well, we'll have both, but I don't want to scare her with that conversation right now.

"I'm starving." I pat my middle, happy to see her. "I'll help."

"I've got it." She slips back into the kitchen, and suddenly, I'm transfixed by the glimpse of her toned, sun-kissed legs.

My place is small, and her humming filters through to the washroom as I clean up. I'm rarely here in my one-bedroom Malibu beach home, usually only to sleep or change. And even though we're mostly at her place—it's bigger and easier with all of Henry's things there—Daisy has a key to my home. What's mine is hers.

"So you just decided to come and cook for me?" I saunter into the galley kitchen and she's at the stove, swaying her hips to the music in her head, long blonde waves swishing across her back.

"Yes, we haven't really spent any time together in days." She turns in tiny cut-off denim shorts and a sheer pink blouse. The outline of her black bra teases me. "Dinner sounded like a great idea."

"Awesome." An easy smile feathers across my face, and I scan the open concept room, with the kitchen spilling into what is both the dining room and living room. "Where's Henry?"

"He's, um, he's spending the night with Silas and Pansy." She averts her gaze, staring into the pot.

"Oh?" My brows rise.

I started my day with Henry, watching him for a few hours while Daisy worked and Pansy had class. It isn't unusual for him to be with her sister but it is for Daisy to have not brought him here.

Sometimes he stays over at Pansy's if she's got a deadline for work, but if that's the case now, why is she here, making me dinner?

"Did I forget you're on deadline or something? I mean, I can always watch him."

"No, no, nothing like that. I wanted the two of us to talk, have dinner like you mentioned, and I thought this would give us the chance." She stirs and lifts the fork toward me with a mound of fluffy basmati rice. "Taste. Does it need anything? Salt?"

"Hmmm." I chew, inhaling the spicy flavors of the sea and earth. "It's great. Stir fry shrimp?" I peer into the wok on the other burner. Plump coral shrimp simmer in a light sauce of onions, garlic, yellow and red tomatoes, zucchini, and corn.

"Uh-huh."

"Looks good." I lick my lips and she looks on, apprehension clouding her features.

"Why don't you settle in, get changed or whatever." She flits about picking up and putting down a dish towel. "Dinner will be ready in about ten minutes."

"Okay. Let me set the table. You want wine?"

"Sure." She nods, attention back on the stove, and I lean in to kiss her cheek, squeezing her waist.

Not long after, we sit to eat at a small table shoved against a wall of the room. She's lit a candle, and soft music filters through the speakers.

My place is a bachelor pad and not that well put together. Sparsely furnished with a mishmash of things, most people would hardly believe a famous musician lives here. I'm not one for décor and would rather spend my money on family or where I spend the majority of my time, and that isn't here.

Daisy loves it because the beach is in walking distance and my bedroom has a magnificent view of the Pacific

Ocean. I'd readily switch places with her so she and Henry could have their ocean. I own it outright, but it's too small for the both of them. Only one bedroom, one bathroom.

"This is delicious. Thanks, Daze." A forkful of rice, veggies, and shrimp goes into my mouth. The plate's almost empty as I devour the food, not realizing how hungry I was.

"You're welcome. The last week or so has been so busy, and it feels like we're in contact every day but it's about planning for Henry or just checking in with each other, and while the award dinner is in a couple of nights, I just thought..."

Her chin lowers as does her gaze and the fork to the plate. She fidgets, tapping out a rapid rhythm with her foot against the floor. She's nervous. Why?

"What?" My fingers entwine with hers, and I tighten my grip until she meets my eyes. "I feel the same way. It has been hectic, and the awards dinner doesn't count as time together. That night is going to be busy, and you'll be mingling and, in some ways, working."

"Oh, ugh, when you put it like that I don't want to go." She laughs. "Do you still want to be my plus one, knowing all that?"

"Absolutely." I put down my knife and fork. "Just so you know, as much as I love this meal"—with my elbow, I nudge the now empty plate away—"this isn't the kind of dinner I was talking about when I asked you out at Pansy's."

Eyes dazzling and confusion coloring her cheeks and wrinkling her brow, she cocks her head to one side. "What do you mean?"

"Daze, I did a shitty job of it, but I was asking you out on a date." Wow, I'm really doing this, telling her how I feel.

I won't stop and contemplate how this could ruin our friendship. What it will mean if she recoils at my confession, at how I've always wanted more with her.

The thought is paralyzing and while a massive risk, baring my soul after three years of family and friendship and possibly bringing a world of hurt and pain...I can't live my life like that.

Regrets are my demon. I have a lifetime of regrets for what I should have done in my childhood. For how my indecision, despite my age, caused irreparable damage and loss. I won't let Daisy and Henry be another regret. Even if it means destroying my heart.

"You were?" She straightens but doesn't pull away, and I take the moment to gather every ounce of courage within me.

"Yes. You said you were ready to date." My pulse quickens. "And I didn't want to lose my chance."

"Your chance?" She smiles tentatively, tongue darting out to lick at her ripe, rosy lips.

I want to nibble on her smile, and my fingers ache to touch her flaxen tresses. Pushing back from the table, I slide my chair nearer to her, closing the distance, and our knees are now touching.

Swallowing, I hold her gaze steady with mine. "Yes. I don't want to freak you out—"

"You won't." The words tumble from her mouth on a breathy exhale, and it's like she's connected with me more so than at any other time this evening.

I can't explain it, but there's a sense she already knows

what I'm about to confess. In fact, she may *want* me to say it, to declare my true feelings.

"Daisy, I can't remember a time when you weren't a big part of my life." There's no going back now and she sucks in a ragged breath. "It's always been you. You became my best friend overnight and your son...the first time I laid eyes on him—he stole my heart. I swear." A shaky hand rakes through my mess of hair. "It sounds corny but it's true. And every day with the both of you is a gift. It's all I've ever wanted. You're my family."

Something shifts in her gaze, a flash that causes her shoulders to deflate, and I've lost her. That connection is gone and when she speaks, the sensation of loss doubles.

"Oh." Just one word but it carries so much meaning. A weighty disappointment.

What was it? My use of friendship? Or family? I have the distinct impression she is taking something completely different from what I've said.

"No, I don't think you get it. Yes, you're my best friend and family, but you've always felt like more to me. More than platonic, more than...you're everything to me. Do you under-stand what I mean?"

She nods, flushes, and then her head switches to shaking side to side as she releases a jagged puff of air.

"I'm sorry, I'm not trying to be clueless, I just don't want to get this wrong." Trembling, her wobbly smile twists my stomach into knots. "You're important to me too, and I... I've..."

Ending our misery, I cup the sides of her face and draw mine closer to hers. Sugar and spice invade my senses.

Delicious.

Her scent isn't easy to describe. Fresh, feminine, rich...
and sultry.

My smile spreads with every intake of breath, her scent
filling all of me. "Words are clearly failing me, both of us, so
let's try this."

I brush my lips softly against her sweet, warm mouth,
easing her into a kiss. I can't even begin to remember how
many times I imagined tasting her.

Daisy shivers, slowly licking my bottom lip until I open
for her. She grabs the back of my neck, and goosebumps
spread down my spine. Our tongues tangle.

She tastes like Shangri-la. A never-never land of utter
perfection and bliss.

Still too far apart, she squeals as I hoist her onto my lap
and her silky thighs straddle me. Hands firmly on her waist,
my thumbs languidly sweep in an arcing motion across her
lower abdomen, not daring to roam any farther. I want to,
damn I do, but if I venture any more than this, I'll lose
control.

Our mouths plunder and ravage, countless kisses, over
and over again, and I can't say how long we sit like that. Hot
and frantic, slow and sweet, we are tongues and teeth and
stealing...everything—our breaths, moans, heartbeats, all
of it.

Finally, I pull back, panting, struggling not to cave to the
urge to keep going. Her kisses blow my mind, my head spins,
and my need for her intensifies. I press my forehead against
hers, catching my breath.

"Gray." Soft hands rest on my cheeks, thumbs gliding over my stubble. "Why did you stop?"

The confusion and plea to her tone and the push and roll of her hips, pressing her core into my groin, does wild things to my heartbeat, stopping and starting all in the same second.

Holy sweet mother. My toes curl.

She tugs on my face, trying to recapture my mouth, and I force myself to push away, needing the space to think straight.

Hands on her hips, I lift her off me and only let go once I'm certain she's steady on her feet. She watches my every move, bewildered and irked.

"What are we doing?" Frustration carries her voice and I meet her heated stare.

"What do you think we're doing?" I ask, not to be difficult but needing to hear her say the words.

"We're finally admitting our feelings for each other." Even as she hits the nail on the head, there's a dissatisfaction to her countenance.

"Yes. I want us to...argh, date sounds wrong but I want us to explore more of a relationship. We already have the friendship, shared lives, our love of Henry..."

"I want that too." Cautiously, she steps toward me as if she doesn't want to scare me off. I was the one to back away but not because of doubts. Never.

She pulls at my wrist, and I relent, edging closer, needing her as much as she needs me. Her hands slide around the nape of my neck, and a rush of blood rages through my body.

Her mouth covers mine and this time, I'm the one to slip

my tongue between her sugary lips, sliding across her teeth. Tasting her is my new favorite thing.

Daisy whimpers into my mouth, and her sound slams into my chest and tightens my balls. Her fingernails dig into my neck, piercing the flesh, and the mix of pleasure and pain is the sweetest perfection.

"Hey." My lips rip from hers and she groans, exasperated. "We've got plenty of time. If we keep going, I won't be able to stop."

"That's the point. I don't want you to stop. I want you, Gray."

I grunt as every word out of her mouth brings a hedonistic delight and sheer agony. "Daze, I'm trying to do this right. We should take this slow."

Burying her head into my neck, she gives me a quick kiss and steps back. "Yes, you're right. Okay. So now what?" She prances around the small room, wrapping her arms around her middle like she doesn't know what to do with them.

"We could watch something." I glance at the loveseat, and images of Daisy and me entangled in each other flicker through my mind. Nope, bad idea. I won't be able to keep my hands to myself. "Or we could go for a walk."

As if reading my mind, she nods vigorously. "Yes, a walk sounds good."

We take the back door that leads onto the beach, and Daisy stops me on the step. The outdoor light shines down on us so we can see each other's faces.

"Gray, what if this changes everything?" Lowering her eyes, the tips of her lashes, an almost white-blonde, fan the crest of her cheeks.

"It will." I'm solemn but confident in my tone.

"But what if—" She stops talking when I press my thumb into her bottom lip and her chest heaves.

"I believe in us. We're already great together. Just think about the new ways we get to learn about each other. Deepen our relationship." I raise a brow and offer a lopsided grin in hopes of lessening her fears.

She lets out an infectious laugh, causing me to chuckle as the hint of tightness loosens in my chest.

"I can't wait." One quick kiss and she takes my hand, pulling me onto the sand toward the water's edge.

The night is cool, and the hypnotic sound of the waves lulls us into a comfortable silence as we walk hand in hand under the milky glow of the half moon.

"India asked me to play drums on her new album." It comes out as a blurt more than a statement.

I wanted to tell Daisy sooner, but I wasn't sure which way I was leaning. I'm still not decided, and time is running out. India needs an answer tomorrow.

"Really?" At first, she's silent and I wonder if she's concerned about India or if it's more. Then she steps in front of me, releasing my hand to bring hers to my face. "Gray, this is great. You love the drums, and it's been too long since you've really played."

Her fingers glide across my cheekbones, and her touch lights me on fire. I stifle a groan, shifting uncomfortably as my jeans tighten.

"Yeah, I'm honored she asked me. I mean, the songs are brilliant, and the album's going to do well, but I've got SG Productions and you and Henry to think about."

"What are you talking about? Working on the album is for SG; I don't get the problem there. And as for Henry and me, we won't hold you back."

"Daze, if we're recording an album, you know what that's like. The days are long, and I won't have the flexibility I have now to watch Henry."

"It's okay. I'll figure something out." She worries her bottom lip. "You know what this means, right?"

"What?"

"No more excuses, I have to find a nanny." She casts a far-off glance out at sea, maybe putting together the list of things she has to do to make that happen.

"Let me do that..." I slide an arm around her waist, bringing her into my chest. "I kind of already got started."

"Seriously?" She tilts her head to look up at me, wrinkling her brow.

"Yeah, I called an agency a few days ago. They're sending candidates we can choose from to interview."

"Gray, this is my problem. You shouldn't have done this."

"Well, I have." I ignore the reproach in her tone. "Only to help."

"I know...and thank you, but next time talk to me first. I keep meaning to do it and somehow it gets pushed to the side. It's like I'm deliberately putting it off."

Her vulnerability slips past her reproving veneer, giving me an explanation for her disappointed reaction.

"Because it'll change what your days look like with Henry but not by much. You won't see him less." I rest my chin on the top of her head, and she burrows deeper into my embrace.

"I guess you're right. You should do the album. When would you start?" Her voice is soft and definitive.

"Two days."

"And you haven't said anything to India yet?"

"Well, I did tell her I had a few people willing to do it if I decided not to. I'll tell her tomorrow."

"Good." She squeezes my hand. "And I'll see if Lucia can pitch in and help with Henry just for the next little bit."

"Hey, even if I'm recording, I want to see him every day. And you. I'll make that clear to India before I agree to anything."

"You better," she teases, spinning in my arms to face me.

"What are you doing tomorrow night?"

"I'm editing all day so it's my schedule to make. Why?"

"Go to dinner with me?" Guilt gnaws at me when I think of Henry. "I want to take you out, but since Henry isn't here now, we could have dinner with him and then hang out once he's asleep."

The gleam of the pale moon reveals a sexy grin, playing on her lips. "No way. I'm with Henry for most of the day tomorrow, and you're still seeing him for a few hours in the morning, right?" I nod and she curls her fingers around my waist. "So yes, I want to go to dinner with you. Is this a date-date?"

Her gaze is soft and hazy, hopeful, and I press my lips to hers. "You bet it is."

11

DAISY
OVERWHELMS AND TERRIFIES ME

We stand behind a beautiful couple, Hollywood A-listers, waiting to be seated. We're having dinner at Catch LA, an acclaimed rooftop restaurant in West Hollywood, frequented by celebrities.

"Wow, this place is supposed to be amazing," I whisper, leaning into him.

"We both love seafood, so I figured, let's check it out." His comment is so casual, as if he made reservations at Red Lobster, that I giggle.

Even without what promises to be a spectacular meal, the open-air dining room offers breathtaking views of downtown Los Angeles and the Hollywood Hills.

Gray angles his head and kisses me, lips firm and confident. He is minty fresh like his favorite gum and masculine in ways I can't explain. What's meant to be a quick, chaste kiss turns into something more when he parts his lips, and without a moment's hesitation, I slide my tongue into his mouth.

The taste of him overwhelms and terrifies me. It's too easy to get lost in him, and no kiss has ever been as good. Gray is an excellent kisser.

Last night, when we'd kissed for the first time, I never wanted it to stop. And now, I feel much the same way, turning into his body without any regard for where we are.

We're no sooner chest to chest than he groans, leaning his forehead against mine. "Behave yourself." His voice is a low, pained rumble.

A smile blitzes my mouth, and I love how I affect him as much as he does me. I'm lit up from the inside at our strong, fiery connection.

"I could kiss you all night."

"Daze." He grabs me by the waist, hauling my body hard against his, and his head bends to nip at the column of my neck. "You're killing me."

Smashing my lips together, I suffocate a squeal and lower my head, suddenly conscious of the petite hostess, looking on with a neutral expression. She doesn't give away a thing, whether amused or appalled with our public display of affection.

My date doesn't miss a beat, and before I know it, we're following the woman through the intimate, yet relaxed candlelit dining room. She deposits us at a table for two in one of the many nooks and crannies scattered throughout the room. Perfect for privacy and romance.

The table settings are across from each other, but Gray

unceremoniously picks up his silverware and puts it next to mine before lifting his chair to do the same.

"There's no way I'm sitting across the table from you."

Again, I find myself giggling like a lovesick teenager and take my seat beside him. His hand rests lightly on my knee and I'm home. His touch is natural and right.

"Yes, this is much better." I stare at his lush lips and want to kiss him again. It's my new favorite pastime and I feel like I *am* a lovesick teenager.

Someone clears their throat and my gaze snaps to our server, a young man standing at the edge of the table. He smiles, takes our drink order and leaves us to look at the menu.

At first, I'm silent, eyes glossing over the array of delicious choices to eat. When Gray picked me up tonight, I nearly swallowed my tongue.

I mean, he's gorgeous and definitely a rock star with the longer hair on top, constantly tousled and flopping onto his forehead, tall, lean, and tattoos everywhere. He usually completes the look with his timeless attire of jeans and a T-shirt.

His wardrobe is basic yet he's devastatingly sexy. His ass is a thing to drool over. Women have literally been brought to screaming tears. No one wears jeans like Gray.

Tonight, I get a different version of him. He's wearing a Tom Ford black suit, without the jacket. Instead, he's in a waistcoat, or like us common people would say, a vest, and the sleeves of his white button-down shirt are rolled up his forearms.

I've seen Gray dressed up before, but because we're now

dating, it's like I have permission to fawn over all the things about him I'd forced myself not to notice when we were in the friend zone.

He stood at my door, and I was speechless yet also filled with a happiness I'd only ever felt with my son. And now, I'm *with* him, tolerating sneaky glances from strangers at other tables, barely able to contain my joy.

"Do you think it's weird that this doesn't feel weird?" I squeeze his hand, almost as if to make sure he's real.

He glances up from the menu, and under the table, one callused finger rubs lazily along the inside of my knee. Suddenly, I'm on fire.

"You mean the date?"

"Yes, also…all of it. You and me."

"What does it feel like to you?" He's intrigued, blue eyes never straying from me while he closes the menu.

"Perfect," I blurt and at first, his eyes smolder. "It feels right. Comfortable." But it's a poor choice of words as his flame fizzles.

He frowns. "Oh, great, so boring."

"Oh, God, no. I'm excited." My heart is a racehorse, thundering in my chest and ears. "I just mean, I don't have the questions or uncertainty that come with a first date. Usually, it's nerve-wracking with so many unknowns. Things can seriously bomb." My stomach backflips at his warm chuckle. "But with you, I know it won't."

"Oh yeah?" One side of his mouth kicks up, eyes twinkling. "And you've been on many first dates?"

Arching a brow, I shake my head and smirk. "Not really. I've maybe had half a dozen. In high school, I had two boyfriends, and once I went to Europe, there were a few first dates but nothing serious. I just know they aren't comfortable, in a good way, like this," I rush to add. "I don't like first dates. What about you? Have you had many?" No sooner do I ask than I regret it.

Jealousy sinks its claw into me at the thought of Gray with another woman. I'm not naïve enough to think his Trojan days were tame. All the guys in the band were sought after, and I'm sure he's had his share of groupies.

But we're talking first dates, not random, casual hookups. Ugh. Okay, maybe this wasn't a good topic. Nothing about Gray and other women is comfortable.

"Nah, I didn't really date. I had one girlfriend in high school for two years and then we parted ways when we graduated. And when I was with Trojan, there really wasn't a chance to have any dates." He shifts awkwardly in his chair.

I wonder if he's thinking what I am. A model and a rock star—we both led what some might think are self-indulgent and excessive lifestyles...and it can be if you let it take hold.

Did he give in to all of that—sex, drugs, and who knows what else? I could ask. He'd tell me the truth. Although does it really matter? I'm not a virgin nor a saint, and I wasn't one before modeling.

He cuts through my thoughts. "You said you know we won't crash and burn. How can you be so sure?"

Before I can answer, our server returns to take our order. I've barely looked at the menu, and I ask Gray to choose for me. He knows what I like.

Once alone, he turns to me. "I want you to answer my question. How are you so sure our date isn't going to tank?"

"Because I already know everything about you that matters. Dating is a way to get to know someone. To see if there's something beyond a physical attraction, if you're lucky enough to even start with that. You know, to see if you click. That isn't us."

A smile buds on his closed mouth, and I can't tell if he's interested in what I'm saying or amused or maybe both.

"Are you making fun of me?" I pull back to get a better look at him.

"No. Never. I feel the same way. Nothing about tonight feels weird or unsure but it's also...what did you say? Exciting." He lightly pecks my cheek.

This feels good and while I don't want to ruin the mood, my curiosity gets the better of me. "You know I don't need this, right?"

"Need what?" Confusion swims in his eyes.

"The fancy restaurant. Dates. I love being with you no matter what we're doing."

"Yeah, I feel the same way, but who doesn't need a night out? I love spending time with you and Henry, but this is for us. And I didn't want this shift in our relationship to just be more of the same."

"Oh, it isn't going to be." I grin and my hand slides under the table to squeeze his hard thigh, taking a liberty I never had before—to touch him whenever I want to.

Now that we're dating, he's mine. And I'm bombarded with sensations and tingles just thinking about our kisses and our touches and the way his muscled thigh heats my palm.

His lips part, eyes darkening, and the air stops moving in

my lungs. I can't seem to bring myself to remove my hand or go any farther. Not that I should be groping him—we're in a public place for crying out loud.

He heaves out a long, ragged breath and closes his eyes for a blink. "I'm going to an early grave because of you."

"Don't say that." I start to breathe again as my hand, with a mind of its own, squeezes his toned leg once more before sliding down to his knee and letting go.

"It's true. Your hands on me..." He leans in close, wrapping an arm around my shoulders, and his warm lips brush the shell of my ear. "Fuck, I want you so badly. When you touch me...the fragile control I'm trying to keep a hold of... Daze, I'm about to snap."

"And that's what I mean." I turn my head anda our lips are now a breath apart. "Even without this amazing dinner, we're discovering each other in new and just as exciting ways."

He swallows thickly and I prepare for a kiss, the one I so desperately need. But sadly, once again, we're interrupted by our server with our appetizers. I jolt away from Gray, hands in my lap as I sit up straight and force a casual, *I'm not doing anything inappropriate* smile.

For most of the meal, we stay close but manage to keep our hands to ourselves. We share the king crab tempura while sipping on champagne, and for our entrees, Gray has the seared yellowfin tuna with a beer. I have the grilled salmon, and we share the parmesan truffle fries—to die for.

"Did you tell India you'll play for her album?" I place the last of the fries in front of him.

"Yeah." He shoves a golden potato into his mouth.

"And? Was she happy? When do you start?" I ramble and my nerves are sparking, still a little troubled by the sexy songstress.

"We start recording tomorrow, and yes, she was happy. So was Silas."

"That's great." I nibble on my lip, playing with the edge of my napkin, trying not to think about all those hours he'll be with India.

I trust Gray, that's not my concern. I don't trust her, and I wouldn't put it past her to make an even bolder move now that she'll have him for hours on end.

"Hey." His warm hand rests on top of mine and I lift my gaze to meet his. "This is strictly business, always has been, and I'll make sure she understands that. I've been more than easygoing where India's concerned but I'm not interested."

"I know." And I do, but it's a relief to hear him say the words yet I don't leave well enough alone. "But you haven't exactly stopped her from groping you."

He raises a brow and drops the French fry back onto the plate. "India loves to make a scene, and telling her to back off would definitely bring one. That's why I haven't bothered until now."

"Now?" I cock my head to one side, hands clammy in anticipation.

"Yeah, before, I was single, and she didn't do anything beyond touching in friendly ways to let me know she was interested. She didn't exactly grope me." His smile is wry and while I could argue the point, but it isn't worth it. I want to hear what he has to say more. "If she had taken it too far, I would have said something. I didn't want the drama. And now I will make it clear to her that I'm with you, and I'm pretty sure my girl doesn't want another woman making any moves on me."

I don't miss the hint of a question to his tone, not wanting to assume I'm territorial or give a damn. Damn, I do.

"You got that right." I snatch the fry from his plate and pop it into my mouth.

I'm full, and eating the last bit of potato is difficult, but I'm making it known that he's mine as are his fries. It's silly, but also my way of lightening the mood. He laughs, smiling as he brings my greasy fingers to his lips to lick them clean.

My insides combust, toes curling as his tongue strokes and sucks on my fingers. I quiver with need, my core pulses, and I'm hungry, ravenous for this man.

Fortunately, the server comes to take away our plates, and I excuse myself to the restroom where I run cool water on my wrists.

12

DAISY

THIS FEELS HOLY

*D*inner is divine, and we pass on dessert. I'm sinfully full by the time we leave at well after ten o'clock. Henry's sleeping at Silas and Pansy's again so we don't have to end our date here, and I wonder what Gray has in mind.

His car pulls up in front of my house, and I shift in the seat to face him. "You going to come in?"

"I shouldn't." His hand grips the gearshift so tightly, his skin whitens.

"What if I said I want you to come in?" I place my hand on top of his and slowly, I pry his fingers loose, one at a time.

He laughs and with the now relaxed hand, he gently pushes my hair off my face. "I meant it when I said we should take things slow. If I come in..."

"And what if I don't want to go slow?" I can't believe I'm whining, but it doesn't stop me from leaning into him.

My mouth covers his, hard and fast, and I deliberately pull away before he can deepen the kiss. If he feels remotely like I do, a quick peck isn't enough. It's a match to gasoline. He'll burn with a want for more. I want more.

I hop out of his car, sauntering to my house, hot and aching in places I've neglected for far too long. I don't need to check if he's behind me. The heat of him, his fiery need, is at my back as I unlock the front door.

He follows me in, shutting the door behind him, and like a tornado, he grasps my hips, twirling me clear off the floor. My head spins and heart thumps in my throat while he carries me through the dark house toward my bedroom.

Yes. Has he finally let go of his silly notion of slow? Is he finally giving in to our mutual desire?

He tosses me onto the bed, and shocked, I release a yelp and a laugh, not pausing once my backside hits the mattress. I scramble up to the side lamp and turn it on.

The dark is nice, but I want to see him. I need to see him. Unknowingly, I've wanted this for so long, this man, and now I don't want to miss a thing. I want to see it all. All of him.

Tugging on my ankle, he pulls me down the bed and I give in to him, dropping my back onto the bed so I'm now sprawled out for him. The mattress shifts with his weight and Gray's now kneeling above me as an exciting thrill shoots through me.

Every inch of me aches for him, and while he's so close, he also feels too far away.

His beautiful eyes smolder as they skate over me. "Daisy, I told myself we'd take this slow."

"Fuck slow," I blurt out on a saucy grin, and he grunts a laugh, eyes widening.

"Why Ms. Dobson, you shock me." His teasing tone does wicked, twisty things to me and I rub my legs together, fruitlessly trying to satiate my need. "I might just have to do something about that filthy mouth of yours."

"I think you should." It isn't a taunt but more a plea because just one look from him sets me on fire.

One hand curls around the back of my neck, lifting my head to bring my mouth to his, and the other caresses my breast through the material of my dress. At his touch, my nipples harden and he makes a satisfied sound, but it isn't enough for me.

I whimper, thrusting my chest into his palm, and his lips fasten onto my neck, tongue darting out for a teasing lick. Then he sucks hard, but it doesn't hurt—not much anyway —and it's more pleasure than pain. Delicious pleasure ziplining straight to my core.

My hips buck off the bed, and he releases a deep throaty moan, catching my bottom lip between his teeth. His fingers grab fistfuls of my hair, knuckles kissing my skull, and his hot mouth scorches a path along my jaw and chin.

Together, we grapple to remove his vest and shirt and my dress and bra without pulling away from each other. Now on my knees, only in panties, my hands glide over his defined chest, broad shoulders, and around his neck.

My breasts press into the heat of him, his hard lines and unyielding muscle. My nipples are pointy peaks, sensitive and blazing, and my fingers tangle in the ends of his hair.

Fingers hooking into the sides of my panties, he drags them down my legs, and I'm completely naked, bared to him. He pulls away to gently place my back flat on the bed.

Then he drops down onto his elbows and forearms, sliding onto his stomach like some kind of military maneuver. The lower half of his body hangs off the bed, and opening my legs, he's face to face with my sex.

Jesus, Mary, and Joseph.

I'm not a religious person, but this feels holy. Prayer feels like something I should do. I fist the sheet, suddenly conscious of how exposed I am to him, truly bared. But I don't want to shy away.

"Everything about you is beautiful." His voice is husky and reverent and my girly bits clench with arousal.

Blond hair falls forward, hiding his face from me, and I need to see all of him. I push onto my elbows and slide my gaze down my body to where he is, between my legs.

A hand reaches for him, fingers threading into his hair as I push the locks away from his face. He stares at me, eyes intent and blazing, before he breaks the connection to dip down to my core.

"So fucking pretty. Your pussy is so pretty." A hand cups my sex, and the press of his fingers sends a hot flood of arousal through me when he runs his fingers through my cleft. "I want a taste. Do you know how long I've wanted to taste you?"

All I can do is whimper approval, or at least I hope that's how he understands it. I want that too—his mouth on me, tasting me.

My legs are aquiver as he kisses his way up the inside, all

the way up from my knees. Up and up, first one leg and then the other. His warm, firm lips and wet tongue pave a path along my inner thighs.

He presses his face against my mound, inhaling my arousal and kissing my sensitive flesh once. I flush from the inside out, and everything within me short-circuits. Mouth molding to the lips between my legs, the tip of his tongue drags through my folds.

Every single part of my being narrows to that single sensation. His mouth and tongue on me. Nothing else registers or matters. Nothing exists but this right here, Gray and me, in this room.

His lips suck on my clit, and one finger pumps slowly and purposefully into my body. It's glorious and not nearly enough. Then two fingers slide in and out of me, and the need for him, for more, surges within me like a tsunami.

My fingers scrape along his scalp, knotting in his hair, and he releases an amused chuckle. I'm not shy about what I want.

With my thighs clamped on either side of his head, my hands hold him to me. He sucks on me, hooking his fingers at that one spot inside me, the one that reduces me to a bundle of nerves, sparking and tingling with every stroke of his tongue and kiss of his lips.

I writhe as the warmth of his breath sends blissful goosebumps skittering along my spine, and he wraps his hands around my thighs, holding me to him as his fingers gently press into my flesh.

His lips never leave my sex and he's full-on kissing me there with mouth, tongue, and teeth, and I'm a mess. Pressure mounts, churning and coiling within me, and I close my eyes, not wanting to look away but unable to keep them open.

My body is tight, every molecule primed, and then it happens. It's the harmless sweep of his hair and the graze of his stubble against me—both at the same time as he eats me out like this is his only reason for living.

Pleasure gallops through me, and I come with his name a scream on my lips. Behind closed eyes, everything is bright and sparkling like a starburst, and my body trembles, breathing choppy.

Slowly, I come down, tremors and convulsions waning, and all the while, Gray doesn't stop until my body lets go, limbs loose, my hold on him slackened.

He crawls up the bed, stopping at my head where he drops down beside me, planting a kiss on my damp cheek. "You're the sweetest thing I've ever tasted."

"God, Gray, that was..." My voice is a low, lazy rasp, and I turn to face him, blinking until he comes into focus.

A strong hand smooths over my hip, settling there, and his warm touch is sublime. These feelings between us are undeniable, more than just physical, and I wonder at how we were able to suppress them for so long.

I lick at my lips and glide my hand over his chest, traveling toward his belt buckle. I'm spurred on by the impressive bulge in his pants, and my appetite isn't satiated.

He grabs my hand, entwining our fingers, and leans in to kiss me, groaning as the tips of our tongues tangle. I taste myself on him and if possible, I'm more turned on, needier and hungrier for him than just a second ago.

I can't explain it but my taste on him is as much a claiming, me of him, as anything else, and I'm flying high, thrilled at the thought.

"Soon, but not tonight." He smiles, kissing at the lines that I'm sure wrinkle the tiny space between my eyebrows.

"Gray." His name is a whine, and I wince internally, not liking how impatient I sound.

"Daisy," he mimics me, but it's warm and teasing.

I watch as he quickly removes his pants, chucking them onto the floor before lying back down to face me. This time, he brings the covers up to our waists.

Overcome with emotion, a need for him to understand my desire for him is more than lust, I mesh our fingers together again.

"You're my best friend, like a father to my son, and I want you to be my lover." I hold my breath, heart pounding.

"I want that too. All of you. Everything." He pulls me to him, lightly kissing my forehead before he rolls me until my back is to his front and we are spooning. "And soon, Daze. Soon." He gently kisses the back of my neck. "Sleep now."

I sink into him, and his hold tightens. The scent of Gray, the feel of him, warm and strong, are the last things I remember.

When I wake in the morning, he's gone. He had an early start at the studio and a long day ahead, and when I make it to the kitchen, there's coffee warming and oatmeal for me. On the counter, Gray's left a note for me in blue crayon.

Daisy,

Last night was everything.

You're everything.

I can't wait to see you later.

xo, Gray

I tuck the note into my pocket and spoon out a bowl of oatmeal and sprinkle nuts and berries on top, all the while smiling. So full, so happy, I'm not quite sure how I'll keep grounded today. I feel like I'm floating on air.

Work...that's what I'll do. It's one sure way to keep me focused. I pull up emails on my phone and think about the day of editing ahead of me. I have a lot to get done before Pansy brings Henry home at four.

And the day won't be over then. Tonight is the awards dinner, and my sister will have my son for another night. Maybe tonight, Gray and I will continue what he started last night.

There are so many unread emails, but one subject line grabs my attention. It reads: **We need to talk. Today.** I click on the bolded text and almost choke on my breath.

It's Costa, Henry's father. The email was sent late last night. He's in LA and doesn't say much more than that he wants to see me today, concerning Henry. No...correction, he *will* see me today at my house in two hours.

The hairs on the back of my neck prickle as the oatmeal makes its way back up my throat. This day was always a possibility when we parted ways. Yet I can hardly believe it's here.

At the time that I became pregnant, I was one of the most sought-after fashion models on the runway. In fact, the ink hadn't even dried on a deal I'd just signed to be the face of a well-known luxury fashion house.

Costa was also a model, successful in his own right, and

my boyfriend, if that's even accurate. We weren't a couple in every sense of the word, but we were together when possible.

Whenever our schedules synced, meaning we were in the same city, we were a couple. I can't speak for his fidelity, but I had been faithful. Costa was the only man I'd slept with for nearly two years.

The last time I saw him was a five-day stretch in Paris, where we spent nearly all of the time together. One night we'd argued, and he'd stormed out. Then we went back to work and separate lives.

Everything changed once the nausea started. I found out I was pregnant, and I was a mess. But even scared, not once did I consider any other option than having the baby. I loved modeling, but I also felt adrift and lonely. A baby felt right.

Of course, with a child on the way, my future career was questionable. If I were to model once more, it would mean jet-setting all over the world, and how would I do that as a single parent?

And I had to tell Costa. I had no illusions we'd get married and be a family. If he wanted to be part of the baby's life, then maybe we could make it work and I could continue to model.

But that wasn't meant to be.

When I told him about the baby, I might as well have told him I had the common cold—no big deal and nothing to do with him.

And to add insult to injury, he had the audacity to claim the baby wasn't his. Bastard.

We haven't spoken since that phone call, and while a paternity test did cross my mind, what was the point? Costa wanted nothing to do with the child, and I knew without a doubt he was Henry's father.

All the while, in the back of my mind, a small part of me held my breath, wondering if one day he might regret his decision. Come claim his son. Is that what this is about in some roundabout, twisted way?

13

DAISY
SPOUTING LIES

I stare at my phone, wanting to talk to someone about this but not sure who I can call. Gray isn't available. He's recording, and while I could interrupt him if really necessary, this isn't an emergency.

Pansy is also out of the question. She has Henry, and if I call her, she'll want to come over, and I don't want Costa and Henry in the same room. At least, not yet—not until I've heard what Costa wants.

Then there's Sasha, but she's somewhere over the Atlantic or the eastern seaboard on a flight to LA. Her last text to me was at four this morning when she boarded the plane.

I'm on my own. That's okay. I can do this.

While I wait, I attempt to edit my last shoot and accept the delivery of my evening gown for tonight's award dinner.

Until the delivery guy showed up at my door, the awards ceremony had slipped my mind. Not in the frame of mind to think about tonight, I hang the garment bag in my closet and send a quick text to Gray. I doubt he's forgotten about tonight, but I send it figuring it's better to be safe than sorry.

When all is said and done, I barely make a dent in my workload. My head isn't in the game, and I will have to start from scratch when I'm in a better headspace.

The doorbell rings and with it, my stomach plummets to my toes. Several deep breaths later and on shaky legs, I open the door to Henry's father.

Despite our differences and my lackluster feelings for him, which are likely mutual, Costa beams at me. His white teeth are blinding and yet his smile doesn't quite reach his eyes. It's forced.

He may be nervous—I sure am—but he hasn't changed a bit. Jet black hair, olive complexion, dark eyes, chiseled jaw, full lips and muscles. Yes, definitely a model.

"Daisy." He holds out his arms, stepping closer to me, and his familiar, Davidoff cologne hits me like a speeding train, ripping down memory lane.

All the time we were together, how we met, the way things ended—it all comes at me way too fast to digest or appreciate yet definitely bound to make me feel sick.

His hands cup my elbows, and he kisses my cheeks three times, stepping back to draw his gaze over my face. "As beautiful as ever. I always said you were like sunshine."

There was a time when I would bask in such a compliment, and now, I strain to muster a smile, stepping back from his grasp.

"Costa, come in." I lead the way into my house, nerves battling it out in the pit of my stomach. "To say I was shocked to get your email is an understatement, and you hardly gave me any notice nor did you let me know how to reach you. What if I'd been out of town? Or working on location?"

I'm not starting our conversation off on the best foot, but I'm also pissed. He's a selfish prick and wanted nothing to do with our son. And suddenly, when he deems the time is right, he thinks he can waltz into Henry's life and play daddy?

"I know. I'm sorry to drop in on you like this. My trip was very last minute. I came in late last night and I'm not staying long."

"What do you want?" My arms fold over my chest, and he shoves his hands into the pockets of his crisp, white linen pants.

"I'm not really sure how to say this." His uncertainty softens a bit of my ire, and I smile despite myself.

Something about the tension in his tone and rigid lines of his frame remind me of how my conversation with Gray started the other night. At first, we were both anxious and that turned out okay. Maybe this conversation will too?

"I'm not sure how much you know about my life now." He motions to the couch as if seeking permission to sit, and I nod.

"Costa, contrary to what you might think, I haven't kept up with your life. We broke up and went our separate ways."

He pauses in crossing one leg over the other at the sharp edge of my tone. It isn't intentional, but I don't like the implication that I'm waiting for him or stalking him for crying out loud.

"Sorry, I'm not doing this right. Look, Daisy, there's no easy way to say this. I got married a year ago."

I'm not sure if he's expecting me to be upset or shocked or indifferent. The timing is curious considering that when I got pregnant, he swore he'd never settle down.

Not that we should have gotten married. We weren't a good match in the long run and how things turned out is proof of that. He made a point of letting me know a baby would hamper or more likely ruin his lifestyle.

"Congratulations." My tone is neutral.

"I married my long-time girlfriend." Now this gets a reaction out of me as I open my mouth and he holds up a hand. "And before you say anything. Yes. She's from Athens and we've been together since high school."

"High school...but you were with Zelda when I first met you and then...me."

"I wasn't exactly faithful to her, but I was honest." He raises his chin as if proud.

I scoff, rolling my eyes. He wants a medal for telling his girlfriend when he couldn't keep his dick in his pants. Oh, please. What did I ever see in this man?

"Costa, I don't care about your marriage, but you weren't honest with me. And that's in the past, so what's your point?"

He nods, looking somewhat sheepish. "We've been trying for a year to get pregnant."

My stomach churns with remorse. He now wants a child but rejected the news of Henry not even three years ago. I'm hurt, not for me, but for my son. He's a wonderful little boy and it truly is Costa's loss.

"Okay." I shrug, not understanding why he's telling me

this unless he wants to make sure I'm not pining for him or have any plans to dump Henry on him.

I am seriously stumped as to why he's here, and I'm losing my patience. To think my stomach was in knots all morning and for what? This garbage.

"We recently found out that I am the problem." He avoids my gaze.

"Problem?" I run my fingers through my hair, from the top of my head to the base of my skull, grabbing at the back of my neck, frustrated and confused.

"Yes. I'm sterile." He looks over my shoulder, still unable to look at me.

"Okay. And what does this have to do with me?" Bile rushes up my throat, preventing the suggestion that he might want Henry now that he'll never father another child.

"You're not understanding."

"No, I'm not. Tell me why you're here?"

Did he have some kind of accident and now that his sperm count is low or nonexistent, he wants my son? He can have time with Henry—after all, he is his father—but my heart spasms. He won't get sole custody.

"I'm not the father of your son."

"Not this again." I throw my arms up in the air and let them fall heavily to my sides. "You may have slept around and had a girlfriend back in Greece, but I wasn't unfaithful. Costa, you are the only man I slept with when we were together."

He's shaking his head vehemently, and his long, dark waves fall around his face. "I'm not suggesting you slept with other men. But I can't be his father."

"Fine. Don't be his father," I yell, stomping around my small living room. "I don't want you to be his father. Let's call you an unwilling sperm donor and leave it at that."

"No, Daisy." He steps in front of me, firmly grasping my arms to hold me in place, and stares intently into my eyes. "Listen to me. It is not scientifically possible for me to be his father. I am not newly sterile. I have been since I was a child."

It takes me several beats to fully comprehend what he's saying, and even at that, I feel like I'm missing something. "What?"

"I had the mumps as a boy, and while the odds are relatively low, it can cause infertility in men. That's why I cannot father children."

His words come at me in slow motion, not necessarily lessening their overall weight but the cadence at which they sink in. And when that happens, my knees buckle, and fortunately, Costa is there to catch me.

Carefully, he moves me to the couch and sits next to me, taking my hand. The heat of his stare burns, and he doesn't say a word until I meet his eyes. His countenance is solemn, and I quiver.

"It was a shock to me too. I was an asshole when you told me about the baby. What's his name, Henry?" He waits for me to say something, but I can only nod, pressing my lips together to hold back my scream.

This is a sick joke. Why is he doing this?

"And then when Sousanna and I couldn't conceive, I had to tell you. Even when I'd denied the baby, I'd known you believed it was mine." He laughs nervously. "I believed he was mine even though I said otherwise."

We sit in silence, and my head is in a fog. Nothing makes sense, and all the while, there's a push and a pull, like a tug-of-war, going on inside my head.

"I won't push you into telling me who you might think the father is—it's none of my business." He holds a hand to where his heart is, all benevolent as he insinuates I'm a liar.

I slap at his chest, filled with so much anger I could level Los Angeles. "Shut up. Shut up."

On my feet, I hustle away from him, my need for distance intense. "Are you insane? You came here and thought I'd believe you? This is crap. Why are you lying to me?"

"I'm not." He rubs at where I hit his chest, and I should feel bad for doing so, but I can't bring myself to care one iota about this man.

I thought I knew him. Even if we never had a future together, nothing more than what we had, I'd never thought him capable of something like this. Something so cruel. And why? Why is he fucking with my head?

"There was no one else, Costa. You don't get to come into my house and call me a liar. That's more than insulting. Why are you doing this?"

"Daisy, we should get a DNA test." His smile is faint and sympathetic.

He makes me want to scrub it off his face with a steel wool pad. Asshole. I never thought he could be so cruel.

"Yes. I want a DNA test." I square my jaw and narrow my gaze on him. "I didn't sleep around. I was a lot of things, selfish most of all, but I slept with only you."

Why do I have this intense need to defend myself?

Profess my fidelity? The urge irks me. He's the one out of line, coming in here and spouting lies.

Costa shakes his head, wavy dark hair bobbing with him. "I thought maybe..." He looks me in the eye, dark eyes imploring. "You can tell me the truth."

"What truth?" I grit out between clenched teeth, rage bubbling deep inside me at what I think he's implying.

"I thought once I explained things...that this would make sense. You'd tell me there had been someone else but you figured given we were together more, it was me. I was the father."

He infuriates me, and I grab for the nearest thing to me, a vase. I clutch it in my hand, ready to toss it, but I get control of myself. I'm not trashing my things because of this jerk.

"I want a DNA test." My tone is unforgiving and cold, and he snaps his head to me as if surprised I might be angry and insulted by this conversation.

"Yes." He nods, defeated. "I found a lab in LA that can perform the test, and we'll have the results in three days. You just need to bring Henry in so they can get a DNA sample. I've already submitted mine."

"I'm not subjecting my son to anything like that." Suddenly the word *my*...he's *my* son and that realization never had greater impact than now.

Is Henry really not Costa's? And if so, who is the father?

"I'll give you his hairbrush and toothbrush. They can do the test with that, can't they?"

His face is drawn and expression disappointed. He shrugs again, and I want to shake him for that stupid, meaningless gesture.

"I don't know. Maybe." He shrugs once more, and I growl. "A fresh sample would be best, but I'll take it in and see what they say."

"Fine." I dash to Henry's bathroom, already making a mental shopping list to get him another brush and toothbrush.

He's always wanted one of those special character toothbrushes, grabbing at them as he sat in the shopping cart at the store. Maybe I should give him one. I was waiting for Christmas, to put it in his stocking, but why?

Why am I waiting to shower him with simple, special things like that? Suddenly, this overwhelming sense of being less than—not a good mother—bowls me over. What's the harm in getting him what he wants?

Costa is pacing in my small living room when I return with Henry's things in separate plastic sandwich bags.

"Thank you. I'll take them right now. I'll text you once I have confirmation for when we'll get them back." He steps toward me, and a small smile breaches his wary mouth as he opens his arms.

What? He wants a hug? He's insane. I'm quick and jump back from him, holding up a hand and shaking my head vehemently.

I can't touch him. I'm filled with rage and bewildered as to why the hell he came here to drop this lie on my lap. Hurt glints in his eye as if I slapped him across the face.

Suddenly, I'm cold and raw, and I haven't an ounce of remorse for this man. I thought I knew him, and now, I'm not so sure.

Without anything left to say, Costa leaves, and I stare at

the spot where he was standing. Dampness registers on my cheeks and I sniffle. Shit, I'm crying. It's so hard to believe any of this.

The man wanted nothing to do with Henry, and at that time, I struggled to make peace with the notion that my son would grow up without a father.

I spent time thinking and worrying about what I'd say when the day came and Henry asked about his dad. And yes, there was a small part of me that hoped Costa would one day come to his senses. One day, he'd want to meet his son.

Even when I saw his email this morning, that's what I'd hoped. I had the greatest confidence that once he met Henry, he wouldn't be able to turn his back on him.

But Costa blew all of that up. He's taken this entire situation one step further. Not only did he walk away from his son, but now he claims he isn't Henry's father. If that's true—and I don't even know why I'm considering it may be a possibility because it's impossible—but if he isn't his father, then who is?

14

GRAY

STRICTLY BUSINESS

*T*his morning, when I left Daisy in bed, cute, warm, and cuddly, I wanted nothing more than to hold her. I liked holding her. Leaving her was hard to do. I was hard. Forget morning wood—my dick never softened after she fell asleep, and I slept with a semi.

Last night was perfection. Daisy's response to everything I did made me feel like I'd single-handedly slayed a dragon. And kissing her...fuck, my tongue sliding into the heat of her sweet mouth, her hot pussy, drove me out of my mind.

I grip the steering wheel and pull myself together. No more thoughts of Daisy until later. Tonight we have her awards dinner, and afterward, I'll have her to myself.

Now outside the recording studio, I gather my things from the car. India's in the sound booth when I arrive, studying a sheet of paper as our recording engineer sets up the microphones in the room. Despite it being soundproof, she must sense something, because she glances up from the song sheet and locks eyes with me through the glass.

Like a little girl showing off her party dress, she holds the sides of her skirt and twirls around so the yellow fabric balloons around her. Beaming, she rushes from the booth, and my gut clenches. Yeah, I have to talk to her.

"Gray, you're here. Yay!" She claps her hands together, and Silas walks in behind me with coffees in hand.

We met at his house before coming here to go over a few things for today, and it gave me a chance to have breakfast with Henry. I don't know how long today will be, and I wanted to see him before anything else.

"Hey, India. You ready?" He hands her a bottle of water and me a coffee.

"Hi, Silas. Hell, I've never been more ready." She pats my arm, and I step out of her grasp. "And I'm so excited to have Gray playing with us."

"Yeah." He leans against the wall, an annoying smirk plastered across his face.

We talked about India this morning. I pushed on how we should manage her because she can be a challenge, but he kept bringing it back to the more personal side of things. Like how I have to talk to her about how things are and will be during the recording of her album. I'm not flattering myself to think she wants some epic romance with me, but she definitely has designs of more than just recording her album.

And Silas was all too happy to keep the focus on that would-be drama like some gossiping high school girl rather than get down to business. Frustrating.

Eventually, to get off the topic, I told him that while there's nothing wrong with India—she's smart, talented, and pretty—I'm not interested. I meant what I said to Daisy. There's no one for me but her.

"India, we'll get started as soon as everyone gets here." Deliberately, I make a wide berth around her.

If I get too close to her, she's like a tornado and I'll be lifted into her destruction-seeking path. My chin tips for Silas to follow.

We may have talked about India, but we never actually talked about what playing on the album would mean. While I'm recording all day and for weeks, which is my choice, Silas needs to understand it changes nothing about our company. I don't want him thinking he can singlehandedly call the shots while I'm otherwise occupied.

He assured me I have just as much say as he does while I'm working with India. Like he needs to say that we're partners. As much as I want to trust him, and I do for the most part, how this will unfold remains to be seen.

We've both done what we said we would that day we were at his house. I went with the realtor to see the land for sale where Silas wants us to build our own studio, and he came to this place, the recording studio we're leasing for India's album, among others.

I want us to sign a one-year lease so we're no longer scrambling for recording space all the time.

"So, what do you think?" I sip at the hot beverage, studying his blank expression.

"About what?" He glances back to India who's talking on her phone.

"This place. Are you good to sign the lease?"

"Yeah, I told Fred we're good." He scrubs at his stubbled jaw at the mention of the owner of this studio. "He's drawing up a contract. We'll have something in a few days."

"Yeah?" My eyes widen. He's coming around to the idea of waiting, and I smile. "You're on board with leasing this place for the next year?"

"Yeah. I like it. You're right."

"What?" I cup my ear and lean toward him. "I'm sorry, could you say that again? I liked the sound of it."

"Shut up, jackass." He pushes at me, chuckling. "Listen, I thought about it, and it does make sense for now. I talked to the realtor about keeping us in the loop about any movement on the land. This way we can make an offer before it gets snapped up."

He was also right about the property he found with the realtor. It's a great location with lots of space to build not only a studio but our entire operation, which would be perfect. Right now, we're renting office space off Melrose, and it's a pain to have more than one location.

And lastly, the price isn't that insane. But it doesn't matter. Timing is everything, and now isn't the time.

"What?" I put down the coffee, surprised at what he's saying.

"I mean, I'm willing to put up some of my own money in the short-term to buy it. And I'd even front some of the costs to start building."

My stomach sours. "This isn't what we discussed. I thought we agreed to be partners on this? I can't have you put up your own money."

I gnash my teeth together, tension shooting a painful jolt through my head. Why the hell does he always pull this crap? It's always his way or no way.

"Easy, Gray. I'm not going around your back or disagreeing with you, but you said so yourself, the property is sweet." He pats at my shoulder. "C'mon, don't tell me you can't see how sick it would be to have everything in one place. On that piece of land. It's perfect."

Nodding, I inhale slowly, willing my frustration and anger to take a back seat. We can't get into this right now. I need to focus on relaxing. We're going to be recording soon. But Silas makes all of that difficult.

"Hey, guys, everyone's here." India sidles up beside me, knocking her hip against mine and winking. "You ready to make some rock 'n roll?"

It's now or never. Time to have the talk. Shaking off Silas's surprise, I turn to her.

"I need to talk to you before we get started." I glance to Silas. "And we'll talk later."

"I'm going to round everyone up, and yeah, let's talk." There's an edge to his tone and he leaves the room.

"What is it?" She picks at something on the shoulder of my T-shirt. I doubt there's anything there—just another excuse to touch me.

"Listen, I want to make sure we're on the same page with the album and everything else."

"Sure, okay." She drags a finger down the center of my chest.

This is the shit I'm talking about, and I remove her hand from my body. "My involvement with the album is strictly business as is everything else we have to do with each other."

"What do you mean?"

I step away from her, putting more than enough distance between us, and she frowns. We aren't in touching range and maybe she's finally getting it.

"I'm not interested in anything more than a professional relationship. And if I'm reading you wrong, sorry. I'm not trying to be an arrogant prick." I give her a self-deprecating smile and also an out, a chance to save face by stating we're only colleagues.

I'm cool with looking like the ass and too full of himself if it prevents an awkward conversation or any drama.

"You could never be an arrogant prick," she coos, and it's evident that a big scene is still a possibility.

"I like hanging out with you, and I'm very flattered and honored to be given this chance to jam with you. But that's it. Nothing else."

She huffs, folding her arm over her chest and thinning her lips. "What are you implying?"

"I'm not implying anything. I just want to make sure we understand each other. No more touching and other things like that. I'm with Daisy."

I can't believe I'm having this conversation with a grown woman. That I need to have this talk. But she's too touchy-feely, and truthfully, I should have done this ages ago. That's on me, but I really did want to avoid any kind of drama.

"And Daisy? You're with her? What does that even mean?" Now she's snarky and put out.

"We're together. It's serious." Daisy and I haven't talked about things like that, but this is what I want.

"How serious? Were you with her at the beach the last time we saw each other?" The way she asks suggests we did something more than talk that day. We most certainly did not.

"We're exclusive." That's all she needs to know.

"Fine." She sulks out of the room, bouncing her hair and skirt behind her.

Fortunately, when I enter the sound booth to play through the first song, everything is cool. India is her usual bubbly, life of the party self.

While she does love the drama and can be over the top, India is also one damn good artist and knows how to focus on what's important. After all, if she produces an epic album, she'll be the star, and that's what matters the most to her.

The day is long, grueling, and...awesome. We cover several tracks and make a couple of tweaks to a few songs. We're off to a good start, and it felt amazing to play again.

Whenever I get a break, I text Daisy to check in and tell her I'm thinking about her. Apart from her first reply this morning before we started, there's been nothing in response to any of my other texts. That isn't like her.

I force myself to ignore the nagging in the pit of my stomach. Does her lack of response mean she regrets last night? This whole dating thing? Or is something wrong?

No, she must be busy. When she gets deep into work, she's single-minded and likely hasn't checked her phone. But even that potential explanation doesn't quiet the unease.

She's a mother. Going off the grid isn't an option. She always makes herself reachable for Henry.

Fuck, by the time five rolls around, it's quitting time for me. I've got to talk to Silas and then get ready for tonight's award dinner. I find him perched on the desk, thumbing through papers.

"Hey, I'm heading to Daisy's, but I wanted to talk about the land for sale."

"Gray, for fuck's sake, why can't you let this go?" He drops the stack of papers onto the desk and stands, pulling at the waist of his jeans. "Today was a good day. Just celebrate that and move on."

"Listen, I'm not here to argue." I release a ragged breath, exhausted and truly not wanting to go another round with him. "You've given me something to think about with the land. I'm not saying no, I just need some time. I understand where you're coming from, and the location is fantastic."

Silas watches me, expression stern and maybe even a little pissed off, and I feel like I should give him more. I do plan on thinking about what he said in more detail.

"Who knows if something like that will be available when we want to build..." Conceding that point shouldn't be as hard to say as it is.

Why is it? Silas is my partner and my friend, and maybe I'm just a little bitter that we're both right.

A slow smile, too triumphant for my liking, plays on his mouth, and he runs a hand through his blonde hair. "All right, I like the sounds of that. I'll wait. You think about it."

He walks closer to me, placing a hand on my shoulder

and squeezing. "Listen, we are partners, and I'm not trying to do anything behind your back. I think we both have solid approaches on this studio thing. I just think we need to compromise."

His final word hangs between us. He lets the silence breathe life into it, and he's a bastard. And I mean that in the nicest way possible.

I can't help but smile, shaking my head because he knows how to get to me. I've said from day one of our joint venture that compromise would be the secret to our success. We both have vision, the know-how, and the drive, but sometimes our egos get in the way. We need to know when to get out of the way.

"Fucker." I lightly punch him in the arm, and he chuckles. "Yeah, compromise." I nod, smiling. "I'm out of here. Have a good night."

I'm halfway through the door when he calls out, "Hey, Gray, what's going on with you two?"

There's more interest than concern to his tone. He is Daisy's future brother-in-law, and while the two of them are a mirror to the other, making sure they see things as they are even if they don't want to, he does care a great deal about her. And the same goes for Daisy when it comes to him.

"Why'd you ask?"

"Pansy mentioned you guys had dinner at your place the other night, and you're going to that awards dinner." He shrugs, suddenly uncomfortable. "It's none of my business, but Daisy is great. I'm,"—he hangs his head, eyes on the ground, and I want to laugh at how much he squirms when talking about feelings and shit—"I'm glad you're finally together. She's perfect for you."

A warmth spreads through my chest, and I'm gratified and humbled at his honest, while maybe difficult, insight. It means a lot coming from him.

"Thanks, Silas. I think so too."

15

DAISY

ALL THAT MATTERS IS HERE AND NOW

The dress is beautiful. A one-shoulder, lavender lace and tulle evening gown with an embroidered bodice of tiny sparkling flowers.

I sway from side to side, staring at my reflection in the cheap full-length mirror hanging on the back of my bathroom door. It's hard not to marvel at how the beams of light filter through the tulle, making the gown glow.

When I'd heard I'd won the photography award, on a crazy impulse, I ventured to Rodeo Drive. Truly, it was insane since I couldn't afford anything designer—hadn't since my modeling days—but that didn't stop me.

I found the dress at an exclusive boutique and that was it. I was a goner and didn't have a chance to stop my reckless splurge. My poor credit card—I grimace at the hit to my bank account.

In the mirror, frown lines pop around my mouth and at the corners of my eyes, and I immediately force a blank expression, erasing those bothersome wrinkles. What is done is done.

It isn't every day you're named photographer of the year, and the dress is more beautiful than I had imagined.

My blonde hair falls in loose waves around my shoulders, and my makeup twinkles, giving my face a natural glimmer. It's perfect for the awards dinner. Too bad I'm no longer looking forward to tonight.

After Costa left, his words weighed heavy on my mind and heart. Even though it was total bullshit, it made concentrating on work difficult, and I only got more riled when he sent a text hours later to confirm we'd have the results couriered to each of us in three days.

Then Pansy came over with Henry this afternoon, only to get some more of his things and so I could spend time with him. I managed to keep it together, enjoying the time with my son and sister, although relieved once Pansy left with him. I will have to tell her and Gray...even if it's for nothing.

I hope it's for nothing.

"Fuck me." A deep husky tone of appreciation causes me to twirl around.

Gray stands in the doorway of my room in a tuxedo. He's gorgeous, the perfect mix of celebrity handsome with his all-around good looks—blond hair and blue eyes—and bad boy danger with dark ink peeking out from the edges of sleeves and his shirt collar.

"Daisy, you look amazing." His blue eyes glitter admiringly, and he drops a small duffel bag onto the floor.

He's staying the night, and until now, I hadn't given it any thought. Now, the boulder-sized knot that's been sitting heavy on my chest all afternoon lessens at the sight of him.

"You look gorgeous too." I'm done with the questions and doubts about Henry and Costa and launch myself at him.

My arms wrap around his neck, and my Erotic Dreams-covered mouth crashes onto his, and suddenly everything is right with the world again.

Costa and his stupid lies melt away, and all that matters is here and now. Gray.

"Hi." He pulls back, eyes heavy-lidded, and his smile slays me. "I was going to ask if you missed me, but I think that kiss just about covered it."

"I did miss you." It's true. Despite how messed up this day was and how scattered my mind is, Gray and Henry are the only ones to keep me sane.

There's a knock at the door as he leans down to capture my mouth once more. He groans, fingers squeezing into my waist.

"I was going to ask if we could be late to this thing," he murmurs against my lips. "I wanted to taste you again."

As if on command, my panties are wet, and my core heats at the thought of his hot mouth and skillful tongue on me, in me.

"You're horrible," I moan, pushing away from him. "Now all I'm going to think about tonight is your mouth on me."

A wicked grin takes over his face and he chuckles. "That makes two of us."

I laugh, grabbing my purse and taking his hand. "You ready? That is probably the driver here to take us to the dinner."

"Lead the way." His hand tightens on mine, and an animal-like growl erupts from behind me. "Damn, Daisy, I'm not going to be able to take my eyes off you in that dress."

Well, that right there justifies the outrageous cost of the dress. I'd spend ten times what I did to hear the blatant hunger in his voice I just so clearly heard.

Tonight's event organizers arranged for a limo, and as we slide into the back, I mull over when best to mention Costa's visit. I can't keep this bottled up for much longer, but tonight is supposed to be special.

How do I not mix the two in my head? The day my stupid ex basically called me a liar, and I received the most coveted award any up-and-coming photographer dreams of.

Despite traffic, our driver gets us to the event on time, and the dinner is fantastic. I graciously accept my award, pulling off my practiced speech flawlessly and smiling for the camera so many times I lose track.

Of course, Gray's presence makes everything bearable. At my side all night long, he silently smiles at the many strangers who approach us to introduce themselves, talk shop, and give me their business cards.

It's more than I could have asked for. Future photography gigs come at me from all directions, and in some ways, it's overwhelming. When we get back into the limo several hours later, I lean into Gray and close my eyes.

"Thank you for being there tonight." My hand squeezes his bicep, and my head nestles onto his shoulder. "It must have been boring for you."

"Nope. Not a chance. It was amazing to see you get the

recognition you so deserve." He kisses my temple. "You okay?"

I pull away, gazing up at him. "Sure. A little tired, that's all."

His brow furrows but he doesn't say anything, and I rest my head back onto him. When we get to my house, Gray opens the front door, ushering me in before him.

No lights are on inside, but the place is alight with candles. Tealights line the hallway and soft music comes from the speakers.

"What the..." I glance back at Gray who's grinning before heading into the living room.

Almost every surface is covered with vases of flowers. Tulips, hydrangeas, roses, and my favorite and namesake, Gerber daisies.

"What is this?" I stare at Gray, incredulous.

"This is for you." In the dim light with the soft glow from the candles, his lips twitch with amusement.

"For me?"

"Daisy, you deserve to be celebrated." He takes both my hands in his and pulls me to him.

Leaning his head into me, he nibbles on the side of my neck, eliciting a flurry of shudders, and I ask on a breathy moan, "You did all this for me?"

He nods, tongue laving at my pulse point, and I curl an arm around his waist, turning in his embrace to look around at the room once again.

Flowers. Candles. Champagne chilling in a bucket. When did he have a chance to do all this?

"But how?" I dip my head back to get a good look at his face.

He flashes me a sexy, crooked grin, and my eyes drop, drawn to the strong cords of his neck. Everything about him fascinates me.

"I have my ways. I wanted tonight to be special since it's just the two of us. But before that, we need to talk." He pulls me to the couch and picks up the remote to turn off the music.

"Talk?"

"Yes, you're awfully quiet tonight. Something's bothering you. What is it?"

God, why does he have to be so attuned to me? I want to tell him about Costa and had planned to once we got back to my place after tonight's event. But the candles, the music...I don't want to ruin this.

But I won't lie to him.

"I had a visit from Costa." My tone is flat even as my stomach churns, reliving the near hour of turmoil with the man earlier today.

16

***

GRAY
SUCKER PUNCH

*C*osta. I can't bring myself to say anything. I'm totally surprised and hadn't seen that coming.

Henry's father. What about him? Why did he come to see her? I've never met him and only know what Daisy's shared, but it's enough not to like him. And if I'm being truthful, I never really gave the man much thought.

The one and only time she talked about Costa was when Henry was a week old. Late one night, the baby was finally able to latch onto her breast for a full feed, and she cried tears of joy. It was one of those standout moments in parenting.

As much as she'd wanted to breastfeed, Henry took his sweet time to latch, and she supplemented with baby formula. Despite it being less than a week since she'd given birth, she beat herself up, feeling like a failure at motherhood because of using a bottle.

Anyway, that night, something shifted, both in Henry and

in Daisy, and they've been in sync ever since. I'm forever grateful I'd been there.

Since his birth, I'd taken to coming over daily to help her, knowing caring for a baby was a monumental undertaking. I was caregiver to my younger sister once she started walking, although I was only a year older than she was.

That night, Daisy told me how Costa had denied being the father and wanted nothing to do with the baby. She hadn't spoken to him since then but sent him her contact information in case he ever changed his mind.

Is that what's happened? My heart pinches. Does Costa not only want Henry but Daisy too?

"What about Costa?" The words are heavy and clumsy in my mouth, but I need answers.

"He came here...today." Her fingers tremble, stroking lightly over my jaw.

I lean into her touch, my mind clouding with the heat of her. "Yes, you already said that."

"Yes." Her palm rests on my cheek and she straightens. "He emailed me sometime last night when he got in and said he needed to see me. He said it was about Henry and then he showed up today."

I lay my hand on top of hers, staring into her eyes and willing my heartbeat to slow down. "What did he want?"

"He said...he couldn't be Henry's father." Her lips tremble, and the tips of her fingers press into my face.

"Okay. We knew he didn't want to be part of Henry's life." I don't get what has her so upset, unless she was hoping he'd change his mind?

I can understand even if there's an ounce of...what is it? Jealousy? Fear?

Something dark and ugly struggles to take root in my gut at the idea I could be so easily replaced by Henry's biological father.

You know what they say—blood is thicker than water.

"No, he says he isn't his father." Her tone is hard, and I'm confused. "Costa says he is sterile and has been since he was a kid. He only just found out now that he and his wife are trying to have a baby."

"Seriously?" Our fingers entwine and she nods her head, pressing her lips together.

The next logical question slips from my mouth of its own accord, without thought. "Is there someone else you were seeing at the time? Someone else who might be his father?"

I'm not judging, and as much as I hate the thought of Daisy with any guy but me, she had a life before we met. And her relationship with Costa and her modeling career are a mystery to me.

"No. You don't understand. I wasn't seeing anyone else. I didn't sleep around."

"Hey." I lift my hand from hers and stroke the side of her face. "I didn't mean to suggest that. I only asked if maybe you'd been seeing more than one person. It happens and it's all right. No judgement."

My fingers sink into her hair, curling around the back of her neck, and she releases a small whimper.

"Sorry, I shouldn't have taken it that way. I'm just a mess right now. Costa was the only one I had sex with."

"I..." Puzzled, I have a hard time processing what she's saying. "I don't know what to say."

There has to be someone else. She had a baby and that takes two people, and one has to be a man. This isn't the Immaculate Conception or something.

"Daisy." I pause, and she must sense my hesitation as she pushes to her feet.

"This is why I'm freaking out. It doesn't make any sense." She shakes out her hands at her sides as if numb, needing to get the blood circulating again. "Costa and I were together for a couple of years, and I was monogamous." She slips off her heels, one hand running through her hair. "I didn't sleep with anyone else."

"So you think he's lying?" I also get to my feet, needing to see her face. The turmoil in her tone is too much without looking into her eyes, offering some kind of reassurance that this will turn out okay.

"It's the only explanation, but I don't know why he's doing this. It's...no, he is fucking with my head." She slaps at the side of her head in frustration.

Her physical blow to her body is a sucker punch to my gut. No way. She won't hurt herself any more than this is already hurting her.

I bring both her arms to her sides, banding them with mine. "Shhh, we'll figure this out. Don't ever do that."

My hand strokes the side of her face, needing to erase the hit, but my attempt to soothe isn't enough...for me. My lips kiss the side of her face, holding there longer than I should but not wanting to pull away.

A tear slips from the corner of her eye, and she starts to

bob her head. The reality of what she did, of what this is doing to her, sinks in, and even still, she doesn't believe me. She doesn't believe it'll be okay.

"All I keep coming back to is...maybe he wants Henry, and this is some twisted way of getting to me. I don't know." Her voice cracks, and a wintry chill burrows into my heart.

Exhaling a harsh breath, she wriggles her arms until I loosen my hold and steps back. I try not to take her retreat as anything more serious than what it is—a need for space. To think.

"When you talked to him, how did he seem? Was he drunk, high, angry?" My head hurts from puzzling over this. "Did it feel like he was being cagey with you?"

Maybe there's something else at play, although I'm coming up blank as to what it could be.

"That's the thing. I could see he didn't know how to tell me, and when I thought he was lying...that's when things got weird." Daisy slides her arms around her middle. "He truly believes he isn't the father, and even when I didn't want to, I believed him."

"Well, there's one way to find out. A DNA test."

"Yes." She nods and starts to pace, her dress swishing with each step. "I gave him Henry's toothbrush and hairbrush for a DNA test. He figured I'd insist on a test and so he arranged one. We'll know in three days."

"Can you trust him?" I take her hand, stopping her from another walk across the room.

"I thought I knew him, but now I'm not so sure. His wife is a girlfriend from high school. He was with her the entire time we were together, even when he was with other models before me. So I don't know, but I'm not subjecting Henry to any of this."

The news of the wife and Costa's lies tweaks a thought. "Do you think the wife has something to do with this? Maybe she wants Henry out of the picture and is lying to Costa about his sterility?"

"Really? I mean, I guess it's a possibility, but who does that?"

"You'd be surprised what people will do. If she thinks you or Henry are a threat to her marriage, especially if Costa was unfaithful to her, then she may have lied to him."

"Should we get our own DNA test?" She nibbles on her lip, and her hands land on my waist, fingers digging into my sides.

I welcome her nearness and kiss her once more, this time on the lips. It's quick and gentle, not looking for anything more than to show her I'm here. She isn't alone.

"Yeah, let me take care of it." I sweep hair away from her face.

"I'll have to ask Costa for a DNA sample."

"No, I'll handle it."

"Gray, but—" I cut her off with a finger to her mouth, and her warm breath skates over my skin, causing a shiver along my arm.

"But nothing. Let me worry about this. I'll figure it all out tomorrow. We should get some sleep." I glance around the room, dejected that the night didn't go as planned.

She stops at the mouth of the hallway. "Aren't you coming?"

Beautiful. The candlelight causes her dress to shimmer

more than it already does, and even with her hair tousled and expression glum, she looks like a princess.

I smile. "Yeah, in a minute. I just need to blow out all these candles and make a few calls to get things started."

"Calls? Like what?" She rests her head against the door-jamb, studying me.

"I'm going to go in a little later tomorrow, so I need to let Silas know, and I want to get the ball rolling on the DNA test, Costa...all of that." I blow out a breath, already weighed down just by the thought of this.

"Can I help?"

"Hey." I saunter over to her, hands now cupping the back of her neck, and I bend to press my lips to her forehead. "Relax. Do me a favor and go get changed. Get ready for bed. Oh, and maybe you can blow out the candles in the bedroom."

Her eyes widen. "There are more candles in the bedroom?"

I nod. "Yeah, and flowers. I may have gotten a little carried away, but I wanted this night to be magical for you." My thumb sweeps over her collarbone, and she trembles, her eyelashes fluttering closed on a blink.

"Thank you. Thank you for tonight. For being here. For everything." She wraps her arms around my back and plants a long, slow kiss on my mouth.

She pulls away, studying me, and I can see it in her eyes. The worry and questions. Oh, how I wish I could take them away.

"What if the DNA results come back and Costa is telling the truth?" she murmurs, stepping back farther into the shadows where I'm unable to see her expression and can only judge her mood by her frail, doubtful voice.

"Do you think that's going to happen?" My hand wraps around her wrist, pulling her back to me.

"I don't believe it will. No, it won't. But..." So much uncertainty laces that final word. "It's hard to make any sense of this."

"Come here." My arms wrap around her, and she nestles into me, placing her head on my shoulder.

"Gray, despite this thing with Costa, you did make tonight special. You make everything special."

My chin perches on the crown of her head. "Try to get some sleep. I know this is hard to believe right now, but it's going to work out. I'll be in bed as soon as I can."

She kisses the base of my neck, and my heart does a back flip. "Please don't be long." She turns toward the bedroom, and I watch her for a bit.

In the gown, she glides down the hallway, and it takes everything in me not to go after her. To make her forget about all the bullshit of Costa.

But first I have to deal with him. I check the doors are locked and text Silas about a change in plans for tomorrow with India's album. He replies right away. He's got questions but he doesn't object, only agrees to my request. Thank fuck.

I'll give India and her album a few hours in the morning. We've only just started, and I can't bail this early in the process. Besides, I'm up tomorrow for a drum solo. So I'll do that before I talk to Costa. But first I have to find him.

Then I place a call to my resourceful and tenacious

lawyer, stressing the importance of finding Costa and giving him until noon tomorrow to do so. No excuses.

During the call, I also ask him to arrange for a DNA test, stressing I wanted the results as soon as possible. We're going to get to the bottom of this.

What Costa hopes to gain by messing with Daisy isn't clear, but I'm putting an end to this. And if I have to, I'll put an end to him.

17

GRAY
IMPATIENT TO GET NAKED

Soundlessly, I slip into the bedroom, expecting the lights off and Daisy in bed. I'm mistaken. Slack-jawed and tongue-tied, I just stand there, staring. Any thoughts of Costa or all that I have to do tomorrow vanish like a puff of smoke.

Daisy stands at the edge of the bed, a dark and sexy butterfly in black and iridescent purple. Utter temptation.

Lace bows, mesh, and crystal buttons fashion bra and panties that are near life-like butterfly wings. My cock hardens at the jaw-dropping vision. It's like she's stepped from the pages of a French lingerie catalog.

Golden tresses dance around her heart-shaped face. Big blue eyes shimmer like sapphires, and a naughty grin skates across her pouty mouth, a pale shade of pink. She's only got eyes for me.

"What's this?" The question comes out like a croak as if

I've lost my voice, and it's a dumb question. It's pretty obvious what this is.

"Isn't this what you planned for tonight?" Hips seductively swaying, she strolls toward me like a coy feline. "What you expected. The candles, the music, the flowers."

"I didn't expect anything." The urge to touch every inch of her smooth, silky skin burns my palms, and I flex my hands, shoving them into the pockets of my pants. "I only want to spend time with you. Celebrate your award, the recognition you so deserve."

"So you didn't want to have sex with me?" She halts, only a foot or two from me, and places a delicate hand on her cocked hip.

"I'd never say that." I bark out a raspy laugh, shaking my head in disbelief.

This woman is killing me. Slowly. And I can't say that I object. What a fucking magnificent way to die—Daisy, the last thing I see.

"I've wanted you for a very long time." My stare is fierce, locking on her bright eyes, filled with excitement, lust, and maybe something more, something deeper. "But tonight, it was never about that. We'll only do what you want, Daisy. It's what you want. Always. You choose."

"I want you." She cups me over my pants, wicked lust tugging at the corners of her mouth. "I want all of you, tonight. All the time."

She doesn't have to tell me twice, and my hand grasps the back of her head as my mouth crashes onto hers. Our tongues tangle, and her hands dive for the buttons of my shirt and my pants.

Reluctant to break our kiss but impatient to get naked, I rip my mouth from hers, shucking my shirt, dropping my pants, and slipping off my shoes.

I drink her in, watching me. Her eyes are heavy-lidded and dazed, lips swollen and pink.

"That's better." A hand scores a path down my chest, resting at the band of my boxers. "But these have to go."

My fingers wrap around her wrist as hers dip below the waistband. "Uh-uh, you too." I flick my eyes over the sexy lingerie I might destroy, tear from her body if she isn't naked soon.

Amusement sparks in her jewel-colored eyes and she nods, pulling her hand away from my body. She slides one bra strap down, and before she can go any further, I bring one hand between her legs, pressing into the barely-there fabric.

Her panties are soaked, and my balls tighten, cock twitching, and I almost come from the sheer heat of her, throbbing with need against my palm.

"Fuck, Daisy. You're so ready."

She nods, teeth sinking into her bottom lip. "I need you."

"I need you, too, but are you sure?" I won't say anymore, not wanting to ruin this moment with all the shit we left outside this room.

But if she needs more time, I want to give it to her. I'll wait for however long she needs.

"Absolutely. I want this. Us. Now." Her lashes flutter closed, and she tilts her head back on a whimper as I grind the heel of my palm into her core, feeding from the steady pulse of her need under my hand.

Together, we remove the last of our clothing—bra, panties, and boxers piled on the floor—and again, my mouth crashes onto hers before she can say another word, stealing her breath.

I scoop Daisy up and spread her flat on the bed. Hovering above, I lower my head to hers and she lifts up, opening her mouth to me. My tongue slips in, stroking, and she wraps her legs around my waist, hooking me closer.

"Not yet." I pull back, the weight of my body on my forearms, sinking into the bed. "Do you have any condoms?"

My jaw clenches, and I hold still, cursing internally for not coming prepared. But I meant what I said. I hadn't planned anything tonight.

Tonight, like any other time, is about what Daisy wants. Sex isn't my goal. Sure, I wanted it, her, but the only thing I needed, demanded, was to be with her, in any way she allowed.

"No." She shakes her head, and my heart sinks and cock cries. "But I don't want anything between us. I'm clean and I'm on the shot."

Bare. She wants me bare inside her. *Fuck.* I'd never done that with anyone.

"I'm clean too, tested, and I don't do drugs." I hadn't had sex in ages—more than a year.

Before, when we were becoming the best of friends, I had casual relationships. And while I didn't hide this, there was never anyone I cared enough about to have them meet Daisy and my friends.

Then when I realized Daisy was it for me, the one I wanted, casual sex no longer held any interest. It felt like a betrayal, not to Daisy, but to me. And it had been long months of no sex. Well, I jacked off to thoughts of Daisy, maybe an unhealthy amount of times, but nothing more. And even with all that, I still got tested regularly, more out of habit than for any real reason.

"Daze." I rest my forehead on her to still my wildly racing heart. "It's been a long time, and I've never been without a condom with anyone."

"Oh, if you don't want to—"

I kiss her to stop her rambling. "No, I want to...with you. I just might not last long." I feel the heat of my blush creeping up the back of my neck, and I kiss her again.

How fucking embarrassing. It's like I'm a teenager again and lasting a few minutes is the best I can hope for.

She laughs quietly into my mouth, and I pull away, sliding down her body to her ankles. She shudders as my hot breath shadows the trail of my lips, working their way up her thighs.

"So pretty and pink." The tips of my fingers tease her pussy, coaxing her open.

She giggles and writhes as I hold a hand to one of her thighs. Lifting her head, Daisy stares down at me.

Heat spreads within me at just her look, as if I've just downed a bottle of scotch, burning and tingling all of my nerve endings, stoking the fires of need low in my belly. My cock is hard as steel, pushing into the mattress.

She widens her legs, granting me full access, and my lips kiss a trail up to her flat stomach, gently kissing and stroking the faint and few silvery lines.

"I love all of you," I murmur into her flesh, loving the signs of Henry on her body.

My body looms over her, and she arches her back, moaning at the sight of my hand fisting my cock, edging myself between her legs.

She reaches between us before I can slide inside and grasps my erection. Hard. Stars. I see stars.

Everything is bright and blazing, then hazy and electric as my toes curl at the feel of her long, slender fingers pumping up and down my shaft. Her thumb swirls the bead of cum around my tip and then she guides me inside of her.

Her hips rise from the bed, her breathing heavy, and she cries out as I thrust into her as deep as I can go. I drop my head to the crook of her neck, planting open-mouthed kisses on her skin.

I taste salt, vanilla, and Daisy. My mouth latches onto her flesh and sucks, dragging my teeth and tongue along the tender spot between her neck and shoulder and then across her collarbone.

"Gray, I need..." She pants, nails digging into my back. "I need you to move."

Nodding, I push up, rotating my hips in a slow circular motion that causes her back to bow and lips to part on a breathless groan.

My tongue swipes over one taut, pink nipple, and I grind my hips against her, teasing. Although I'm not sure if I'm torturing her, or me, or more likely, both of us.

"I love these." I flick at her nipple, and she plunges her fingers into my hair, holding me to her breast, and I oblige, taking it into my mouth.

I release a low laugh against her flesh, loving how readily she responds to my ministrations, telling me what she likes without words.

Moving inside her, slow and sweet, I draw out the pleasure, not wanting this to end. Daisy moans, meeting me thrust for thrust. And when my hands blaze a trail down to her ass, fingers cleaving the sweet flesh apart, she tenses.

Still pounding into her, I capture her gaze, seeing the question in her eyes. Do I dare go to that taboo spot?

"Not tonight," I murmur against her lips, and her body relaxes.

"Okay." Her mouth hovers near mine, bedazzled eyes set on mine. "I want you everywhere. I'm yours."

As if striking a match, her offering ignites my already pounding tempo. I'm relentless, and the slap of skin against skin only feeds the chase of the climax, thrumming and coiling at the base of my spine.

"I need you to kiss me," she whimpers, hands reaching for my neck to bring me to her.

I claim her mouth and rock my hips upward, deep into her, aching to get closer as if it's possible.

"Yes. Yes. Don't stop." Her fingernails sink into my flesh.

"Come for me, Daze."

Her body goes tight and liquid at the same time, and her arms and legs shake as she cries my name. I feel every glorious bit of her warm, wet pussy clenching around me and hiss.

Ecstasy tunnels its way down my spine. I pump, hard and fast, in and out of her. My climax, like a massive tremor, explodes and burns my insides like lightning singeing the earth.

18

DAISY
HELLO, CRAZY, I'M OVER HERE

*L*azy and more alive than I've ever felt, my hands slide into his hair, grabbing fistfuls, and I pull his head closer, closing the only inch between us.

The weight of him on top of me is indescribable, and that alone makes my toes curl. I don't want to move. He chuckles into my neck, and his tongue sweeps long and languidly against my skin.

"Daisy." His voice brushes over me like a lover's caress, and I release my hold on his hair as he lifts his head to look at me.

His stubble scrapes along my palm and the inside of my wrist. I tremble. "That was amazing."

My body still quivers, and I moan as Gray slides out of me. "Fucking incredible."

He plants a quick kiss on my temple and ducks into the bathroom, coming back with a washcloth to clean me up. Then he slides in beside me, arm draping over my waist.

"I'm hungry again." My confession brings a flush, heating my cheeks.

"Wow. You're ready so soon?" His hand rests flat on his abdomen, still rising and falling faster than usual.

"No." I gently hit his solid chest, not wanting to move my hand from the warmth of him. "Not for that, although maybe later. I'm hungry for food."

"Really?" He arches a brow, and I narrow my gaze.

"Yes, really. We just burned a gazillion calories and dinner was hours ago."

"Hey, I'm with you. I could eat. What do you have in the kitchen? I'll grab something."

"I've got popcorn." I wink, wondering if he'll remember. "Oh, and bring the champagne."

"Popcorn and champagne. Yes." He's already up, sauntering to the doorway in all his naked glory.

Damn, his ass is one fine piece of muscle. I just want to gawk at it, maybe even sink my teeth into that hard globe.

"Or maybe you've changed your mind? The popcorn can wait?" Gray's staring at me over his shoulder, a naughty glint in his eye as he turns around to face me, already semi hard.

I huff out a laugh and throw a pillow at him. "Food and drink first, then more of that." I wave my hand at him, knowing if he comes any closer, any thought of food will vanish.

Minutes later, he's back with a tray, laden with a big bowl of hot, buttery popcorn, two flutes of champagne, plus the bottle, and two water bottles.

He sets it on the table, handing me the bowl and bottle and my glass before slipping in beside me. We sit with our back against the headboard, sheet only covering from the waist down as we munch on the salty, kernelly goodness.

"Do you know what this reminds me of?" I ask between bites.

I think back to the time I first visited his bachelor pad on the beach. He'd just come back from Trojan's final tour. He had invited me over to check it out.

"How could I forget, although I must say this time is better." He eyes my bare breasts, licking his lips, and I giggle, ogling his lean inked torso.

"Fair enough, I have to agree." I lean in and kiss his cheek.

"You came over with Henry asleep in his car seat. You looked beautiful but exhausted."

I gasp, surprised to hear his take on that night. He looks to me and holds my gaze. "I was a mess. Exhausted for sure. I was hungry, and you didn't have any food. Come to think of it, you didn't have much of anything."

"Hey, I'd just moved in. I offered to order something, but you had popcorn and I had champagne. Pansy had brought it over when I'd bought the place. It was chilled and unopened."

"And delicious. The good stuff, like this one." I sip at the bubbly drink.

"Yeah, it was good. And we ended up watching a movie after what felt like hours of trying to decide what to—"

I interject, hitting the bed with my palm. "Hey, you kept insisting on watching that scary ass movie, *Us*."

"It was a good movie that I ended up watching without you." He straightens his spine as if he has superior taste, and

I roll my eyes. "And what was it you kept coming back to? *Little Women.*" He mock shudders. "I'm just glad you agreed to watch *John Wick: Chapter Three.*"

"Hey, I was the one to suggest it."

"And smart choice at that." He winks, tossing a handful of popcorn into his mouth.

I toss a kernel at him, and he grabs at my body, bringing us to a lying position with him half-lying on me. His fingers are possessive on my body, coasting up one side.

His kiss is gentle, and he tastes salty and buttery mixed with the toastiness of the champagne. "Yum, you taste delectable."

Kisses, one after the other, are at first gentle and warm—firm lips against mine as if he's testing my willingness. Or maybe, if he's like me, wondering if this is real or just a glorious dream.

"Gray." My arms slide around his neck, and I roll my body fully into his, telling him with my body that I need more. Want more.

He shudders, and from the back of his throat a strange sound erupts. Sort of like a gasp and it causes a shudder and half growl, half moan from me.

My need for him, the love I feel for him, all of it sends shivers of panic darting through me. The hunger behind our kisses scares me just a little, because it feels like us, together —we're too much and not nearly enough.

*H*is nose nuzzles into my shoulder, and the warmth of his chest against my back is heaven. Last night was amazing, better than my wildest dreams. Only Gray could salvage my heart—take the horrible ordeal with Costa and make me forget, if only for the night.

He's amazing. Where would I be without him? The thought scares me, and I snuggle closer and he murmurs into the crook of my neck.

I could stay here forever. Forget about the world and all that's waiting for us once we leave this bed.

"Good morning." His voice is a sleepy rumble, sending a hot shiver up my spine.

"Morning." I wriggle once more into him, and he groans in a way that makes me smile, loving what I do to him.

"Hey, stop that." His grip tightens on my hip and he grins, planting a quick kiss on my cheek, then bounds from the bed.

"Where are you going?" I already miss him, and he pauses at the bathroom door.

"I've got to shower and get out of here."

I grab my phone from the side table to look at the time. "But it's only six thirty."

"Yeah, but the studio. I'm only going to be there half the day." His hand slaps on the doorframe and he disappears from the room.

Seconds later, the shower is on, and I flop back onto the bed. I could join him, try to distract him or keep him hostage. As much as the idea is tempting, I can't. He's rearranged his entire day for me because of my problem with

Costa, and I can't make him late to the studio on top of everything else.

I can only imagine how pissed both Silas and India would be at him. As tempting as it is, I can't do that to Gray.

In under ten minutes, he's out of the bathroom in faded jeans, and one hand tugs down a well-worn white T-shirt that now covers some of his ink and muscled glory.

His light hair is damp, slicked back from his face, and he studies me, still in bed.

"What have you got planned for today?" He rummages through the small duffel bag he brought with him, pulling out a pair of black socks.

"I've got more editing to do, and then I'm visiting Sasha before I pick up Henry. She got in yesterday."

"That's great. It'll be good to see Sasha again. You excited?" He's now on the edge of the bed, back to me as he puts on his socks, and a hand grabs my ankle through the bedsheet, squeezing.

"Yes. I can't wait to see her and to tell her..." I stop myself before dampening the mood. Until we get the results, it's insanity to keep running through my conversation with Costa.

Hello, crazy, I'm over here.

"About Costa?" Socks now on, Gray stands and turns to face me.

"Yeah." My eyes drop to the bed before flicking back to him. "She knows him, too, and she was there back then, so she might be able to shed some light on this."

I don't believe she'll know something I don't, but it will be good to talk to her.

"Hey, I've got to go." He gently pinches my chin. "But call me if you need me...for anything. I don't care."

His gaze is laser focused, waiting until I nod, then he smiles, kissing me, gently, almost reverently before releasing my chin.

"I'll be back tonight, and if you want, I can bring Henry with me."

"Oh, thanks, but it's okay. I'll swing by Pansy's and get him."

"K." He leaves the room.

I lie down and squeeze my eyes shut for a beat or two, holding back the tears. Gray is still at the forefront of my thoughts as Henry springs to mind followed by the bombshell courtesy of Costa.

Everything is so right and also so wrong. My confusion brings anger. I'm angry at Costa, at the situation, and perhaps most of all at myself.

Doubt whispers in my ear, incessantly chipping away at what I once thought to be true. Costa is Henry's father. Now I don't know, but isn't that stupid? How can I not know? Costa has to be the father. Anyone else is inconceivable.

Shaking my head, I jump from the bed, grabbing Gray's tuxedo shirt, lying on the floor. I slip my arms into the sleeves and wrap the fabric around my naked body. His warm citrus scent surrounds me and spurs me on as I run to the door.

"Gray. Gray." My frantic tone mirrors my insides, and I can't get to the front door fast enough.

He's almost out the door when he glances over his shoulder and pauses at the sight of me. "What's wrong?"

His gaze sweeps over my bare legs and the haphazard

wrapping of his shirt around my body. His crystal-blue eyes darken to cobalt with each second that ticks by as he stares at me.

And as cliché as it sounds, time seems to stand still. The war between doubt and fear, battling it out in my stomach, ceases. Gray is everywhere, dominating all my senses.

"Nothing's wrong. I just..." I inch closer and he watches my every move like a dangerous predator, raw and electric, ready to strike. "You mentioned getting a DNA test. What about Costa? How are you going to do that?"

"I'm going to talk to him today, and I'll get his DNA. It doesn't hurt to get two sets of results."

"How? I don't even know where he's staying?"

"Don't worry. I'm on it." He now steps inside, letting the door swing to almost closed.

"I don't want you to go to the troub—"

"Daze, don't try to talk me out of this. I'm not doing this to cause you stress, but I need to see him for myself. I think it's a good idea for me to get a read on him too."

I nod. It does sound like a good approach, but my stomach knots at Gray and Costa butting heads.

My concern isn't for Costa but for the man in front of me.

The one who my son looks at like he hung the moon.

The one who has my heart.

19

DAISY
WORD VOMIT

"I'm not trying to stick my nose in where it doesn't belong." He rests his hand on my shoulder, fingers gently massaging my muscle and then up to cup my cheek.

"No. No. I don't think that."

"Good. Daisy, this is my business." One thumb sweeps down to my jaw, and I shiver at his raw adoration. "You're my business and so is Henry. I love you."

He bends his head, mouth on mine, and his teeth catch my bottom lip. Goosebumps spread, my insides coming alive, and my toes curl.

"I love you too," I mumble against his mouth as my hand wraps around the back of his head, nails scraping through his hair.

There's so much I want to tell him, so much more I need to convey, and those three powerful and endearing words are only the beginning.

He pulls away on a groan and one hand rests on my bare thigh, caressing, and I shift the fabric higher up on my leg. I'm giving him better access to where I want him most, and he chuckles, shaking his head and gripping my leg firmly but gently.

"No panties," he groans, and I almost wince from how painful it sounds. "Why are you deliberately making this hard?"

"What's hard?" I cup his groin, smiling and widening my eyes like saucers at his growing arousal. "Ooh. Gray."

"Daze." His other hand cradles the back of my head, and he tugs me toward him, our foreheads now touching. "I've got to go. If I didn't care about what time I worked till tonight, I'd stay but...fuck...I want to be here with you and Henry later."

Nodding solemnly, I attempt to pull away. Let him go. He holds on tight. And it's my turn to moan in frustration. "Gray, how can you leave if you won't let me go?"

His husky laughter tickles my lips, and one hand slides around my back to bring my chest flush against all his hardness. Then fingers slide down my back and slip under the hem of his shirt until his hot hand rests on my bare ass.

"I'm never letting you go." He tightens the grip on my head, as the fingers on his other hand sink into the flesh of my bottom.

He kisses me hard, tongue sweeping into my mouth, and I consume the guttural sound he makes. His other hand moves down from my backside, digging possessively into the underside of my thigh as he lifts my leg to curl it around his waist.

The heat and outline of his hard cock presses into my stomach and I growl, not amused with how he's now playing.

"Gray." I rip my mouth from his, breathless, chest heaving. "No fair."

"Now you know how it feels." One more quick kiss and he's gone, leaving me slick and bothered, my arousal coating my inner thighs.

My morning is busy and for the most part, my mind doesn't wade too deep or for too long in the doubt and confusion.

At one point, my phone buzzes and I glance down, frowning at the name on the screen. Jerome. I hit the 'I can't talk right now' reply option, not able to handle his needs and whining on top of everything else.

My phone vibrates, and he's sent a text, asking for a date for his photo shoot of me. Running on no patience for him, I send back a one-word text—No. I can't coddle his ego right now. It may be wrong or a mistake, but he doesn't know how to take a hint.

Then I send a text to Sasha.

Me: Welcome to LA. You're likely passed out and jet-lagged, but I'm reminding you that I'll be there at 2. I want margaritas.

I stash my phone in my bag and get back to work, not expecting a reply from Sasha. She most probably took a sleeping pill and passed out. The woman doesn't handle jet lag very well. I mean, who does? But she gets nasty, so it's just as well she rests.

By early afternoon, I head over to the hotel where Sasha is staying, feeling more like myself. For the most part, Costa is relegated to the back of my mind, and even when I texted Gray to see how he's doing, I refrained from asking if he'd spoken to Costa. That can wait until tonight.

I knock on the suite door, and as if waiting eagerly on the other side, Sasha swings the door open immediately, throwing her arms around me.

There's squealing, laughing, and out of nowhere, I burst into tears. Obviously, my internal words of encouragement didn't work. On my way to the hotel, I told myself to keep it together until we'd caught up.

Seeing Sasha will be hard in light of my conversation with Costa, but also amazing. I've missed her, and after all, she's the only person that was in my life at that time. We were inseparable and often tried to get work in the same cities or on the same shoot. We were always together, and if anyone can help me make sense of this, it's Sasha.

Face to face with Sasha, I can barely string two words together. My lips tremble and a fierce burning ruptures at the back of my eyes.

"Honey, I know it's been a long time since we've seen each other, but don't cry."

I can't stop. Hot, fat tears roll down my cheeks, and Sasha's once happy face shifts into distress as she wipes at my face.

"No, Daisy, tell me what's going on." She pulls me in for another hug, and I sniff and snort into her chest.

"Shoot." I pull away and gratefully take the tissue she hands me. "I didn't mean to do this."

"What's going on?" She pulls me toward a loveseat in the small sitting area of her suite. "I know this is more than being excited to see me although I understand my mere presence could bring you to tears."

A harsh, uncontrollable laugh bursts from me, and I'm grateful for Sasha and her attempt to lighten the mood.

"I'm sorry about crying like this." I wipe under my eyes. "I told myself to keep it together."

"Honey, it happens to the best of us. Now tell me, what's wrong?"

All of it rushes out of me like a waterfall tumbling over the side of a mountain. There isn't any order to what I'm saying, and I'm not even sure if it makes any sense. It's word vomit, and my desire to get it out supersedes anything else.

For the most part, Sasha is silent, nodding, frowning, and sometimes growling, and only interrupts once or twice to ask questions for clarification.

"Holy shit. That's a lot of bullshit."

"What?"

"You don't believe him, do you?" She squeezes my hand. "He's screwing with you."

"Why would he?" I sound defensive almost as if I'm upset on Costa's behalf that she's suggesting he's lying.

"I don't know, but Daisy, you weren't with anyone else. Costa is the father." She pauses, sharp dark eyes studying my face to the point of discomfort. "Was there someone else?"

"What do you mean?" I snatch my hand from hers—call it an automatic reflex or an internal defense. It's a fair question. Costa asked the same thing, and she doesn't mean anything by it.

If it were her telling me the same story, I'd ask the same question, but it still stings.

"No. There wasn't anyone else."

"Fine. So you weren't double timing him, not that I would say it was wrong because the asshole would deserve it." She puckers her brow, likely shoving thoughts of Costa out of her mind. "But honey, did you sleep with someone else? Say a one-night stand."

I don't know how to respond without sounding insulted. Again, her question is valid and even plausible, but she knows me. She was there when Costa and I were together. There was no one else.

"Honey,"—she softens her tone and expression—"I mean, is there a possibility that Henry is someone else's child?"

"No. No, I swear." Needing distance before I lash out, I leap to my feet and start walking around the room. "This is crazy, I get it, and it feels like Costa is messing with me, but I don't know why. Gray wondered if maybe it was his wife. Maybe she didn't like the fact that Costa and I share a child together and was somehow trying to sever that tie."

"Hmm, that's a good theory." She taps her long, beautifully manicured fingernail against her lush red lips. "He's still a fucking bastard. I never liked him."

"Sash...not helping." I roll my eyes, frustrated with her hate-on for Costa. It all started when he got another male model booted off a shoot.

Sasha had been close with the other model, and it had infuriated her that Costa did such a thing. Although it does happen.

"I don't care." She waves a hand at me. "I can't help it. He's a piece of shit and now look what he's doing to you. The only way to put a stop to this is to prove him wrong. Get a DNA test."

I nod, running a hand through my hair. "Yes. We are doing that and should have the results in two days."

"Daisy." She's now on her feet, coming toward me with concern oozing from her every pore. "Darling, if he isn't the father, then what the hell happened?"

I burst into tears once more, and this time, they are even more out of control. I can't bring myself to say the words, but that's where I keep getting tripped up. As I play out how this could go, if Costa isn't Henry's father...

"I-I can't go there." It's all I'm able to say, looking away from her.

There's only one other explanation if I can't produce another potential...man. It means I was... I could have been...

"Honey, it's okay. It's going to be okay." She holds both my hands in hers, so tight that it almost hurts. Yet in some strange way, I need it. I need the pain to ground me.

"Okay, let's back up a bit. We're going to figure this out together. You know when Henry was conceived, right?"

"Well, give or take." Immediately, I'm back at that time in my life, and Sasha stares, urging me with her dark gaze to go on. "It was the week after Paris Fashion Week. Costa and I had worked the week before and we then had five days in Paris off."

"Oh, I remember." She drags me by the hand back to the couch. "The two of you stayed at a hotel."

"Yes. The George V."

Sasha and I lived with a few other models in a beautiful apartment with a spectacular view of the Eiffel Tower. The place was owned by the modeling agency we worked for, and we were the only two there that week. Most of the others had either gone back to work or taken off for Ibiza or some other paradise.

"Why didn't you stay with me?" She tilts her head to one side, scrunching her nose.

"Mickey was in town, don't you remember?" That's all I needed to say for her to understand why I wasn't at the apartment.

"Ah, yes. Mickey." She says his name with such nostalgia that I can't help but smile.

She had been so gone for that guy. It wasn't love but profound lust. Whenever the two of them were in a room together, I was so turned on that I had to change my panties.

They couldn't get enough of each other, and as a result, one day I'd had the misfortune of walking in on them having sex at the apartment. That's why I usually stayed in a hotel or at someone else's place when he was in town.

"Didn't we throw a party one night that week?" Sasha's eyes glitter with mischief, and it's clear she's reliving the memory of several unmentionable moments.

"Yes, we did." I nod. "Costa and I were together for most of those five days. Well..." Some of it is hazy but I recall there being a fight. "I think the night of the party we argued, and Costa left."

"Why? What happened?"

"He was angry because I was on him about drugs. He was high that night, stumbling around the place, breaking things."

"Yes. Yes, I remember. I was so pis—"

I cut her off, not wanting to hear how much she dislikes him. I know. "Anyway, so he left."

"Did he come back?"

"I think so." I rub at my temple as if that somehow helps with the memories. "Yes, when I woke up that morning, he was beside me in bed."

"All right. Anything else?"

"I can't think of anything else. Like I said, we were together all the time. And that week was the last time we'd had sex. Then I found out I was pregnant."

"Okay, think back to that week. Do you remember feeling off? Like not yourself? Or out of it?"

"What are you trying to say?" My question is futile and dishonest. I know what she's getting at, and I can't bring myself to say it, much less dwell on it.

"I don't know." She shrugs and looks away. Lies. "I'm just trying to think of something that might have happened to explain this. Did you hit your head? Is there something you could have blocked from your mind?"

As if running through a maze, I go through the week. Some of it is unclear and vague recollection, and with every turn, I come to a dead end. Nothing clicks, nothing makes sense.

"No. There's nothing."

"Okay, sweetie. Give it some more thought. We'll figure this out." She wraps her arms around me.

We spend a little more time catching up before I have to leave, promising to talk later and see her soon.

In my car, before I head home, I check my emails, still playing catch-up on the less important things I neglected yesterday. A text pops up from an unknown number with a picture of Gray and me from our date.

It's a great picture, and I'm immediately drawn to it although a little uneasy. We're close, intimate, looking intently at one another. There's also a link to an LA media gossip site with more pictures from our date.

Along with the image is a short article saying we're an item. It ends with a bit about models and rock stars as well as a list of other famous pairings of that kind.

I don't know how to feel about it. I don't feel anything looking at it. I'm not one to shy away from the media. And yet when I study our picture, I remember that night and how good it was. How amazing I felt.

I have this strange feeling. Who sent this to me and why? What are they trying to say with it?

It's weird, but the first person that comes to my mind is Costa. And it doesn't make any sense but nothing has. He doesn't care about me that way.

But then why would someone send this to me? Unless it's just another way to mess with my head.

20

GRAY
WASN'T EXACTLY FAITHFUL

"Gray, come on." India bursts into the sound booth, banging the door against the wall. "What is going on with you?"

"I know, it's shit." I drop my drumsticks and stand, huffing out a long, aggravated sigh.

We've been at this one part in the song for nearly an hour, and I'm the one screwing it up.

Last night when I'd texted Silas, I didn't provide much of an explanation but agreed to give them five hours in the studio, until noon. India was none too pleased and didn't say a word to me this morning, but she's making up for it now as she rants about my piss-poor performance.

I've got nothing, and there's no point correcting her or defending myself. She's right. I'm not focused and not getting it right. I played it perfectly a few days ago when I'd suggested the change up in the music.

"India, I'm sorry. I'm just not..."

"You're not here, and you're wasting my time. Why, Gray? Why? Is this your idea of a game?" Her nostrils flare, and her long dark hair flies behind her as she stomps around the small room.

Silas folds his arms across his chest, expression blank but observant through the glass. I can't tell if he's disappointed in me, India, or the entire situation. I'm guessing the latter given every minute counts and I've fucked us over and wasted everyone's time this morning.

"Hey, guys, let's take a break." Silas interrupts through the speakers, and India glares at him through the window.

Then once again, she makes her grand exit with a scream, lifting her hands into the air. Silas watches from the other room and shoots me a not amused glower. I'm the one to get up, feeling more than responsible for her outburst, and I go to him.

"I'm sorry. I just have something to do and I'm—"

"Your head isn't in the game. She's right." His jaw tenses and he nods.

"And you're too easy on her. Maybe if we called her on her bullshit we wouldn't have to deal with her tantrums," I lash out, bitter that we tiptoe around her. "Everyone did that shit with you and look where it got us. Trojan's dead."

He staggers back a step as if I've shoved him, and truth be told, I don't know where that came from. I loved Trojan but don't harbor any resentment toward him for our retirement.

"What the hell, Gray?" Silas narrows his gaze, lips thin, and he crosses his arms over his chest. "Is this about whatever it is you have to take care of this afternoon?"

"No. This is about you cutting me out of shit." I'm vehement, refusing to let him off the hook and admit Daisy's news last night is weighing on my mind.

"Seriously."

"Don't be an ass." I plant my hands on my hips. "We need a firmer hand with India, and I'd do it but I'm in the shitty position right now since I'm straddling two roles."

"What are you talking about?" Dismissive and irate, he starts to pace.

"I'm one of the band for all intents and purposes. I can't be the one telling her to cool it and be professional and then get in there and play the drums." I shut up and let what I'm saying sink in.

If I take on the role as producer, giving orders and calling the shots, it'll only create tension between the band and me. Especially if I'm telling India to stop acting like a diva. It could impact the quality of the album.

"Fine." He tenses his jaw even as he relents. "I'll talk to her about cooling it. She can be exhausting, but Gray, she isn't wrong. You're distracted, and I don't know what's going on, but my gut tells me it's about whatever is happening later today."

Now I'm the one to relent. "Yeah, it is. I can't say more right now but when I can, I will." Daisy planned on talking to Pansy, but this mess with Costa isn't mine to share.

I got a text from my lawyer not even an hour ago. The fucker is staying at the Chateau Marmont. Of course he is.

And now I'm consumed with thoughts of speaking to him. I can't deny I'm also raring to see this motherfucker in person. Forget I already don't like him because he was with Daisy, but I downright despise him for what he did to Henry.

Before all of this garbage, the spineless bastard had the balls to deny his own son. I don't like the guy.

"Go. You're of no use to me like this."

"But we've got another hour."

"Forget about it. I know you're good for it, and the sooner you take care of whatever this is, the sooner I can have you rockin' this album. We won't waste the time. We'll focus on India and the others." He slaps my back, and I've got no words to adequately express my gratitude.

Thank you doesn't feel like it even begins to do the job.

"Thanks, I owe you."

He nods and saunters down the hall, likely to face the drama queen.

The drive to the Chateau Marmont is forgettable and I can't say much about how I got here. I don't bother with the front desk and head up to the floor where Costa is staying. My lawyer not only found out the hotel but also the room number and confirmed that the asshole is here.

I bang on the door, not going in under any pretenses.

"Who is it?" a man asks from behind the closed door.

"Open the door now." I slam my palm against the metal door, and I can see an eyeball looking through the peep hole.

"Costa, this is about Daisy and Henry. Open this door now."

The latch turns and he opens the door, stepping back to let me in. He's everything I thought he would be. Calvin Klein perfect, yet a darker, more mysterious version stands before me.

Chiseled features, thick, black curls, sulky mouth, and a

smoldering gaze that with one look, a would-be admirer believes the man only has eyes for them.

I'm not insecure about my body or looks, but something about this guy bothers me instantly. Maybe it's because he's the father to the little boy I wish was mine. Heck, maybe he isn't the father, but he had the chance to be and pissed on it. That I can't forgive.

"What the fuck are you after?" I charge at him, hand grabbing at his jaw and pushing him back against the wall.

"Hey, watch it. Don't hurt me." He cowers, closing his eyes.

"Then start talking."

"What do you want from me? Who are you?"

"I'm Gray, Daisy's boyfriend and your worst nightmare. I don't know what you're after, but you can't come here and mess with her like you did."

"I didn't lie. Look, please stop. You're hurting me."

I can't be. My grip is firm but hardly tight. If he wanted to, he could try to knock me off him, but he really is a pretty boy. I release him and let out a disgusted snort.

"I've got to work. I can't show up bruised or bones broken."

"I didn't plan on touching you unless you gave me reason to." I'm not prone to violence, but right now, all I want is to draw blood. "Start talking." I widen my stance and fold my arms across my chest.

He straightens his shirt and pushes his dark hair off his face, looking me in the eye. His tale is much the same as Daisy's account of the conversation, and as much as I hoped for something more, something to indicate what Costa is up to, I get what she meant.

This guy is a stranger to me and yet I believe him. He's sincere and comes across as though he believes every word of what he's saying. And may even be a little broken up about it, although that could have nothing to do with Daisy and Henry and everything to do with discovering he's sterile.

I even press him about who asked for the testing. Can the doctor in Greece be trusted or his wife? All his answers assure me nothing underhanded is going on here.

No, scratch that, something is off. Someone is Henry's father and if not Costa, then who? I believe Daisy believes Costa is the father. How the fuck did this happen?

My heartbeat pounds in my ears like the ominous drums in some slasher movie. Every time my mind takes me down that dark path, I just...I can't. It can't be...

"Now do you believe me?" Costa's frustrated tone pulls me from my perplexing thoughts.

"Why did you come here in person? Why didn't you call her?" I partially figure his response before I've even fully formed the question, but it needs asking.

"I'm an asshole but not that much of one." His jaw tightens, and he bares his row of perfect, white teeth. "I have work in New York in a few days. Then when I found out..." He drops into a chair, leaning forward so his arms rest on the tops of his thighs. "I tried to think how I would feel if I were Daisy and got a call out of the blue from an ex. And not just any ex, but one who was a jerk to her."

He snorts and I join him. At least he admits he's a jerk—that's definitely one point for him.

"I figured she most probably slept with someone else and maybe the news wouldn't be shocking...and I wanted to be angry at that."

He runs a hand roughly through his dark waves and tips his head up to look at me. "I had no right to be. I wasn't exactly faithful to her, and despite everything else, I care about her. We had good times together. If it were me, I'd want to be told in person, so that's what I did. I decided to come to LA first."

The more he says, the more satisfied I am with his version but also insanely irritated at having more questions with no answers in sight.

"We'll have the DNA results in two days. Daisy and I will each get them delivered to us us."

"We're going to get our own tests done." I steady my stance, preparing for an argument or outburst.

"What? Why?" His dark eyes search my features, looking for some reason or explanation.

"It's nothing personal. As things stand right now, I believe you, but I want to make sure. So I've arranged for another test, and it'll be ready in the same amount of time. I need your DNA."

I pull out the kit I'd picked up from the lab on the way here and hand it to him.

"The instructions are in there. From what I understand, it's quick and painless."

He's already nodding and standing. "Yes, yes, I know. I did the same for the tests I am having done. I really don't understand why this is necessary." He isn't challenging me but sounds more resigned as he takes the package from me.

"I'll also need your email, and you'll get a link to a secure site when the test is completed so you can also have access to the results."

He reads the instructions and places a long stick that looks like a big cotton swab into his mouth. The stick scrapes along the lining of his mouth, collecting DNA cells, and when done, he places the stick into a sterile container.

We exchange email and cellphone numbers, and I slide the container into the bag provided by the lab. Then I walk to the door of his suite.

Costa trails behind, fidgeting. I sense his need to say something more and pause with my hand on the doorknob.

"Gray, ah...I don't know." He scratches at the back of my neck. "Daisy seems shocked by this. Like none of this makes any sense to her."

I nod solemnly, swallowing hard. That nasty lump of understanding lodges in my throat, blocking air from getting into my lungs.

"If she didn't...didn't sleep with someone else, then..." He hangs his head, hands clasping at the back of his neck on a long, torturous exhale.

His confusion and uneasiness are felt deep in my gut, and even though I can't bring myself to fucking fathom the other possibility, I let him off the hook.

I'm with Daisy. I will be the one to get her through this no matter what the outcome is. "Yeah, it means something far worse happened. Something she either knows about but won't speak of, or she has blocked it."

"What? Blocked it?" He cocks his head to one side, brow wrinkled. "Does that really happen?"

"I don't know, but I'm going to find out." I open the door all the way. Suddenly the room feels too small, too hot, and I need to get out. "Look, you were there around the time of conception. I don't expect you to answer me right now but think about it. Think about that time. Was there anything unusual? Anything that stands out now that things have changed?"

"What do you mean?" He folds his arms over his chest, fingers digging into his biceps.

"I don't know what I'm asking. All I know is Daisy doesn't understand what happened. If you're not Henry's father, then someone else slept with her around that time...and likely without her consent." I clench my jaw, gathering strength and composure from deep within me.

"Fuck." Costa's expression is grave, and he nods. "I'll give it some thought. If anything comes to mind, I'll text or call you."

"Thanks."

My feet can't carry me fast enough from the hotel. Hopefully that's the last time I see Costa, because if it isn't then he's lied and put Daisy through a lot of turmoil for nothing.

On the drive to the lab to drop off his DNA sample, I do the same as I asked Costa to do. I think back over times when Daisy would talk about her pregnancy and her time in Europe during those final days before she left for LA.

I'm no expert, but she has never shown any signs of distress or anything like that. Is it possible that she doesn't remember anything?

21

GRAY

ONE FINE BEAUTY

*A*fter I drop off the DNA sample to the lab, I visit my lawyer to go over what else needs to be done. I arrange for a private investigator, actually several, to look into Costa, his wife, and that period of time in Paris when Henry was conceived.

I hadn't planned on any investigations, but after meeting Costa—and I believe he's genuine and legitimate—I want to make sure we haven't missed anything. He clearly loves his wife, and that makes him the last person I should trust to judge her character.

And like I asked Costa to think back to that time in his life, the answer lies in the past, so that's where I'm looking.

My heart stumbles, hardly imagining what Daisy is going through. I'm in knots and anxious as shit, and in some ways, I'm a bystander. But not for long.

I may be quiet, and some people might even say reserved,

but I don't like sitting idly by, doing nothing, especially where Daisy is concerned.

After my lawyer, I switch gears and focus on hiring an agency to find a nanny, as well as stress the urgency of sending résumés so we can set up a few interviews as soon as possible. It's another way I can help even if it doesn't feel like enough.

Hiring a nanny is big, and the search has taken far too long and stalled far too often. Daisy is busy, and while she won't admit it, my guess is the expense of a nanny might put a bigger dent than she would like in her bank account.

Sure, her business is doing well and will be doing even better now that she's gaining prestige in the industry, but the cost holds her back. I will help her with that too, and slowly I'll make her see we're in this together.

We've been texting all afternoon and every single message from her has included some question about how things went with Costa. She's obsessed with knowing the outcome.

I get it and would likely be the same—an incessant drumbeat until I got answers—and I will tell her, in person, tonight. At that time, I'll also tell her about the PIs.

Before picking up dinner to share with Daisy, Henry, and Sasha, I go to my place and grab more clothes. I won't be sleeping anywhere but with Daisy. We haven't talked about it, but I always intended on moving in once our relationship advanced. You see, I was patient, waiting for Daisy, but there was no question or doubt we would be together.

Dinner in hand, I walk through the front door of Daisy's

house, and girly squeals of laughter punch at my chest. The buoyant joy of it tugs at the strings of my heart.

I walk into the kitchen, glimpsing Henry out of the corner of my eye, sitting on the hardwood floor of the living room. Vroom, vroom comes from his little imaginary race-track or roadway as he plays with his toy cars.

Sasha is finishing up a story, and Daisy almost chokes on her giggles. Both sets of smiling blue eyes land on me. I deposit the takeout bag of Lebanese food on the counter, and my gaze sweeps over Daisy.

The uncontrolled hammering of my heart against my ribcage intensifies when her perfectly bow shaped lips slant upward at the corners into a slow, contagious smile.

"Holy fuck." Sasha places her wine glass onto the table and gets to her feet.

"Sasha!" Daisy's admonishing tone and stern expression gives her friend pause.

The fashion model looks to Daisy, and there's no denying the two of them could easily pass for sisters with their blonde hair, blue eyes, and tall, lean frames. Sasha's grin widens as something naughty flashes in her eyes.

"Sorry, but how can you expect me to behave when all this deliciousness is in the house?" She sounds like a DJ and waves her long, manicured fingers in my direction.

"I know, I know, it's hard, but keep it clean and no swear-ing. We have a child." Daisy bites at her mouth, suppressing a smile—Sasha needs no encouragement—while trying to pull off a serious glare.

My smile eclipses my face, and warmth blooms and

spreads throughout my chest. It has nothing to do with Sasha's compliment and everything to do with Daisy saying *we* have a child. I'm pretty sure the *we* she's referring to is me and her.

"Fine." Sasha accepts the reprimand and opens her arms to me.

"Hey, Sasha, good to see you." I wrap my arms around her waist for a hug, and after a bit, I try to pull away, but she continues to hang on.

She whispers in my ear. "Just go with it. Let me have a little fun."

Her hands roam freely along my back as she titters with laughter, and Daisy playfully bats at her friend's touchy hands.

"That's enough. Leave him alone." Daisy pries her friend off me, and I chuckle, more than amused to be the center of attention.

My woman slips into my side, bringing my arm around her neck, and hangs on tight. As if she has anything to worry about, but I can't deny I love how possessive she is about me.

"Grayson Bennett, you are one fine beauty," Sasha purrs, running a hand over my heavily sleeved arms.

My tattoos chronicle my life in one way or another with images, quotes, and symbols. Some have meaning and others, I just liked, but now they hold memories.

Her touch isn't in the least bit sexual, just friendly. Sasha's trying to get a rise out of Daisy, but my girl isn't taking the bait. Well, she's trying to act cool and unfazed but the fact that her hand is digging into my waist makes me think otherwise.

"It's been too long, and you're looking as gorgeous as ever. How are you?" I bring Daisy with me to the fridge for a beer.

"Darlin', I'm so happy to finally be here." She reaches out and takes one of Daisy's hands. "Especially right now."

The solemn note to her tone tells me they've talked about Costa and all of that. I nod and look to Daisy who has taken the bottle from me and is popping the cap before she hands it back to me.

"Hey." My lips brush over hers, tasting the fruitiness of the wine and the sweetness that is all her. Electricity pulses through my body.

"Hi." Her fingers wrap around the sides of my T-shirt, holding me to her. "Sasha is right, you're delicious."

She presses onto her toes to reach my mouth with hers, teasing the seam of my lips with the tip of her tongue. I wait, anxious for her tongue to delve into my mouth, but she doesn't. She licks once more and ends the kiss. Something changes her mind. Maybe it's Sasha's presence, or more likely, Henry's.

"Yes, delicious." She murmurs appreciatively as her thumb wipes away any moisture on my bottom lip.

She leaves me thirsty but no longer for the beer, and Sasha chuckles behind me, clearly amused.

"So how did it go with Costa?" Daisy washes her hands in the kitchen sink, glancing at me over her shoulder.

"He didn't say anything different from what you told me." I recap the rest of the conversation and how Costa assured me that we could trust his wife and the doctor in Greece who gave him the news of his sterility.

"And do you believe him?" Sasha's voice is sharp and challenging as if there's no other answer but no.

"I do." I open the bag, and Daisy stands beside me, hands out for the first container.

"You do?" Daisy's tone is flat, and in those two words there's so much more going on. Her demeanor infers if I believe Costa, how can I possibly believe her?

"He's a lying son of a bitch," Sasha snaps, downing the last of her wine in one long gulp.

"Hey, I can't explain it because I believe Daisy, and Costa is the only one who could be"—I lower my voice—"the father, but when I spoke to him, he looked and sounded sincere."

Daisy nods, maybe not satisfied with my response, but accepting.

"Even so, to be safe, I'm having him investigated and his wife, and I've arranged for them to also look into that week in Paris."

"You are?" Daisy's alarmed, blue eyes round like dark moons, and a frown shadows her brow.

"Now that is smart." Sasha lays out the cutlery and pours herself another glass of wine.

"Why didn't you talk to me about this first?" Now Daisy sounds a little ticked, and I open my mouth to explain but I'm cut off by her friend.

"Honey, Gray's not only gorgeous but smart. Don't be upset with him." She removes the lid from a large container and sets the Fattoush salad down.

"I'm not upset, it's just that..." She rakes a hand through her tousled blonde hair.

"Daze, this morning when we talked, I hadn't planned on getting a PI. It was only after meeting with Costa that I realized we need more answers to the countless questions we have."

She nods, folding her arms over her middle. Unable to stand the posture, how she's closing herself off, I grab at her arm and bring her to me. I cup her face in my hands and lean my forehead against hers.

"We'll get the test results which will hopefully put an end to all of this, but there's still the question of why he would suggest something that can be disproved." My gut clenches, because what I'm saying is a strong argument for Costa telling the truth.

There's no logical reason why he'd lie. Even if he wanted Henry, sole custody, ultimately the courts would have to get involved, so why lie?

"And if Costa isn't the father..." She blinks at the water gathering in her eyes. "We may have something to go on from the investigation." She pulls away, staring down at the table. "We should eat, let me get Henry."

"No." I rest my hand on her arm. "Let me get him."

"Gray, it is the smart thing to do." She pushes a processed smile onto her tight lips. "Thank you."

I nod and go get Henry, returning to a table full of food.

"Wow, how many people did you think we were feeding?" Daisy takes Henry from me and gets him set up for dinner.

Platters of kibbeh, hummus, tabbouleh, beef and chicken kebabs, lamb chops, and other Middle Eastern delights are laid out before us.

"I was hungry." I pat my stomach and shrug. "I'll eat whatever's left over tomorrow."

She laughs, securing the highchair tray in front of Henry before sitting down to fill her own plate.

"Everything looks delicious." Sasha tears off a piece of her pita bread and dips it into the hummus. "Hey, flower girl, you better hang on to this one." She winks at Daisy and pops the garlicky goodness into her mouth.

Throughout the meal, we laugh, share stories, and I even mention how I hired a nanny agency and she'll have résumés first thing tomorrow to look at.

She drops the pita onto her plate, and both Sasha and I stop eating. "Gray, I said I'd handle anything to do with hiring a nanny."

"Yeah, but I had the time and figured I'd get the ball rolling. You'll still get to go through the résumés and interviews. I'll only help when you want me to."

"What if I wanted to use another agency?"

"I used the agency you'd short-listed as your number one choice." My defense does nothing but rile her up.

She pushes her chair back a bit and folds her arms over her chest. "What if my schedule doesn't allow for interviews right now?"

Her questions and body language are like one sharp jab to my chest. *Ouch.* I screwed up.

"He's only helping you." Sasha wipes her hand on a napkin, perplexed at Daisy's reaction.

While I appreciate her support and the backup, Daisy's rigid, almost closed off posture suggests it isn't helping.

"You know what, forget it. Thank you for doing this. Really." She slides back to the table and takes my hand in a reassuring squeeze, but I'm not convinced.

She's most probably pretending to be okay, and with Sasha here, I don't push it. But I will if I have to.

Fortunately, it doesn't take long for the friction to fade. The rest of the time spent eating and talking helps Daisy shake off some of the gloom hanging over her.

A little later, I take Henry out back to play, then bathe him and get him ready for bed. Once again, I fall asleep with the little guy and wake up about an hour later, groggy.

Daisy and Sasha are in the living room when I return.

"We thought we had lost you." Daisy tugs at the edge of my shirt which is riding up as I yawn and stretch. "If you'd fallen asleep with him, I would have kicked you out."

I chuckle. "Yeah, his bed gets me every time. As soon as my head hits the pillow, it's a grueling battle to stay awake."

Sasha laughs. "Well, I'm going to leave and give you two some alone time."

"Don't leave on my account." I plop down beside Daisy, pulling her into my arm.

"No, it isn't you. I ordered an Uber and it'll be here any minute. Seriously, I'm exhausted. The jet lag is kicking in." She grabs her handbag, slipping her arm through the handle, and stands. "But I'll see the both of you soon."

We walk her outside onto the front lawn at the same time the Uber pulls up. Daisy and Sasha hug, make some more plans, and she gets into the car.

Daisy stares after the Uber disappearing down the street and I'm about to drag us back into the house when movement from my peripheral vision causes me to stop.

Across the road and a few houses down, a man gets out of a car. It's too dark to make out who it is from this distance but there's something about him that's familiar, maybe his build or gait.

And there's also something about this person that sets my teeth on edge. Then he calls her name, stalking toward Daisy, and that does it. Jerome.

Why didn't I notice his car parked along the curb? How long has he been waiting out here? This is most probably about his bullshit portfolio. He won't let up on insisting she model for his photo shoot.

"Oh, no," Daisy mutters under her breath and looks from Jerome to me.

"Go inside." I edge myself around her as a barrier between her and the approaching man, but she doesn't move. I feel the heat of her at my back.

"Gray, let me talk to him." She presses her forehead to the center of my back briefly and the urge to revel in her nearness is overwhelming, but now isn't the time. I'm not moving and would go to great lengths to protect her. "I'll get him to leave."

"No. I'll get rid of him." I turn to face her, leaning down and pressing my lips to hers. "Go."

She nods and twirls as a hand reaches out to tag her shoulder. I grip his forearm and growl. Jerome tries to shake me off, staring intently at Daisy who is partially facing us.

"My beautiful, are you avoiding me?" His tone is forced cheerfulness, but he's doing a terrible job at hiding his annoyance. "Or are you too busy with your boyfriend?"

And there it is—his sneer as his beady eyes flick to me, expression now glacial.

"Hey." I push at his chest, then turn to rest a hand on her hip and kiss her once more.

Yeah, the move isn't necessary and is deliberate, but since when has kissing the woman you love been a bad thing or a waste of time? I can be a caveman when I need to be, and I make no apologies for it. This bastard won't leave her alone, and he needs to understand she isn't his.

"You go inside." I release her.

"Bye." She peers around me at Jerome but that's it. No smile or lingering. She's gone, and the man at my side snarls, his displeasure radiating off him.

"Daisy," he calls, no longer hiding his agitation. "Dai—"

"Look here." I poke my finger into his chest again, and his head snaps down to where I'm touching him.

Slowly, he raises his head back up, eyes narrowed on me. "What is your problem?"

"My problem? What are you doing here?"

"I came to talk to Daisy."

"Well, now isn't a good time. She'll get back to you when she has time." Hands on my hips, I glare at him, and if he were a cartoon character, there would be smoke rising from his ears.

"What the hell? Who do you think you are? You take her to an awards dinner and now you think you own her?"

If I were a lesser and maybe smarter man, I might recoil from the fury in his tone, but this man only infuriates me. I'm not in the least bit intimidated.

"I don't own her. No one does." I get into his face, making

sure he sees my aggravation at this little visit of his. "Daisy and I are together, and not that I owe you an explanation but it's after ten at night. She's tired, and now isn't the time for her to listen to you whine about your career and other bullshit."

"You little piece of..." He clamps his mouth shut, maybe thinking better of his insult or how getting into a verbal or physical match with me will not help his cause.

Jerome stares beyond me at the house as if trying to figure out how to get past me. How to get to Daisy.

"Leave." My nose practically touches his, but he doesn't budge.

"We're not done here." Despite his warning, he spins on his heel, fuming as he marches back to his car.

Oh yes, that's where Jerome is wrong. We are most certainly done. If I get my way, Jerome will be out of our lives soon.

22

DAISY

IT'S A DARE, A PLEA, AND A PROMISE

"Y ou didn't have to—" Chest tight, I suck in a breath as the words catch in my throat.

Gray comes for me, his gaze filled with an unfathomable intensity. "Don't make excuses for that man." The words are strung tight, sharp like the glinting blade of a butcher's knife. He's upset, furious even, but not with me.

Hungry eyes sweep over the flimsy tank top down to my panties, and before I know it, he's in front of me. He lifts one of his large, callused hands to rest flat on the half moon of exposed skin above the scooped neckline of my top.

His thumb toys with the hem, skirting the top of my breast, and his fingers drum against my thrumming pulse. With his hand splayed between my breasts, his fingertips curl around the base of my neck and he nudges me until my back hits the wall.

"Do you have any idea how badly I want you?" He pins me to the wall, and my heart hammers in my throat.

"Take me. I'm yours." It's a dare, a plea, and a promise.

My fingers thread into his hair and I pull him down to my mouth. Rough-skinned hands make fast work of discarding my top and panties, and I shiver at the cool air against my skin, or maybe it's his touch.

Nipples instantly puckering, I lean into his possessive hands, drunk on his kisses and needing more, something only he can give me. His hard erection grinds into my stomach and my hips move, back arching as I'm frantic to become one with him.

Reading me so well, or because he craves the connection as much as I do, he releases his buckle, button, and zipper seamlessly, never stopping the insatiable stroking of his tongue in my mouth.

Then, with one hand, he shoves down his jeans and boxers to just below his ass. His long, hard cock, so perfect, juts out toward me, and he runs two fingers through my slick arousal.

"Daisy." His voice is a hoarse rasp, blanketed in devotion as he pinches, swirls, and strokes my clit. The tight spiral of fire in my stomach is both exhilarating and paralyzing.

He lines his crown with my entrance, eyes boring into mine, and all I see is a healthy dose of desire and uncondi-tional love. With one blinding thrust into me, the world fades away and there's only Gray and me. Us.

᠂᠁᠂

ray's hand dances along the underside of my breast, causing tingles throughout my body. "Did you sleep o—"

"Mommy. Mommy." Henry bursts through the slightly opened door, bounding onto the bed with Jellycat in hand. "Gaga?" His name for Gray comes out like a question but also a happy surprise.

Shit. I tense, not knowing if I should explain to my two-year-old son why Gray is in my bed or let it go. I had wondered how best to approach this with Henry, in a way that he could understand, but he is only two. Do I even have to say anything?

Gray is already so much a part of his world. He sees him every day and would love to see more of Gray, even if the man no longer sleeps on the couch but in my bed. Henry may be young, but he's smart, and sometimes, with some things, words aren't needed.

"Hey, my little man." Gray tries to untangle us without revealing we're naked beneath the sheets at the same time my son launches his little body at the man.

Jellycat, the stuffed octopus, whacks him in the head. *Oof.* Gray catches Henry with ease. In one smooth move, his arms close around the little boy while he rolls away from me, avoiding what could have been a head-on collision, literally, between Henry's and my own. Ouch.

Henry laughs, arms and legs wrapping around Gray, and my insides fill with something warm and gooey. The sensation, this right here, is keeping the Costa turmoil from slowly seeping into the forefront of my mind.

"Let's go make breakfast and Mommy can get dressed." Gray pulls him from the bed, placing Henry on his feet. Then he nabs his jeans from the floor and drags them up his California-tanned and toned thighs.

Henry's already halfway to the door when I get a glorious view of Gray's magnificent ass as he goes commando beneath his denim. I groan, rolling my face into my pillow, and he chuckles, hand pressing into my back and lips at my ear. "Like what you see, perv?"

I nod, fingers fisting into the edges of my pillow and kicking my feet out like a petulant child that can't have what they want.

"Take your time." His warm lips press into the back of my head. "Let's go, Henry."

Grudgingly, I roll onto my side, and Gray tosses me a robe with an easy grin before grabbing Henry's hand. My son bounces on his little feet, all too eager to play chef. My heart stutters, and I'm sure the smile that blooms on my face is brighter than the sun.

"I'll be out as soon as I have a shower." I force myself to look away, get a hold of myself before I jump out of this bed and join them. All I want right now is to be with them both.

I pick up my phone from the table and inwardly groan at the time—barely six o'clock. My son is an early riser. That explains why my muscles feel like blocks of cement.

Then one look at my notifications, both text and email, and I want to go back to bed as a cranky grunt pushes past my closed lips. Jerome.

"What is it?" Gray, practically out of the room, stops and frowns.

"Just stuff I have to get to." My hand pushes back a mop of hair from my face, and I wrap the robe around me before getting out of bed. "I completely checked out yesterday afternoon."

If I dare say his name, tell Gray Jerome's hounding me, I'm not sure what he might do. Whatever took place between the two of them last night wasn't good, judging by the way Jerome has blasted my phone with messages.

I should feel bad for him, but I can't bring myself to do much more than move forward. I'll deal with him...later.

"Hey, don't be so hard on yourself. There's nothing there that can't keep until you have a shower, food, and coffee." He strides to my side of the bed and curls his hand around mine, the one holding the phone. "Ma'am, do I have to confiscate the device?"

His voice is suddenly deeper, more imposing as he impersonates a police officer or someone in a position of authority. I laugh, a welcomed heat blossoming on my cheeks.

Henry has no clue what's funny, but he joins in, wrapping a chubby arm around my leg and staring up at us amused.

"No, sir. I will leave the phone right here." I drop it onto the mattress before leaning in to press a quick kiss on Gray's cheek. "You want one too, Lovebug?" I bend to pick up Henry for a hug and he squirms, shaking his head from side to side.

While my son tolerates kisses, he'd rather be off exploring, playing, or something else. And right now, I'm pretty sure all he's thinking about is getting his hands on some food.

But the little guy relents, allowing the kiss, and he even

rests his cheek against mine afterward. No sooner than I start to nuzzle him, he's wriggling once more to be free.

I put him down and follow them to the doorway, stopping to lean against the frame. Two bedheads, hair in disarray, laugh and scamper out of sight.

Despite all the questions and heartache the past two days have been filled with, I'm at peace in this very moment. Things are right in my little bubble. No matter what happens, I have them and that's all that matters.

I shower and dress, and once I'm in the kitchen, Gray takes off to do the same. He has to be in the studio by seven thirty and he has another long day. I use the time to rearrange my schedule and answer a text from my sister.

Pansy sensed something about me yesterday when I picked up Henry and she now wants to see me this afternoon. She's worried and has time before class.

My insides spasm with nerves. I could hold her off, tell her nothing is wrong, and I even contemplated not saying anything about Costa unless I have to—if the test results prove he is telling the truth.

But as unsettling and mind-boggling as it is, each time I talk about it, a little more of the enormous and indecipherable ball in my stomach loosens or unravels.

Gray pads back into the kitchen, clean and sexy, smiling at me. "I'm going to see if I can get tomorrow off."

"Why?" I stand from the chair, inching toward him.

"It's tomorrow." His unspoken words fall upon us like heavy pelts of freezing rain.

Yes, when the DNA test results are in.

"Gray, you've got the album. I can't ask you to do that.

India and Silas are going to lose it." My thoughts fray, worrying about his obligations and the burden my problems only add.

"First of all, you're not asking me to do anything. And..." He lowers his voice, leaning into me even though Henry couldn't care less what we're talking about.

He's Picasso, creating his next masterpiece, fingers playing with his milk and Cheerios across the top of his highchair tray.

"I don't want you driving yourself crazy, waiting and alone."

"But the album... Look, you're right. My concentration isn't there right now, so I've moved things around on my schedule to allow for today and tomorrow." My fingers trek the wing of the robin on his forearm. "And I won't be alone. I've got Henry, and Pansy's coming over later today. I'll be busy. And tomorrow I'm going to look through the nanny applications and I'll set up some interviews—"

"I want to look through them too. You aren't alone in this. Let me help." His finger rubs at the inside of my elbow, soothingly, and my insides quiver.

How does he do this to me with just a touch?

"Why don't I look at them first and then share the ones I've selected for your thoughts?" I wrap a hand around his neck.

"I'm not promising anything. Let's see how today goes, and I can always make my mind up later."

"Gray." My voice cracks and suddenly a surge of emotion overwhelms me.

Words can't even begin to express how I feel about this

man. His concern and caring for me, for my son... I can't imagine doing this alone, or with anyone else.

"Yeah?" Traces of concern ring his words.

"Thank you." My face buries into his warm, solid chest, and I'm wholly aware of his fresh, masculine scent.

His hold tightens and kisses the crown of my head, releasing a deep humming sound so like contentment. Before I lose all willpower and take up residence in his arms, I break away.

I've unwittingly invited his scrutiny as he cranes his head to study me, and I turn to Henry, running a hand through his short, soft tuffs of hair. My son smiles, soggy Cheerios sticking to his chin and hands.

Gray chuckles, and the simple sound of his delight infuses me with the same. He bends to say goodbye to Henry and then to me. "I'll call you later. Love you."

"I love you too."

The morning is uneventful, and for the most part, I get a fair amount of work done. After lunch and with Henry down for a nap, I wait for Pansy, and it's in that brief time of nothingness that I find Costa's words running rampant in my mind.

By the time my sister walks through the front door, I'm sick with anxiety and no longer eager to share the story. Intuitive as ever, Pansy senses my distress immediately.

"What's wrong?" She drops her bag to the floor and sits next to me on the sofa. "Sorry I'm late. I forgot my notebook and had to double back for it. But I still have twenty minutes until I have to leave for class."

I can't look at her, my gaze down in my lap. Pansy and I

haven't always been close. Heck, no, we were never close, not until recently.

We've grown into a sisterly friendship only since I wound up on her doorstep pregnant and refusing to reach out to our older sister, Ivy. She's a neurosurgeon and all-around perfect, albeit judgemental, person.

"Hey." She softens her tone, rubbing at my arm. "Tell me what's wrong."

"I thought I could tell you…"

"Is it something to do with Gray? Is everything okay with you two? Or is it Henry?" Her tone is more urgent and insistent and I chastise myself for putting her through this torture.

Time to move past my hang-up and just tell her. "No. Gray and Henry are great. Well, in a roundabout way, this is about Henry."

I settle into the couch, making eye contact with my sister, and tell her everything. As expected, there are times when she interjects with a question, a gasp, or a plain old head shake. It's surreal, and seeing my sister's reactions helps me accept that all I'm feeling is natural.

"Daze." She clasps my hand in hers. "And you get the results tomorrow?"

"Yes."

"Do you have any idea who the father is, if not Costa?"

"No." Tears sting my eyes, and I don't want to cry again.

"Daisy." Pansy's tone causes my insides to quiver, recognizing her all too compassionate yet somber voice. "Honey, you could have been sexually assaulted."

All I can do is nod, pressing my lips together into a

painful line, no longer able to hold back the tears. I haven't been able to say it out loud. Shit, not Costa, Gray, nor Sasha has either but I'm sure we've all thought it.

"Yeah, it's possible. I mean, there were so many moments where...there was always a party or an event...alcohol and drugs."

Shame bitch slaps me across the face and I look away. The heat from my wild days, the carefree binges on alcohol or random hits of coke or who knows what else. It was every-where and given freely, and I took my share.

"But I can't think of a single moment where I felt violated. I know, it's hard to believe when I just told you I may have been drinking or high." The contempt for myself is hard to miss in my voice.

"Honey, don't do that." She slides her arm around me, bringing me into her body. "Having a good time at a party doesn't mean you deserved to be assaulted and taken advan-tage of. Is it possible you were drugged?"

"What? Like the date rape drug?"

It had crossed my mind, but I had immediately killed the thought. Bile burns the back of my throat. I can't consider what that means. That there was a predator among those I worked with and maybe even trusted.

"Yes."

I bite my lip, trying to hold back the tears, but they refuse to go. I wasn't a saint. I drank. I sometimes would do drugs. There was even a time or two where I passed out at parties. So, yeah, it was possible that I could have been drugged and would think no more of it than a horrible hangover.

"Oh my God." I cover my hands over my face, ashamed and sick to think of my recklessness and how I made it easy for someone to take advantage of me.

23

DAISY
TICK, TICK, TICK

"*I*'ll be back as early as possible tonight." Gray's stubbled cheek nuzzles mine as his tongue licks at the base of my ear, and I shiver, hands clasping his lean waist.

"It's okay. Take your time." As I say the words, I'm also dreading all those hours waiting for him once the results arrive.

Last night, we talked at length about how he'd only go into the studio today if I promised to wait for him to open the results. He would do the same with the email from the lab where he got another test done. We'd do it together.

At the time, it's what I wanted, and it was a small concession, easy to agree to. I didn't want to be alone when reading the results, but now, in the brightness of the day, can I wait for him? It could be several hours until he comes back.

"Love you." His lips press onto my mouth, and he strolls into the living room to say goodbye to Henry.

I don't have any plans for today other than to review the more than thirty nanny résumés the agency sent yesterday. Sasha is busy with work despite this trip being a vacation. Her agency booked her for two local campaigns since she's considering moving to LA and putting down roots here.

Between playing with Henry and going through all the nanny applications, the time drags. I've spoken with the placement agency and arranged for four interviews with six more as potentials if none of the first four are a good fit.

Gray texts every couple of hours, and by the time Henry's nap rolls around, I don't know how I'm going to fill the time while he sleeps.

It takes everything not to go out of my mind, and that's why I answer the call from Jerome, despite avoiding him. It's something to do and I can't keep putting it off.

"Hi." I saunter into the kitchen to fix a tea.

"Finally, you answer the phone." He's exasperated and clipped. "Is the asshole nowhere near, is that why? Has he told you not to call me?"

I'm ticked that he thinks Gray or any man has that kind of hold on me, but I don't care enough about him to set him straight.

"Jerome, don't call Gray an asshole. If that's how you're going to talk about him, I'm hanging up." I pour hot water from the kettle into the mug.

"Seriously?" He sounds incredulous. "That...that...he was beyond rude to me the other night, and you haven't called me or responded to any of my texts since then."

"I don't know how to make this clearer but I'm dealing with a lot right now. And now isn't a good time. Gray was looking out for my best interest." Two fingers rub at the crease forming between my brows. "You need to back off."

"Back off? What's wrong?" There's a hint of concern in his tone, but I'm not sure if it's for me or for the fact he's not in on my problems.

"I can't model for your portfolio. I'm flattered that you want to work with me again, and I'm sorry I agreed to do it. At the time, I truly thought I could, but things have changed."

With the tea in hand, I amble into the living room and sit in one of my oversized chairs. "I'm already behind with my current schedule and the future work coming in. I can't fit it in, but I promise to get one or two top-tier models for you."

"But, Daisy, I want you."

I bite my bottom lip, holding in a curse. This man is beyond insistent, but I won't back down. "You aren't listening to me. I want you to succeed—I really do—but this is the only way I can support you."

Silence on his end of the line gives me hope that I'm finally getting through to him.

"What's going on with you?" His voice is calmer, maybe even more caring.

"Just things."

"Daisy, we're friends. I'm here for you. Talk to me."

A sarcastic laughter threatens to break free from my throat, and it takes everything in me to lock it down. My friendship with Jerome has always been one-sided with his needs ahead of everything else.

His offer to help may be sincere, but I'm not sure he knows how to without getting something out of it. I'm not telling him about Costa. We don't have that kind of relationship.

But, since this feels like he's extending an olive branch, I should meet him halfway. If only so we can move past this.

"There's a lot going on, and it's getting harder without permanent care for Henry, so I need to hire a nanny."

"Oh." And that right there, that one dismissive word about sums it up. He couldn't care less about my problems.

As an afterthought or maybe because he realizes how his response came across, he asks, "Can I help you in any way?"

"No, but thanks."

"Okay. Do you want to go for a drink or dinner tonight?"

"No, I can't. I have plans with Gray."

"Oh. Well, call me when you can. I'm here for you."

"I will. Thanks, Jerome." The doorbell rings, and I hope he can hear it rather than think I am trying to get rid of him when I say, "Someone's at the door and I'm expecting a delivery. I have to go."

"All right. Bye."

I drop the phone and march to the front door. It's a delivery guy, holding out a letter sized envelope. "Daisy Dobson?"

"Yes." I nod.

"Please sign here." He shoves a device into my hand, and I sign with my finger. "Here you go, and have a nice day."

The return address is some lab in LA. The DNA results. It's funny how something that's barely a few ounces can feel like the weight of the world in my palm.

I could end the agonizing anticipation and rip this open

right now. I'd have my answer, but I promised Gray I'd wait for him.

Back in the living room, I drop the envelope on the coffee table and sit across from it, staring.

It's a bomb.

There's no real sound emanating from the thing, but an incessant sound lives and breathes in my mind. The *tick, tick, tick,* chips away at my resolution.

Why did I agreed to wait?

24

GRAY

HUDDLED IN A CORNER

On the drive to Daisy's, I try calling her again, but once more, it goes straight to voicemail. I am later than usual and glad I'd seen Henry this morning. Otherwise, I'd have tried harder to speak to Daisy, just to beg her to keep him up.

When I get to the house, I let myself in and I'm greeted by an eery silence. Even with Henry likely sleeping, Daisy always has music on. The quiet is ironically unsettling.

On my way down the hall, I pause at the kitchen. It's a mess, and I survey the disaster. I don't think I've ever seen it, let alone any other part of her house, like this.

The small table is littered with a crumpled takeout bag, and there's a nearly untouched burger and fries on a plate in front of where Daisy usually sits. It looks like she only took a bite out of the burger. A ketchup bottle rests on its side, lid open and red sauce oozing onto the tablecloth.

The removable tray to Henry's highchair rests against the

wall, still dirty with grease and pieces of now dried food sticking to the plastic surface. And his actual chair and the floor directly beneath are scattered with crumbs and chunks of burger and fries.

Henry is a messy eater, but Daisy is the first to clean up any trace of his meal. As if that isn't weird enough, it looks like they had takeout for dinner. She usually saves that for a special treat or if she's had a rough day, preferring to cook his meals.

What happened? Unease creeps into my belly, growing and churning as I walk down the hallway. I was away much longer than I'd planned to be today.

Not a sound comes from Henry's room, and I breathe a little easier at the sight of him fast asleep in his bed. Like a ball, he's curled up and cuddling his stuffed octopus. A book lies on the side table, and his clothes are strewn about the floor. That isn't something Daisy would do, especially when the laundry basket is not even three feet away.

After I quietly straighten up his room—it only takes a few seconds—I head to Daisy's bedroom. The door is slightly ajar, light on, and I knock at the same time I push it open.

She isn't in there, although there are signs of her. Cell phone on the bed, a letter lying on a pillow, and an opened envelope resting on the side table. I glance at the locked screen of the phone and see my last few texts and one from Sasha are unread.

Her room is abnormally untidy, like the rest of her home. What the hell happened?

Then the sound of the shower finally registers. The bathroom door is closed, and the din of running water loosens the intense tightness in my chest.

As much as I want to go in there, see her, I don't want to scare her. I'll wait and tidy the kitchen.

Thirty minutes later, the kitchen's clean and there's still no sign of Daisy. The water is still on, and running out of patience, I carefully step into the bathroom.

What I see nearly brings me to my knees.

My heart cracks. Chest heaving, breath shallow, I grab onto the doorframe of the bathroom. Through the glass doors of the shower, Daisy's huddled in a corner, fully clothed, shivering and crying.

Her body shakes incessantly, almost as if she's in a blender. Yet the way she's trying to make herself so small, head tucked into her chest and arms wrapped around her knees, she looks like a scared animal. Reminds me of a child.

I rush toward her, flinging open the glass door and nearly falling to my knees in front of her. Cold ice water pelts down onto my back, soaking my skin instantly through the thin fabric of my shirt.

A sharp, icy sensation stabs at my chest. My lungs seize and heart stops. It's fucking freezing. How can she sit here like this?

"Daisy." My hand brushes over her wet head. "Daze." I try to get her to look at me, but she doesn't move. "Let me get you out of here."

Her body quakes although she's unresponsive to her name. Can she hear me? Does she know I am here? Only her sobs tell me she's conscious.

Fuck, her sobs are soul crushing. I clench my jaw, tighten

my abs, and inhale as I wrap my arms around her trembling frame and bring her to standing.

Anchoring my feet to the slick, tiled floor, I tighten my grasp around her and carefully step from the shower, wrapping a towel around her.

My mind's scrambled but also slowly letting the pieces slide into place. The letter. She opened it. Without looking at the official results or even the email I received from the lab, based on her current state, I know Costa isn't Henry's father.

I place her on the bathroom counter, and she shivers uncontrollably. Her neck bows, head sinking to her chest, and she is unable to look at me. But at least the crying has stopped.

"Daze. Daze." I run the towel across her drenched head and down the sides of her face, then lift her chin to look into her eyes.

"Gray?" My name is a broken whisper.

She's a trembling mess, and her teeth start to chatter. Her gaze is hazy, unfocused as if she questions if I'm really in front of her.

"Tell me what happened." The question is to get her talking, focused on something more than anything else. I've already figured it out.

Using one end of the towel, I wipe at her neck, removing the water droplets on her. She says nothing.

Fuck. I'm going crazy. I just need her to come back to me.

"Let's get you out of these clothes." At the sound of my voice, she rests her forehead against my chest, fingers now gripping the front of my shirt.

Slowly, almost with difficulty, she widens her legs,

drawing me in between her thighs, and all I can do is hold her tight. I never want to let her go.

But her clothes are soaked, and she's an ice cube. So cold that I'm now chilled just holding her.

"Come on. You need to change." My hands rub up and down her back and arms, the towel drying her skin.

She's waterlogged, and the only solution is to peel off her sopping clothes. I make quick work of it and wrap her in another dry towel once she's bare. My actions seem to settle her.

The last of her silent tears finally cease, and her shaking lessens somewhat. It will take a while for her core temperature to get back to normal and the tremors to stop.

Literally freezing from the outside in, her skin is frosty to the touch with blotches of red and stark white, and her lips are a purply-blue. Her once clear blue eyes are now bloodshot and swollen. Who knows how long she'd been crying?

Dammit, I want to yell and break something.

Once she's completely dry and changed, I drag the chair from her bedroom into the bathroom. She sits in front of the mirror, and it's cramped. The room is small, but that's also good because I'm generating a decent amount of heat.

I rummage around in the cupboard underneath the bathroom sink until I find the hair dryer, and the warm air beating down on her head not only dries her hair but also helps to warm her up some more.

Daisy sits, wrapped in a blanket I snatched from her bed, and stares into the mirror, unseeing. She doesn't even blink.

I haven't tried to talk to her. There's no point with the noise from the hair dryer, and once done, I strip off my damp clothes, down to only my boxers, and put her in the bed with me.

With the covers over us, my body wraps around hers, arms and legs securing her to me. I cling to her, needing her more than anything, even more than confirmation by reading the letter she received or the email to tell me her worst fear has come true.

She doesn't know who Henry's father is or how that happened.

"Daisy." Her name is a silent prayer in the quiet darkness of the room.

She shifts backward into my front and murmurs. Does she hear me? Is she slowly coming out of this trance?

"If you don't talk to me, I'm going to take you to the hospital. You're scaring me." My voice doesn't sound like my own.

I'm already scared, and there's only one other time in my life when I felt like this. Not even the horrific death of my father compares to this. It was a long time ago, another lifetime, when I was just a boy. And I never wanted to feel like that again. Never.

My lips brush against the back of her neck, and she quivers. "I know and I'm here." My arms carefully squeeze her middle, needing her to talk. Say something. Anything.

Slowly, she spins in my arms, turning to face me. My eyes have adjusted to the dark, and her eyes are clear, blinking up at me a few times, and then her hand reaches out to lightly brush the side of my face.

"Costa isn't Henry's father." A single tear rolls from the corner of her eye. "I didn't sleep with anyone else."

"I know." My thumb wipes at her damp eye. I wish I could say more, but there isn't a single thing I can say to make this go away.

"You believe me?" Shock carries her words.

"Of course I do." I'm alarmed at the question or that she even needed to ask. "Why wouldn't I?"

"I feel like I'm insane, doubting myself like maybe I forgot what happened or made it all up." She drops her hand between us on the mattress. "And if I haven't lost it then we both know what this means."

She watches me carefully, her lips parted and eyes shuttered, her expression blank. "I was sexually assaulted."

25

GRAY
A VILE HUMAN

The days and weeks following the DNA news are emotional, exhausting, and interminable...and at times, crushing.

Daisy tries to go back to normal, not quite shrugging off the reality of her altered world. She refuses to talk about what might have happened, of how she became pregnant, or at least, she won't talk to me about it.

Sasha is the only one she'll even broach the topic with and even at that, the conversation usually ends in frustration. Neither of them is able to remember anything of significance, and they emerge from their torturous traipse down memory lane with no further clarity or new information.

For the first week or so after that fateful day, Daisy carried through on already scheduled photo shoots and deadlines, including booking new work and arranging numerous nanny interviews.

She's robotic and numb, but the cracks in her foundation

slowly began to show and spread despite her efforts at grasping normal.

It's been three weeks since the test results, and some days, she won't get out of bed. Strangely, a few photo shoots fall through for one reason or another and she doesn't care. Instead, she fills that time with sleep.

And if she is up, she's zombie-like, going through the motions. Jerome still calls, and I run interference, or at this point, we both ignore him. Given she isn't working, he can't understand why she won't do his stupid photo shoot.

I've pretty much moved in with them, and while that's fine with me, I don't know if I'm helping or making things worse. Henry senses something is different, maybe even wrong, but he's too young to clearly express himself, and I try my best to fill his days with happiness.

Both Pansy and Sasha help out where and when they can. Sasha isn't used to taking care of a child, but she's here nearly every day and spends hours with Henry.

She has even postponed some of her work and plans to relocate. Daisy's current state has only strenghtened her desire to move to Los Angeles.

My attempt to uncover something with the private investigators was fruitless. Nothing unusual or questionable came back on Costa, his wife, or the doctor, which isn't surprising based on the DNA results.

As for reconstructing that week in Paris, the investigator came up with nothing significant. But he did provide an accurate timeline of events which I've shared with both Daisy and Sasha.

Sasha also spends a lot of time contacting people from

back then, trying to figure out what what's missing or to find answers. So far, nothing.

I even took off a few days from the album, which went over really well with Silas and India. For the most part, Silas was understanding, and he even tried to be a buffer with India, but she was out for blood.

Since time is money, I told her to find someone else, and I even gave her a few names of drummers who were willing to make themselves available right now, but she wouldn't agree to it. She insisted she wait on me, that she only wanted me on drums for her album, and while flattering, I'm convinced she also wanted a reason to be angry. A reason to throw temper tantrums and call me, screaming obscenities.

On my way home from what was my first full day back in the studio, I call Sasha.

"Hey, how's it going? I'll pick up dinner and be home in about an hour."

"Hi, Gray." Sasha lowers her voice. "One sec, let me just go into one of the rooms. Sorry, Daisy and Henry are playing in the backyard."

"How was she today?" I inch forward on the highway.

"Okay, for the most part. She went for a run, did some work, and arranged a final interview with Jocelyn."

We've decided on a nanny—Jocelyn Mallard. Both Daisy and I have met with her twice, and we both agree she's by far the frontrunner. All that's left is for an initial meeting with Henry. We want to see if the two gel before we hire her.

Now more than ever, we need someone to take care of Henry during the days, and we can't keep relying on Sasha and Pansy to help out. They have their own lives.

Once I'm home, Sasha leaves and the three of us have dinner. Daisy and I clean up and get Henry ready for bed. At a little after nine thirty, it's just the two of us. Alone.

I lead her to our room. Generally, she's more open, easier to talk to, in the hour or so before we sleep. I think it's the dark and intimacy between us. Naked and in bed.

We get ready for the night, turn out the lights, and meet in the middle of the mattress, lying face to face. A strip of moonlight sifts through the thin curtain, illuminating her soft features enough that I can detect any subtle shifts in her expression while we talk.

"It's time we find a place with more space." My finger trails the arch of her blonde brow and her lashes flutter. "The beach."

She smiles, eyes closed. It's a tiny smile, a little lopsided with a faint dimpling to one corner of her mouth. But I'll take it.

"That would be nice," she murmurs, opening her eyes.

My hand curls around the nape of her neck, and I draw her in, my lips brushing her forehead. We lie like that for a few more minutes, her once serene features tightening and shifting as she nibbles on her bottom lip.

"Tell me what you're thinking." My fingers knead her shoulder, coaxing her to talk.

"Henry." Her son's name sounds both adoring and anguished.

"What about him?" My mind whirs, anticipating what she'll say next or what's bothering her.

"He's my son...but we know nothing about his..." Unable to say the word, her eyes drift shut once more on a shudder.

"True." My hand slides down her shoulder, then her arm, and eventually, it rests on her hip. "It's frustrating not know- ing, but what about it? You don't feel differently about him, do you?"

"No." Her voice is as sharp as a blade, cutting off any doubt of her feelings. "Never and I'll always love him. I don't think there's anything he could do to make me not love him. But his father..."

"No, father isn't the word." It comes out harsher than I intend, and I soften my expression.

"You're right. So right. This is harder than I thought."

"It's okay. You can tell me anything." I'm moved that she's finally broaching the topic and not wanting her to clam up again.

"I don't know who his father is, and while Costa wasn't perfect.... And I'm far from perfect, but at least I knew what kind of man Costa was. Despite how much of a bastard he was to walk away when I told him about the pregnancy, he isn't a horrible person."

I disagree. Costa may have been scared, and I'd even give him a pass at initially walking away, but nearly three years later, he was still out of the picture. And I doubt if we'd have heard from him, ever, if he wasn't infertile.

As if detecting my opposition, Daisy says, "At his core, he's a good person. But Henry's father...he assaults women. I don't know who he is, but he's a vile human being. My son is part him, has that man's blood in him."

"It doesn't matter. Henry will never be like that."

"How can you say that? We don't know for sure."

"I do." Elbow bent, I prop my head in my hand, staring

down at her, and continue with my voice definite. "DNA, biology, that's only one part of who we are, and I don't think it's the most important. I'm going to tell you something about my childhood that I haven't told you before."

She pushes up to my level, now also on her elbow, and her gaze is perturbed and intrigued. "What is it?"

I shift to sit, my back against the headboard, and pull her up next to me. "I never told you this, not because it's a secret but because it's in the past. It happened before I turned seven."

Her gaze snaps to mine. "Seven? You were adopted when you turned eight, weren't you?"

"Yeah. I feel like I've lived many lives. There was the time before the adoption, then the years with my parents after they adopted me, then Trojan, and now."

She nods, expression understanding, and I remind myself that as much as I hate talking about those first six years of my life, even more so than the year in the home, waiting and hoping for a new family, Daisy needs to hear this.

And truthfully, I had always planned on telling her everything. "Now is the best of my life."

My hand cups the side of her face, and the tips of her fingers glide over the scruff of my jaw. "Tell me, please."

"Before the adoption, there's only one thing, one person, I will never forget, and all the rest was worth letting go and that's what I did. And I think it relates to how things are for Henry."

She traces idle circles on the inside of the wrist of the hand still holding her cheek. "Really?"

"My father...my biological father was gone before my second birthday. That was no loss. He was an abusive, violent man and while I was very young, all I remember of him is crying. My crying, my mother's. And things were harder once he left. My mother had me, barely two, and my sister, a baby."

"You have a sister?" This is news to Daisy.

I've never spoken about my birth parents or my sister. Not to anyone, not even Daisy or Eli.

"Yeah." This time the smile on my lips hurts, snagging on the memories of my younger sister. "Her name was Robin. She was just a year younger than me."

"Robin." Her hand moves to the bird inked on my forearm. "Where is she now?" Her question is a dagger to the heart although to be expected.

I rub at the center of my chest and briefly shut my eyes, maybe to shut out the past, but I have to go forward. The door is opened and there is a point to this, a purpose and meaning Daisy needs to understand.

"She's dead. She drowned when she was five."

Daisy lets out a mournful, "Oh no."

"My mom wasn't much better than my father. She had a temper, and her needs came above all else. If money was scarce, which was all the time, she'd sooner spend it on liquor and cigarettes than food for us."

Her body tenses, expression darkening, and I nod, understanding all too well how upsetting it is to hear something like this. Especially when she's the best kind of mother there is.

"We were a burden to her, and when my father left, the

only thing that mattered was finding another man. Another meal ticket. We were left alone more times than not, and even at my age, I took care of my sister."

I roll my neck to lessen the mounting tension. "As soon as Robin could walk, we'd hide out in a little fort I'd made out of cardboard, leaves, and twigs, not too far from the trailer. I also found an old cooler and would hide food in there. It was safer...better to be out of Mama's way."

"Gray, that's horrible." Her touch is tender, and I'm grateful for the light in her eyes—even if it's sad, it's something.

"Yeah, and there were times when I wanted us to run away, but we were too young. And truthfully, I was scared. Robin would have run, gone anywhere with me. She had the ultimate faith in me. Trusted anything I told her to do. My biggest regret is second guessing myself and letting fear paralyze me. We should have run."

I shake my head, not knowing if things would have been better but believing maybe we'd have had a better chance.

"If we had, my sister might still be alive today."

"What happened?"

"My mother hauled us with her on a weekend camping trip. She'd found a new boyfriend. Another asshole." Bitterness sinks its teeth into me. "And she wanted to play house. He didn't care about kids, but there we were, out in the wilderness, and we got put in this small rowboat. Just Robin and me. She wanted some alone time and figured it would get us out of her hair."

Daisy's already shaking her head, hand inching toward

her mouth. She sees where this is going. It isn't hard for anyone to see that.

"Yeah. We had life vests, and at first, we had a great time. We were laughing and singing, then Robin stood up. She was dancing, and even though she was a little thing, the boat listed to one side and then another. I didn't know anything about boats. Shit, I didn't even know how to swim. Neither of us did."

"Gray...no."

"The boat capsized. The life vest pulled me up to the surface of the water, but my sister was nowhere. I waited, thinking the same had to happen for her. She had to pop up from the water, but she didn't and I didn't know what to do.

"I was screaming, waving hands in the air, and I saw my mom on the shore. At first, she was running toward us. But then she stopped and watched as other adults came to our rescue. People dove into the water, and someone tried to free Robin from the boat. The life vest had hooked onto one of the oars, and it was holding her down. She was stuck."

My voice cracks, and I have to pause. Daisy wraps her arms around me, burying her face into that space between my neck and shoulder. Her tears wet my skin, and I want to kick myself. I didn't mean to make her cry.

"Daze, sorry, I'll stop." I tilt up her chin and she jerks out of my arms, gaze boring into mine.

"No. I want to hear this." Her hand splays against my bare chest, right over my heart. "Please go on."

"A man got Robin onto the shore, but it was too late. They couldn't save her. And my mom...she was gone. She must have realized or feared she'd be blamed. Maybe even charged. She'd left two minors unsupervised in the water.

"Later, the police took me to where our tent was, but they were gone. And after, when I'd given them her name and they drove me to the trailer, our home—nothing. Not a trace of her. That was last time I saw her, when she stood on the shore and watched her daughter drown and son scream for help."

"Oh my God, Gray, I don't know what to say." She clings to me, lightly kissing my neck and whispering words of love and comfort.

"I didn't tell you this story to make you sad but to show you just how horrible my birth parents are, and I have their blood in my veins."

"You're nothing like—"

"That's my point. I was exposed to my parents, lived with my mother for six years, and I am nothing like her. I know this as sure as I know I need air to live and breathe. And the same goes for Henry." I cup her face in my hands, and her pale eyes sparkle in the dim light. "Whatever happened to you was horrible and the man who did it, despicable. I wish I could hurt him, give you justice, but know this—your son is nothing like him.

"Henry will not be like that man. He's a sweet, loving, smart, funny little boy, and he's influenced by those in his life."

"That's true." Her tone is relieved, almost happy, and I pull her down with me until we're lying on the bed, arms wrapped around each other. "Thank you for telling me about Robin. When you're ready, I'd love to hear more about her."

"I'd like that." I kiss the top of her head. "Let's try to sleep."

"Night, Gray. I love you."

"Love you too. Sweet dreams."

Daisy falls asleep faster than usual, and I lie there, listening to her slow, steady breaths and let thoughts of Robin wash over me. It isn't often I relive to that dreadful memory, but not a day goes by that I don't think of my sister.

The next day is bright and sunny, and we spend the morning lazing around, eating a breakfast of pancakes, eggs, bacon, and toast. I don't need to be in the studio until ten and only for two hours. Daisy and Henry are coming with me for a bit. Henry wants to see me on the drums, and then we have one last interview, hopefully, with our nanny-to-be.

When we arrive at the studio, India's on us before we even make it down the hallway.

"Gray, you're finally here." She bounces in her flip-flops, eyes glittering and movements frantic. Is she high?

"Yeah, I told you I'd be in around ten and I was bringing Daisy and Henry." My hand, resting at Daisy's lower back, rubs in gentle circles. "India, you remember them both, don't you?" I tilt my head toward Daisy. Henry's run ahead and is chattering with Silas who is crouched to his level, laughing.

"Yes. Hi." She gives Daisy barely a glance and grabs at my forearm. "I've got the most brilliant idea ever." She tugs me forward, urging me away from Daisy, but I'm reluctant to move. "I don't know why I didn't think of it sooner."

"Hey, India, calm down." Silas moseys toward us while Henry squats on the floor, playing with a toy car.

The songstress rolls her eyes and cocks a hip, placing her

hand on her waist. He pays her no attention, nodding at me as he nears. Then Silas takes Daisy gently into his arms and squeezes her tight.

While he hasn't seen her nearly as often as Pansy has, his concern isn't masked very well. His brows crease and lips climb half-heartedly into a faint smile. India wrinkles her nose at the whole display as if she's more than had enough with any and all attention not on her.

"So, Gray, as you know, as soon as the album releases, we're going on tour." India's a steamroller oblivious to anything in her path, and once more, she grasps my arm and pulls me forward.

"Yeah." More annoyed than interested and too slow to dodge her, I dig in my heels.

She frowns, unable to move me even an inch, and eventually, she drops her hand, giving up any attempt to pull me away or get me all to herself.

"I want you on the tour." Her face is a neon sign, bright, garish, and hard to ignore. "You'd be amazing on drums and think about the publicity. Trojan's drummer joins India Holt on World Tour."

Hands up and open, she slides her palms outward in arcs as if imagining a headline. "We'd draw in not only India fans but think of all the Trojan fans who would kill to see you play again. The crowds would go insane!"

26

DAISY
NONE OF THAT COMPARES

*G*ray on tour. India's tour. If memory serves me right and he goes on tour, he'd be gone for easily a year. India had mentioned they'd be stopping on every continent, and she's right. The fans—they would go berserk for a chance to hear from another member of Trojan.

Jared had a brief albeit very successful solo career after Trojan retired. The fans were wild, and yes, it was Jared Grange so there is that to consider, but the fandom was almost more intense than their Trojan days.

My head whips to Gray the second India's done trying to sell him on the tour. His expression is blank, although somewhat stunned. In some ways, I'm sure he'd love to go on tour.

I had agreed to watch him play this morning even though he was only going to be gone for a couple of hours. This visit would be bittersweet. I knew that going in, because Gray gets this ethereal, faraway look to him when he plays. It's like he's in another world and wherever he is, it's the best place on earth.

There's no way anyone can compete with that. I'm almost envious of him, of what he finds when playing the drums or creating music. And when Trojan decided to retire, Gray said he was fine with it and even wanted it, but he misses performing, making music.

And while producing records fulfills some of that, it isn't the same. It doesn't feed all of his passion.

"Tour?" The dreaded word slips from my mouth before I have a chance to get control of it, and I wince.

Maybe it's better this way. The tour would be good for him. I'm a mess. My business is at a standstill. So much so, some of my photo shoots have fallen through for no apparent reason, and I can't bring myself to do anything about it.

The calls for new work keep coming in, and I'm putting off booking anything for the future. I can't seem to move forward.

I'm stuck...stuck on that stupid week in Paris. No matter how hard or how long I sit silently and rack my brain, going back through those days and hours and minutes, trying to recreate every moment...

Nothing stands out.

Nothing is off.

Nothing is different.

"India, ah, that's an amazing invitation, but I can't accept." His tone is grave, leaving no room for misunderstanding.

"What? You can't say no." India is on him again like a fly

to shit. Hand stroking, face inches from his, and I swear she does it to deliberately bother me.

I'm not threatened by her, as much as I hate seeing her hands on Gray. He isn't hers. I trust him, and there's nothing between them.

Heck, even on India's part, she doesn't need to steal someone else's man, nor do I believe she wants to. But she has this need, it's huge and unavoidable, and doing stuff like this, fawning all over Gray, seems to feed it, fill it. *Whatever.*

"He'll think about it," I chime in, and Gray's head snaps in my direction. India starts clapping her hands and jumping up and down like a happy kid at a birthday party.

His gaze narrows on me. "No, I'm not."

I grab his hand, squeezing it and giving him my best, most encouraging smile. His expression remains stern, and sensing the mounting tension, Silas steps in between all of us.

"Hey, India, why don't we give them some time alone." Silas pulls at her shoulder, and she grudgingly turns around to head down the hall. "I've got Henry. You two talk."

It's as much a reassurance as a warning. Gray's crushing blue eyes never stray from mine. In the deep, endless flecks of silver and gold of his irises, I can almost see his deliberation about how best to tackle this...me.

"I'm not going on the tour." He's going with the direct approach. "I don't want to go, and I'm not leaving you and Henry." His hands latch onto the curve of my waist, fingers curling into my skin.

"You should think about it." My tone is composed and

just as direct. "You love to play. Think about how much fun it would be. And Henry and I would come out and visit you."

His head shakes vehemently from side to side, blond hair falling across one eye, as he leans into me. His lips are a breath away from mine, and I stop breathing while his eyes hold mine.

"No." He's close enough for me to see how his eyes glitter with determination. His voice drops to a low growl. "You and I both know what it means to be on tour."

I gave birth to Henry while they were on Trojan's last tour. Our friendship had been young at the time, and we were only just starting to get to know each other. But there had been days at a time when I wouldn't hear from him or Pansy, who had also gone with them on the tour.

Sometimes, it was the time difference plotting against us and never quite lining up, and other times, our schedules would rain down chaos. As a new mother, I had to steal sleep any chance I could get, and his schedule was just unpredictable. *Yeah, I knew what a tour would do to us.*

"It's long and grueling hours, and I'd have hardly any time for the two of you. I barely know what city we're in, and there isn't any time to go out and explore or enjoy the sights." He's exasperated having to remind me and maybe a bit confused as to why I'd even suggest that he go. "You and Henry are the most important thing to me."

His words heat me to the core, turning my insides to liquid. And in the same breath, I'm panicking as my heart leaps into my throat. I can't hold his life hostage, too, while I figure out my crap—and that is if I ever figure it out.

"Gr—"

He cuts me off. "I get to play on this album, and that's awesome. I get to work with amazing artists every day, creating fantastic music. That's awesome. But none of that compares to you. To spending time with you and Henry." He presses his forehead to mine. "None of it. Do you hear me?"

Before I can say a word, he kisses me hard. Then he pulls away and follows Silas and the others, leaving me breathless.

The next few hours go by fast. Gray plays the drums, and Henry loves every minute of it. He's wired, thrilled to see Gray performing, and to be expected, at one point he insists on playing the drums too. Silas, India, and Gray are all too agreeable and give my son free rein of the instruments.

My phone vibrates, and I step from the room when I see it's Sasha. "Hi, how are you?"

"I was calling to ask you that very question." She's become a lioness watching over her cub. "Are you with Gray? At the studio?"

"Yes. Henry is having a blast, and everyone is spoiling him."

"Good. Listen, I have something to tell you but I'm thinking I should do it when Gray's with you."

My feet stop, and I press my back into the wall for support. Did she find something?

Sasha has been ruthless in calling models, makeup artists, designers, or anyone we can think of who might remember anything from that time in Paris.

All my muscles freeze. "Sasha, tell me. I can handle it."

"Fine. Do you remember Apollo?"

"You mean the model from London?" I couldn't forget him. We'd shared many photo spreads and runways.

"Yes. He sort of became the international poster boy for hipsters because of his iconic beard."

"I know who he is. We were friends and worked a lot together. Don't you remember, we had that hugely successful campaign in France for Milton, and after that, all we seemed to get were bookings together."

"I remember. The two of you even went to Sandrine demanding solo go-sees and gigs."

"Yes. We didn't mind working together, but we also didn't want to be pigeonholed as a couple."

"Are you sure he felt the same way?" she asks in a way that causes a shiver to run down my spine.

"Sasha, quit stalling. What are you getting at?" Flutters like nervous snakes slither through my stomach.

"He was at our party that night." She means the night we think something happened. It's the only night where Costa and I weren't together for several hours.

"Okay, but that doesn't necessarily mean anything."

So many memories of Apollo rush through my mind. We were friends. We even flirted, and he'd asked me out once, but I turned him down because I was with Costa.

"I've talked to a lot of people these past few weeks." She pauses and my gut clenches at how much she's done for me, even delaying her return to Paris. "And several people have mentioned how much he adored you. Some even say he had a wild crush and was obsessed. Totally bummed when you went to Sandrine to 'break up your duo' as one person put it."

"What?" I don't remember him like that. Was I blind? It feels like there was so much I didn't see.

"Honey, I know this is a lot to take in, but we need to talk to him."

"To Apollo?" My throat is intensely dry, and suddenly, I feel sick.

Since Costa came back into my life, I've wanted nothing more than to know what happened.

Until now.

Now, the idea of finding out the truth terrifies me. Even as I know logically it doesn't change the past. It's like I can pretend it never happened if I never get answers.

The answers I so desperately seek.

"Yes. I've made some calls, and it turns out he's in New York. He's working one of the same fashion shows as Costa. I've booked a flight for us to go in three days. He'll still be there, and I think we should surprise him."

"Oh my God." My legs shake and I slide down to the floor.

"Daisy, are you okay?"

"Do you think it's him?" The very thought, let alone the words, eats at my insides.

I can't reconcile the Apollo I trusted and worked with, the funny man I spent hours with, sometimes practically naked, with someone who took so much from me.

"I don't know, but it's our first real lead. We'd be stupid not to follow through on it. I'll be with you every step of the way. And you know Gray will be there too."

"Gray." My voice cracks thinking about him and how to tell him we might be toward the end.

The end of what? It doesn't feel like an end, but like another dark passage.

"Daisy, Daisy." Sasha's insistent voice cuts through my thoughts.

"I'm here. What?"

"Where's Gray right now? Is he with you?"

"I'm out in the hallway."

"Okay. Stay where you are, and I'm going to call him. I'll fill him in and you just chill."

I'm nodding and realize she can't see me. "Okay. And Sash..."

"Yes?"

"Thank you. You're really good at this taking care of people thing." A laugh, strangled by a cry, springs from my mouth.

She snorts before getting serious. "There isn't anyone else I'd do this for."

She ends the call and I sit there. For how long, I couldn't say. Even as I dig through the past, unearthing moments with Apollo, I have a hard time with the possibility. The sense of betrayal and shame is overwhelming.

Gray eventually finds me, and he sits with me in the hallway for a while. And like Sasha said, he's already making arrangements to be in New York with me.

Eventually, we leave, and Henry passes out as soon as I buckle him into the car seat. He's still sleeping when we arrive, and Jocelyn, the nanny candidate, waits at our front door.

A flame of wild red hair surrounds the tall, lean lady on the front step. She smiles down at Henry cradled in Gray's arms. Silent greetings are made, and we settle in the living room while Gray puts Henry to bed.

I excuse myself and splash cold water on my face, pushing any thoughts of the upcoming trip out of my mind.

"Henry usually sleeps for a little under two hours," I say as I walk back into the room. "So he could go for a little longer, or his eyes may pop open the second his head hits the pillow." I place the coffee pot onto the trivet before sitting across from her on the couch.

"Yes, that can happen." Jocelyn scoops some sugar into her cup. "Naps are important."

"That's for sure." Gray strolls into the room and sits beside me, taking my hand in his.

Suddenly I'm overcome with panic. To this woman, we look like a family. Are we a family?

I mean, I've wanted that for as long as I can remember, but then everything has changed. Nothing makes sense anymore, and I'm not even sure who I am.

And if Apollo is the person we've been looking for, what changes? Nothing.

My art and career in photography no longer brings me much joy. Sure, I'm still working, even if the pace is slower. But I don't always have the vision that I once had.

I no longer have the ability to see the image before it's shot. Every aspect of a great shot—the angle and the light— used to talk to me. It all came so naturally to me as if a part of me. And now? Nothing.

No, there are days when I go through the motions with everything, all the while stuck in a chamber of what ifs and dark imaginings. Even with a potential answer. A name. A person. I still have no knowledge or recollection of what may have happened to me.

But that doesn't stop me from going to the worst places in my mind. And now, I have a name and face to put to those nightmares. To those conjured scenarios that I don't want to fathom and yet will never forget.

How can we be a family when I don't even know what it means to be me? And all of this is all too easy. Too perfect. Life isn't perfect.

I learned that the hard way more than ever and now... now, I'm filthy, angry, and ashamed.

How can Gray still want to be with me?

"Wouldn't you agree, Daze?" Gray's question cuts into the wormhole of my shadowy thoughts, pulling me back to the present.

"Sorry, what?" I blink a few times, gaze darting from Gray to Jocelyn and back. Both stare at me, clearly aware that I drifted off to somewhere else.

"I was just telling Jocelyn that if Henry takes a liking to her, we would like her to start as soon as possible."

"Oh, yes." I nod, and as if saved from any further awkwardness, Henry, bedraggled and cute, ambles into the room.

He holds Jellycat in one hand, most of its eight stuffed tentacles trailing along the floor, and yawns.

"Hey, Henry, we want you to meet someone." Gray holds out his arm, and needing no more encouragement, Henry's on his lap in no time.

Gray makes the introductions, and Jocelyn and Henry get to know each other. My phone buzzes on the coffee table and I pick it up. I'm waiting for a client's response about a meeting time and hope this is it.

It isn't. I stifle my groan and hit ignore. It's a text from Jerome. Since we last spoke that day I told him I would find a few models for his portfolio, which I have, he texts me at least once a day.

Sometimes he'll even mention that he knows I'm not working as if that's enough for me to agree to his stupid photo shoot. Even if I was in the right frame of mind, I'd refuse to model for him.

He's so persistent, and Gray has tried to get rid of him but with no luck. A couple of weeks ago, I sent an email with details for the models, so he can't say I held up or ruined his shoot. Although I'm sure he'll say that or anything else if he wishes.

I no longer open his texts. Many are unopened on my phone, and I'm tempted to delete them—delete him—but in fairness to him, he doesn't know anything about Costa, Henry, and maybe Apollo and all of that. He can't fully comprehend what I'm going through or why I don't have time for his pettiness.

And I don't want to tell him any of it. We aren't friends. That's becoming apparent more and more. I haven't thought about reaching out to him or even missed our conversations. But maybe it isn't fair to jump straight to ending the friendship when I'm not in the right headspace. How I feel may be about where I am at this moment and nothing to do with Jerome.

"Can you start tomorrow?" Gray asks Jocelyn, and his question yanks me back to my living room where Henry sits on the woman's lap, laughing at something she said.

I turn to Gray at my side, surprised he wants her to start

so soon. He isn't looking at me and is most probably fully aware I checked out of this final interview.

"Oh, well, yes. Of course." She's a bit flustered or surprised at the timing, and I can't blame her. A deep red creeps into her cheeks. "I didn't expect to start so soon, but I can make it work."

"We'll only need you for a few hours in the afternoon. I'll text you the time." Gray shoves a hand into his pocket and secures his arm around my waist.

"We do?" I'm no longer able to stay quiet, intrigued and perplexed at the same time.

Gray's easy grin causes a stir in my stomach. "Yup. It's a surprise." He turns back to Jocelyn. "Thanks again for coming, and we're looking forward to working with you. The agency said they'd take care of the paperwork, and we'll have keys for you tomorrow."

"Wonderful." She shakes my hand and then his before crouching to Henry to say goodbye.

She's very kind and gentle with him, and once she's promised to see him tomorrow, she leaves.

"We don't need her to start until Monday." I angle myself in his hold to fully face him once she's gone. "What surprise?"

"You'll just have to wait and see." He kisses the tip of my nose, wearing a satisfied smirk.

27

GRAY
READY TO BOLT

*D*aisy pulls into the driveway of the beach house along the Pacific Coast Highway. Through the windshield of her car, she eyes me warily, a million questions flitting through her gaze.

I'd left early this morning for the studio and spent most of the day recording. Before lunch I sent her a text, asking her to meet me at this address at two p.m.

Excitement thrums in my veins like an electric current. I've had this surprise for over a week now, and it has been damn near impossible to keep my mouth shut. But the big reveal all depended on Daisy, and until now, she hasn't been ready to receive this gift.

Once I heard about Apollo and what that might mean, I thought about putting this off but changed my mind. After moving forward with Jocelyn and having more and more conversations about making our living arrangements official, it feels like the right time.

Daisy needs something positive to look forward to. This surprise won't lessen what she's going through, but hopefully it'll give her something to fight for—our future.

"What is this place?" She shuts the car door, glancing around the busy highway to her back and then up at the Malibu beach house.

"Don't I even get a hello?" I open my arms and she embraces me.

My mouth presses to hers, and my tongue sweeps across the seam of her lips, delving in to stroke mine against hers. Daisy moans, tightening her grip on the back of my shirt.

"Hello." Her voice is breathy when she pulls away, once more casting a glance to the left and the right of us, and then behind me to the front door. "Are you going to tell me what's going on?"

"Yes. All in good time. Do you want to go in?"

She nods, eyes glittering. "Yes. If we can."

I take her hand and lead the walk through the front doors of the four-bedroom home with four levels starting at the beachy floor, one below us.

"Does it look familiar?" I shut the door behind her, and she stares at the stone fountain wall just inside the front entrance, mesmerized.

The tranquil trickling of water, cascading down the tiny, pebbled stones lining the wall, permeates the large, marble tiled foyer.

"Kind of. I think?" She drinks in the large, open space with wooden stairs and iron railings, leading both upstairs and downstairs.

Buttery sunlight streams in from the large skylight three

floors above, and directly in front of us is the living room with its hardwood floors, gas fireplace, and one wall of windows.

And beyond the glass is the breathtaking view of the Pacific Ocean, literally steps from the house.

"Oh my goodness. This place is beautiful." Daisy takes tentative steps toward the room, drinking in the view, and I stand back silently watching her.

Warmth fills my chest at the awe and wonder on her face. It's the first time in awhile there hasn't been a hint or trace of anxiety, sadness, or anger. Yes, this is the right time to bring her here.

"Is this..." She pauses, looking at me over her shoulder and motioning to the handle of the sliding glass door.

"Yes, you can open it. Go out onto the deck." I saunter to her side, stepping onto the terrace with her.

Warm salty air and the hypnotic ebb and flow of the surf crashing onto the sandy shore envelop us. It's amazing.

I've been here several times in as many weeks, and every time, when I walk out to look at Las Flores Beach, this view, the sounds, and the scents bring a smile to my face. A peace to my soul. I hope it'll do the same for Daisy.

"Wasn't this place for sale?" She rests her forearms on the balcony railing, staring out at the azure waves.

"Yes, it was one of the homes you had in your pile of beach houses."

Her gaze swings to me, eyes widening, and she snorts. "This house was a wild and crazy dream. I could hardly afford the others I'd selected to see. But this one,"—her fingers interlace as if in prayer—"this one was never a reality.

I just loved how it looked and it was so close, no, right on the beach."

I nod, smiling. "Yeah, it's amazing, isn't it?"

"It is, but Gray, why are we here? Whose house is this?" Now looking at me, her gaze is puzzled, some of that worry creeping back in.

"Let me show you the rest of the house and then I'll answer all your questions." My hand wraps around her arm, and once she releases her fingers, I take her hand.

Before heading up, I lead the way down to the ground floor, the beach. This floor is part inside and part outside. She studies the large sandy deck complete with a water grotto-style spa, a natural gas fire pit, bar, and flat screen TV.

Here the sounds of the waves and the gulls drown out any din from the highway. Next, we visit the state-of-the-art kitchen, dining room, and a guest bedroom, which I figured could be Daisy's office.

Then we climb the stairs to the third floor, and she takes in the two bedrooms and bathrooms before we ascend one more floor. At the top of the house is the master bedroom that walks out to a private rooftop deck with coastline views and the bathroom which includes a large oval tub big enough for two and deep enough to fill the water to our shoulders.

"How big is this house?" Her hand runs along the white stone mantle of the gas fireplace along the center of one wall in the bedroom.

"A little over thirty-two hundred square feet." I shove my hands into the front pocket of my jeans and shrug, not wanting her to get hung up on things like that.

The place is big. Way bigger than my small bachelor pad or even her barely fifteen hundred square foot home. Because if she gets hung up on the size, she'll make the leap to the cost, and while it was a lot of money, I hadn't made the decision lightly.

SG Productions is doing really well, I have money set aside for my mother's care, and I have a good chunk in savings. Sure, the purchase of this home did take a fair amount of it, but I'll make some of it back. I'm certain of it, and it isn't like Daisy won't want to contribute her fair share. I know her, and it will be a bone of contention if she thinks I'm gifting this home to her.

She gasps, "Wow. That's big. And the ceilings." She tilts her head back to admire the driftwood with the exposed beams. "It's beautiful. Now tell me, why are we here?"

"Daisy, this is our new home."

"What?" Her tone is flat as if what I said doesn't make sense.

"We've been talking about moving in together, getting a place, and you wanted this place. It's ours."

"No." She scurries past me a few feet and then stops before I can go after her, turning to face me.

I stiffen, pulling my hands from my pockets and inching toward her. She steps back, casting harried glances around the room. It's like she's looking for a way to escape.

"Gray, this costs millions. I can't..."

"Before you go on about the cost, I figured you might have a problem with it. You can put your share toward it. What you can, when you can. And if you want, you can pay all or most of the bills. Whatever you want. We can figure all of that out, but don't worry about it right now."

I reach for her, needing her close, needing to calm the tornado of uncertainty brewing inside her. But she isn't having any of it and steps out of my grasp, head shaking from side to side.

"Gray, I don't need saving." She's annoyed, and I'm confused as to where that came from.

"What are you talking about?"

"Just because you couldn't save your sister, doesn't mean you can make up for that by saving me. I don't need saving." She folds her arms over her chest, teeth sinking into her bottom lip. "Besides, what happened to your sister isn't your fault. You were a child too."

"This has nothing to do with Robin. This is about us, our future. And I'm not trying to save you." Even as I say the words, a small speck of it is a bitter lie, and it burns my tongue.

The lie isn't about Robin. I've long since come to terms with the fact that I couldn't save her. I was only a child too. My only regret is not leaving with her.

No, the lie is about saving her. Until this moment, I only wanted to help, to make sure she understood she isn't alone, but in doing so it may have felt to her like I was trying to save her. Fix something that I couldn't or that she didn't want fixed.

I shift on my feet, willing myself to stay rooted to this spot. Not to get any closer. It's very clear she's ready to bolt at any moment, and I must get through to her.

"I can never fully imagine what you're going through, and

I understand that I can't make it go away as much as I wish I could. But I also want you to know that I love you and I'm here." I press my hand to my chest, our eyes connected. "And I'm not leaving you."

"This isn't me. My life doesn't work out this way." Silent tears spill from her turbulent eyes. "My modeling career ended abruptly because I became pregnant."

No sooner are the words out than she slaps a hand viciously over her mouth. A painful sob breaches the barrier of her fingers.

"Oh God, that came out wrong. I didn't mean it like that. I would never trade Henry for anything."

She leans forward as if her knees might give out. Before I can get to her, she straightens and steps back to ensure we keep our distance.

"Gray, I love you too, and I love how kind and loving you are to think about doing something like this. But the house, the nanny, the amazing, wonderful man that you are"—she points to me and it feels like an arrow to my heart—"I can't... it's too much."

"Daisy, what's too much? You and Henry and I are a family. We stick together."

"I'm a mess. I can't focus on the future or any of this. I don't even know who I am anymore, what I want. Why would you want this with me right now?" Her question plunges into my gut. How can she even ask that?

"I love you. Everything I've ever wanted. And I don't care how long it takes you to figure this out. I'm here for you and will help you."

"And what if I don't figure it out?" Walking backward,

eyes still on me, she edges out of the room. "What if I'm never myself again?" A few more steps away from me, closer to the staircase.

"What if that Daisy"—she points behind her as if there's another version of her standing there, fading into nothing-ness—"never comes back?"

She's now at the top of the stairs. "What if this,"—she waves her hand over her body, a sneer plastered across her face—"what I've become, a shell of who I once was, is all that's left?"

One foot on the step, she grasps the railing. "I won't do that to you, Gray. I won't ask you or expect you to live with this."

"Daisy. Daisy." I chase after her, body shaking.

Turmoil and sorrow pour from her like water from a tap on full force, blanketing not only her but also me in desolation so vast that I feel it darkening my soul.

28

DAISY
THE BRUTAL TRUTH

I fly down the stairs, hand barely gripping the railing. As much as I don't want to tumble down these steps, holding on will only slow me down. All it would take is one misstep and I would break my neck.

"Daisy!" My name is a low, anxious growl from Gray, and his anguish is a sledgehammer to my chest, cracking my ribs, splintering my breath, and pulverizing my heart.

I don't want to hurt him. I don't even want to run, but if I don't, I might drown.

This house—no, not just the house—everything working out, falling into place, and all that it represents is like a sinking ship. And I'm stuck on it.

Like the Titanic, it feels too big to stop from going under, but so beautiful. And all I'm able to do is ruin it. Whether I stay or go, everything is ruined eventually.

My ballet flats hit the main floor, and I glide to the door, fingers curling around the handle. Gray's ragged breathing and hurried footsteps are a shadow's breath away, and I spin to face him.

"I need space. This is all too much." My fingers dig grooves into my once tidy ponytail, nails curling into my scalp. The pain anchors me. "I'll call you. Just give me some space. Please."

Sadness flickers in his warm crystalline gaze but he nods, backing away with his hands up as if to say, *I won't push, I'm not a threat.*

He never does anything to hamper me, hurt me. He could never be a threat even when I feel crowded and confused. It's my doing, not his. Gray always gives me what I want.

"I'm sorry, I didn't mean to go too fast."

"No, this isn't on you, Gray. I don't know what I'm doing. Too many things are still unanswered and may never be answered, and I don't know...I just need time...space."

"Okay. Please call. I love you, Daisy."

Back on the Pacific Coast Highway, the tears fall freely. As much as I want Gray and all that he has to offer, what if it's shattered one day too? That I couldn't bear. I'm hardly hanging onto what of me is broken.

I dare not trust what we have even if it's the most beautiful thing I've ever had. I willingly trusted so much before, trusted that my life was solid, that nothing and no one could get to me, ever truly hurt me. I'd been wrong. So very wrong.

Sure, I'd had disappointments and heartaches before, but nothing indelible, nothing I couldn't get past. And now? Now I don't know.

My phone rings as I near my house, and it's Sasha. I send her to voicemail, and as much as she hates that, I can't talk to her right now. I can hardly make sense of things at this moment, and she'll only tell me how much of a fool I am. This I know.

Once at home, I sit in the car for a few minutes, wiping at my tears and thinking of what comes next. Gray will show up at some point. Maybe not tonight but likely by tomorrow.

There's no way he'll let me go to New York in two days without him even if things are still unresolved between us. He'd worry about me and want to see Henry.

Henry. I don't want to keep them apart. I can't. Okay, so that's tomorrow. What about today? This afternoon? First things first, I can't go in looking like this. Jocelyn will definitely think I'm out of my mind.

I angle the rear-view mirror so I can see my face and grimace at the blotchy cheeks, puffy eyes, and shiny red nose. My hair is a mess, and using my fingers, I comb back the stray strands as best I can, tightening the hair tie.

My phone rings again, and half expecting either Gray or Sasha, I'm momentarily stunned to see Costa's name in bold letters on the screen.

"Costa?" My stomach clenches, and his name spills from my mouth as if I'm spitting out something that tastes bad.

"Daisy? Yes, it's me, Costa."

It's strange, silly even, how hope flutters in my chest at the sound of his voice. It's fleeting but I wonder if he's calling to say all of this has been one sick joke. Ha, ha. Sorry for my bad judgement but hope you can laugh about it.

Stupid because I have two DNA tests that say otherwise. None of this is a joke or anything to laugh about.

"Daisy? Are you still there?" His tone is insistent, almost worried.

"Yes, I'm here." I sniffle, cringing that he might think I'm crying about him.

"I'm sorry to do this over the phone, but I'm still in New York and then heading back to Greece in a few days."

"It's okay, what's wrong?" Yes, something has got to be wrong for him to call me. My pulse speeds up, and I wonder if this is about Apollo.

Why didn't I think to ask if Sasha had talked to Costa? No, she wouldn't. She doesn't like him.

"When I met Gray, he asked me to give some thought about the last time we were in Paris together...that week." He clears his throat, sounding uncomfortable.

"Uh-huh." I rest the back of my head on the seat rest.

Gray said as much to me so this isn't news, but I hold my breath and tense my muscles as if readying for another blow. I'm prepared to hear Apollo's name.

"I remembered something about the night we fought. Do you remember that night?"

He doesn't know how many hours Sasha and I have spent reconstructing that week. He doesn't know we've narrowed down the timeline to the very night he's talking about.

Of course I remember. I'll never forget.

"Yes. We fought a lot, but this one was about how you were always high. I was sick of it."

"Yeah." He chuckles but there isn't anything light or amusing about it. "And I got so angry with you that I left."

"What else is new. One of us was always storming out." My disgust isn't well hidden, and it's okay if he mentions Apollo, or anything else. I can do this.

"True. I ended up going back to our hotel room and drank some more. It was childish, and after a while, I missed you. We only had a couple more nights together, and I didn't want to spend them apart."

"Okay." It's all I can bring myself to say, not even caring about his admission of missing me, which would have meant the world to me back then.

As if sensing my indifference, he says, "I was a selfish asshole. I don't know how or why you put up with me."

"You came back," I offer up a concession, not wanting to hang on to any negative feelings toward him.

Our screwed up relationship wasn't all his doing. We were both very good at fighting and even better at making up.

With all the hours I've spent rehashing the past, I sometimes wonder if that's why we actually spent so much time at odds. I admit, sometimes I even fabricated a senseless argument only so we would have rough makeup sex.

We'd rip off each other's clothes, nip, bite, and scratch at each other, working out our frustrations as we chased our climaxes. As good as the sex was, we were fucked up.

My relationship with Gray is so different. There's no comparison. In addition to mind-blowing sex, he makes me feel cherished, loved, and like his partner.

"Yeah, I did." Costa's low voice ends any thoughts of Gray, and I focus on what he's called to say. "It was early in the morning, like two or three a.m., I'm not sure. I headed for your bedroom at the apartment and someone was coming out of your room. Remember Jerome Pascal?"

Jerome? Not Apollo?

Suddenly, the brutal truth, like a vise-grip, tighten around my throat, choking all the air from my lungs.

Costa, Sasha, none of them from my modeling days know Jerome is here in LA. *Shit.*

"Daisy?" His voice cuts into my fears, and I make a strange, muffled sound, unable to form any words. "Daisy."

"Yes." My reply is merely a whisper.

Costa continues, "I asked him what he was doing coming from your room, and at first, he didn't answer, only brushed by me. He was always an arrogant prick."

Voice cold like granite, losing any grip on patience, I say, "Yes. Go on."

"Right. I grabbed his arm and asked again. He said you were sleeping and that he brought you some water, and that was it. I had a weird feeling at the time, but I was stupid. I was coming down from everything I'd taken that night, and I felt like shit."

Words fail me. Unlike Sasha mentioning Apollo, this is different. Terror grips at my organs, digs into my lungs, squeezes my heart.

"I'm sorry. I never gave it another thought. Even when you told me you were pregnant, I never thought of it again until Gray asked me to think back. I spent time going through every day of that week, over and over again." He sounds like he's exhausted as if he wants a medal for all of the brain power he used in his magnanimous efforts to help me.

I shouldn't be so hard on him, but I can't stop myself. I was the one violated. I was the one who can't remember what was done to her and yet he's the one feeling aggrieved.

"And then it came to me, how I'd found you in your room." His words are a needle prick to a balloon, blowing all air out of my hissing thoughts.

"What do you mean?" I'm light-headed and faintly sick, skin clammy.

"The bed sheets were around your ankles. You were only in your dress, but something about it felt off. Or maybe I'm only realizing that now, with everything we know about Henry and the scandal with Jerome."

"What do you mean?" I demand, nearly yelling into the phone.

"Sorry. Your dress had ridden up to your hips and you didn't have any panties on."

A strangled cry vomits from my mouth, and I try to think back on that night, waking up that morning, of anything similar to what he just described. But everything is a blur, and the little bits I do remember are hazy, not helpful at all.

"Costa, Jerome is here in LA." My head is dizzy. "He has been for over a year. What scandal are you talking about?"

"What? You've stayed away from him, though, right?" His frantic tone snaps something inside of me, and suddenly my mind scatters, thoughts splintering in all directions.

I force out the two words, "What scandal?"

His sudden departure from Paris comes to mind. I never pushed Jerome to tell me why he left. He was so well regarded and pretty much called the shots, picked the jobs he wanted.

It did always strike me as odd that he walked away from Paris, the epicenter of fashion, to come to LA and start at the bottom once more. He is a nobody here. Not even his reputation in Europe matters here, funnily enough.

And why didn't I ask the questions? Because I didn't care. The man is self-centered enough, I didn't want to give him a reason to drone on about how he was wronged. It didn't take much for Jerome to talk about myself.

Stupid. Stupid. Stupid.

"He left Paris, disgraced. Persona non grata. He assaulted a young model, and I think charges were pressed. But I never followed it closely so I can't say for sure."

"Oh my God. Oh my God." I swing open the car door, sticking my head out as I drop my feet to the ground.

"Daisy, are you okay? Is Gray there?"

The phone slips from my hand with a *thud* onto the floor of the car as I race to the house. Henry and Jocelyn slide in and just as quickly out of my mind. There's no stopping to pull myself together.

I burst through the front door, swing open the powder room door, and sink to my knees to retch into the toilet. My stomach is emptied of all its contents, and I heave some more, even when there's nothing left.

Jocelyn crouches at my side and places a hand on my shoulder. I flinch at her touch, drawing away from her and wiping at my mouth with the back of my hand. Unable to look at her, I get to my feet, legs shaky, and flush the toilet.

She steps back into the hallway, worry painting her features. "Are you all right? Do you need me to get you something?"

I wash my hands, splash cold water on my face, and rinse my mouth out several times. In the mirror, my reflection disgusts me.

How could I have been so stupid? My attacker was here all along. In my inner circle. The urge to purge roars with a vengeance as my throat muscles convulse and saliva gathers in my mouth.

My mind races with my options. What should I do first? Call Gray? Sasha? The police? Jerome will pay for what he did to me. Of course, I'll need a DNA test but unlike with Costa, I don't need it. Jerome Pascal is a rapist.

"I'm okay. Just something I ate," I lie, drying my hands and stepping into the hall.

It's bizarre, but for the first time in a while, my mind is clear like the clouds have parted to reveal a bright sun. I feel strong and oddly empowered. The path to justice is within my reach.

The darkness isn't gone, and I don't know if it ever fully will go away, but I don't feel as helpless. I can't change the past and because of my precious son, I would never wish for a life without him, but I deserve peace.

And Gray—his gift today comes to me in a different light. Not as something I may lose at any moment or something to be feared, but like he said, it's our future. He's my future.

"How's Henry?" I follow Jocelyn into the living room.

"He's such a good boy. We had fun playing together and then your friend arrived a little earlier than expected." She stops in the middle of the room, kneeling to pick up the last of the blocks on the floor.

"My friend?" I cock my head to one side, searching for my son.

Henry comes from the hallway that leads to the bedrooms, and behind him, a large hand grabs hold of his arm, hauling my son back against his legs.

Hard eyes glint cold, and a sinister smile captures Jerome's mouth. "Daisy, it's about time you got home."

A dark shroud of fear buds within my heart, black as poison, leeching into my blood, muscles, and bones.

"Mommy." Henry tries to leap toward me, but the man behind him has a tight grip on his arm, fingers sinking into my son's soft, pure flesh.

Henry whimpers, Jocelyn lets out a small rush of air, and my eyes stay trained on Jerome just like his never stray from mine.

"Hey, Lovebug." My veins fill with ice cold dread, and despite my brittle smile, I pump as much joy as is possible into my voice. "Jocelyn, please take Henry and leave."

"No." With a stern expression and terse tone, he lifts my son into his arms. "Jocelyn, you can go."

"Jerome, let her take Henry. Then it's just the two of us." He doesn't like children, and if I can only appeal to that, to the idea of just him and me, maybe he'll agree.

"Jocelyn, it was great to meet you. You can go now." His smile is cold as is his heart, and the woman looks frantically from him to me, sensing something is off, perhaps even gravely wrong and at a loss as to what to do.

What lengths Jerome is willing to go to and why he is willing to let her leave isn't clear. For all the time I spent with him, I never really knew him and can't decipher his motives or what he's capable of.

I must assume the worst. If that's the case, he could kill Jocelyn. Me. Henry. No, no, no. Not going there. Can't.

"Thanks, Jocelyn. You can leave." I barely spare the woman a glance, knowing I may lose my composure if I do.

She may be our only hope to get out of this, and it takes everything in me not to scream for her to get help. Maybe I don't need to convey any of that to her because she already knows we need help.

Help. Remembering my phone, I pat a hand on my dress pockets, looking for it, but nothing. Shit, where is it?

The nanny nods, taking one final look at the three of us before she scurries from the house. Isn't he worried she may call the cops?

As if I spoke out loud, Jerome steps closer and says, "She may call the cops, who cares." He shrugs. "She doesn't have enough for them to come out here any time soon, but we won't be here anyway."

His free hand slides around his back, and when he brings it forward, he's holding a gun. "Let's go."

Henry whines, wriggling in Jerome's arms to get free. His hands are outstretched for me and Jellycat, lying on the couch. I make for the stuffed animal and pause when Jerome releases a low animalistic growl.

"It's his stuffed animal. His favorite." I point to the octopus. "Can I get it? Hold him."

He grunts and hands me Henry. "Hurry. Let's go."

I barely have my son and the toy in hand before he's

wrapped a large, craggy hand around my arm, pinching tightly as he drags us out the door.

The sunlight is blinding and I squint, noticing I left my car door open. Then the moments before I went into the house—the end of my call with Costa, dropping my phone, and vomiting come at me in waves.

Jerome ushers us to my car. I left the keys in the ignition. "Get in. You're driving."

He tries to shove me into the driver's seat with Henry in my arms and I resist. "Wait. I have to put Henry into his car seat."

"No." He wrenches my son from my arms. Henry cries, batting his hands and the stuffed animal at Jerome's chest and face.

"Stop it." He shakes my son so violently, I lunge for him, trying to grab the gun. Jerome anticipates my attack and presses the muzzle into my chest. "I pull this and you're dead. Then where would your precious boy be?"

I stop, frozen at his threat. His stony eyes narrow into thin slits, and his lips become a macabre twist, resembling the thin, sharp wire of a garrote. "Get in the fucking car and don't try a thing or else he's dead. I'll get him in the seat."

Jerome has a hard time getting Henry to cooperate as he stiffens his body, making it next to impossible for Jerome to get him into the seat. The older man delivers a hard slap that shocks my son, and his body goes limp.

Henry then wails, the pain replacing the shock. He releases one of those deep, mournful cries that expands his chest and rents his breath. For what feels like eternity but is only seconds, Henry is silent as his chest heaves and grasps for air.

My heart breaks, and I pounce from the front seat, hitting at Jerome's back. He backhands me, shouting obscenities, and as if remembering the gun, he turns it now on Henry.

"No," I cry, slumping back into the front seat, tears streaking my face.

"Fucking sit down, seat belt on, and shut up."

I do as he says and then he's in the front passenger seat, gun poking into my side. "Drive. And if you so much as give me lip, I blow his head off."

29

GRAY
THE CHILD IS COMPETITION

uck, fuck, fuck. The heel of my palm slams into the steering wheel and I press my head into the back of the seat, closing my eyes to block out the magnificent beach house. Our new home.

I thought Daisy was ready, but I was wrong. Now what?

Eli. I should call him and he'll help me fix this. He'll tell me what to do. The guy might not have a woman in his life, but he's smart when it comes to the fairer sex.

I start my car and hit the dial pad on the car dashboard, but before I can select his number, my phone rings.

"Gray, it's Sasha." Her voice is tight. "I've been trying to get ahold of Daisy, but it keeps going to voicemail."

"What's wrong?" I put the car into drive, sensing urgency despite not knowing what this is about or if anything is wrong. There's a mounting need inside me to be close to Daisy even if it means breaking my word and forgetting about her wish for space.

"I just talked to a friend in Paris, and she was updating me on this scandal with a photographer accused of sexual assault. She said he now lives in LA and as we talked, I started to think about that time in Paris, and I remembered Jerome Pascal was always around, which in and of itself—"

"Jerome Pascal?" Something cold and sharp lodges in my chest. "He's the accused photographer?"

"Yes. You know him?"

"Fuck." I swerve around the slow-moving car in front of me, suddenly wishing I could snap my fingers and be with Daisy. "He's friends with Daisy and has been nosing around her business for over a year. He's like a fucking virus she can't shake."

"No." Her shock and terror echo in my ear, sending a shudder through me. "Is Daisy with you?"

"No, she isn't. Tell me more about these charges. Was he..." My tongue is like a steel beam, heavy and unwieldy. "Do you remember anything to do with him and Daisy during that week?"

I've never liked that man, and it wouldn't take much for me to want to hit him. But if Sasha says what I fear she will, I'll kill him.

"Nothing specific stands out, but he was at most if not all the events we would have been at, and I'm almost certain he was at our party too."

"For fuck's sake," I roar and she squeaks through the line. "Sorry."

"No, no. Do you think it's him?"

It's the closest we've gotten to a solid link between Daisy and someone who could have attacked her. That guy, Apollo, was a possibility but the charges against Jerome and now he's here...

"It's fits. Whoever assaulted her, drugged her and it would explain why she has no recollection of Jerome. Tell me about the charges."

If these allegations are remotely similar to what we think happened to Daisy, then we have our man. Jerome is her rapist. He's...he's Henry's father. *Fuck.*

"Gray, I think it's him. A new model, practically a nobody, said he had assaulted her, and at first, she was ignored. No one wanted to believe her, especially about someone like Jerome. He was revered and sought after within the industry."

My gut roils. Daisy told me about Jerome's reputation when he'd first contacted her upon his arrival in LA. It never sat right with me, how someone with his stature would leave the limelight, of sorts. But this makes sense. He had no choice but to run.

"The girl went home to Russia, gave up modeling. Jerome claimed she was lovesick and wanted a relationship with him and he turned her away. You know, a woman scorned and all that. It was his explanation for why she'd make up such a horrible story."

"No one investigated?"

"No. Then a few more models, well-known and respected, came forth with similar allegations. Again, at first, some shut their ears and eyes to what was fast becoming a loud outcry. It got to the point that some of the biggest names in the modeling world refused to work with him. I suppose with that kind of support, the young woman from Russia pressed charges. Jerome was shunned by the European fashion industry, a pariah in Paris. He fled the country for LA. And now, mysteriously, the charges went away and the model is quiet."

"What?" I brake for a red light, fury constricting my chest at the thought of him getting away with his crimes.

"That's what I learned from the phone call today. The charges have been dropped, and the young woman refuses to speak to anyone. No one knows for sure, but some think that Jerome paid her off. She went into modeling to help her family so money would have gone a long way, and I mean no judgement."

The melancholy and personal touch to her tone tells me the young woman's plight hits a little too close to home. Sasha is Russian, too, and like this woman, turned to modeling, using her beauty as Daisy had put it to me, to help her dying mother and brother.

"Sasha, I'm almost at Daisy's. Let me tell her this in person." I'm ten minutes out and while Daisy isn't in danger, she can't hear this over the phone.

She isn't the best of friends with Jerome, but this will be a betrayal. A violation, no doubt. And it's hard to tell if this will cause her to withdraw even more or not.

"What can I do?"

"Stay close by the phone. I'll need to talk to a lawyer about how we get a DNA test, and I'll likely have to talk to the police."

"Let me know if I can help with that. Any of it. I'm here and I can come by too."

"Great. We might need you to come over. I'll let you

know." I end the call and park the car outside of Daisy's house.

Her car isn't here, and I call her as I get out of the car, making my way to the front door and collecting my thoughts before blowing up her world, yet again.

An automated voice comes on and tells me that this mailbox is full. What the hell?

"Mr. Bennett. Mr. Bennett." I swing around at the sound of a woman's voice, and Jocelyn runs toward me, panicked.

"What's wrong?"

"Daisy and Henry..." She's out of breath, tears brimming in her eyes. "They left with this man. Jerome."

"Jerome was here?" Panic slams into my back and my knees wobble. "He took Daisy and Henry?"

She's nodding, only able to look me in the eyes for a blink or two at a time. "Yes. I'm sorry. She told me to leave, but I knew something was wrong. I didn't know he had a gun."

"A gun?" My heart gallops in my chest and I grab at her arm, willing my breath to slow the fuck down. "Okay, start from the beginning. Tell me what happened."

Jocelyn explains how Jerome showed up looking for Daisy, although he didn't seem surprised that Daisy wasn't there. It sounds like the nanny was his chance to get into the house.

Daisy hadn't seen or spoken to Jerome in weeks. I figured he was pissed, but I hadn't thought he'd do something like this. But that was before I knew about Paris.

"He said he was a friend, and Henry seemed to know him. I wouldn't have let him in, but he said Daisy had arranged to meet him, and I figured she didn't tell me because she thought she'd be back in time. I should have called you, called her before letting him in."

"Don't worry about that. Please, go on," I reassure her, sensing her need to lessen some of her guilt.

"He was fine while he waited."

"How long was that before Daisy got there?"

"About fifteen minutes. Then Daisy came home. She was sick. She ran straight to the washroom and that's where I found her. Then she saw Jerome and told me to leave with Henry. He wouldn't let me take him. Jerome told me to go. I didn't want to."

"And the gun?"

"I only saw it after. Once I left, I sat in my car." She points over her shoulder to several houses away where a small car is parked at the curb. "I wasn't sure what to do, but then they came out only minutes later, and he had the gun on Daisy and Henry. That's when I knew I had to do something."

"Then what happened?"

"I couldn't see everything but there was some kind of argument. He hit Henry."

Her words come at me like a savage beast, ripping at me, and in turn, my rage springs to life deep within me.

"It happened so fast. Then they drove away. I was going to follow them but decided to call the police and then I was going to call you."

"Good. What did the police say?"

Her troubled expression darkens further, if that's possible. "There's no telling when they'll be here. Forty-five minutes, maybe an hour. In terms of importance, no one's hurt and it isn't clear that a crime's been committed. They said someone would come out eventually."

I curse under my breath, staring down at the phone still in my hand. Daisy's voicemail is full. Maybe that's from Sasha and me, but I've got that app where I can find her phone. I bring it up while Jocelyn watches.

Finally, a green dot appears on the screen. It's going east on the I-10. I could wait for the police, but every second counts, and there's no telling what Jerome will do. And if he doesn't know about Daisy's phone and then discovers it, we could lose her location.

"Okay, I've got to go." I scan the front of the house, not looking for anything in particular, and rush toward Jellycat on the ground. It must have fallen from the car or someone's hand when they got into Daisy's car.

"What can I do?" Jocelyn asks.

"Can you wait here for the cops?" I go to the front door, ready to unlock it for her but it's unlocked. "I'm going to call her sister Pansy and friend, Sasha. One or both of them will come and wait with you."

She nods, going into the house, and I get into my car, bringing up the map with GPS coordinates and the green dot on my phone. The dot is still headed east on Interstate 10.

During the more than two-hour drive, I make calls to Sasha and Pansy, both of whom make their way to Daisy's house. Sasha needs to be there so she can fill the cops in on Jerome's time in Paris.

I also get a call from Costa, and as he talks, it becomes clear that Daisy knew about Jerome before going into her home. It explains why she was sick, and it also means she knows why Jerome would take her.

Does he know Henry's his? And if so, is that a good thing or a bad thing? The bastard always hated having Henry around. He acts like the child is competition.

Rage bubbles up from my gut, wondering what he plans to do with them, especially when the map indicates they are now on another roadway, heading toward Idyllwild, a small town nestled in the San Jacinto Mountains.

The car winds up into the mountains, and I'm too restless to admire the sweeping views of the valley below. A call from Silas comes through as I turn onto a dirt road, getting closer to the now stationary dot on the screen. Daisy's car.

If it takes any longer to set eyes on the car, I might run something over in my agitation. And then there's...no, I won't even go there. I dredge up all my fury and determination, and in turn, tamp down the niggling fear that I will find the car, but Daisy and Henry won't be there.

"What's up?" I'm clipped, on edge with my greeting.

"Gray, the police want you to stand down and wait. The LAPD are tracking Daisy's phone too. They've called in the local police, and they're on their way."

"I'm not stopping." I clench my jaw, tightening my hands on the steering wheel. "I'm close. Her car isn't moving. Any minute now and I'll see it."

"Yeah, we know. The cops say there are cabins in the area and Jerome most probably has them in one."

I nod, glancing to the fading light through the car windows. It's a little after six in the evening, and the sun is sinking fast toward the horizon. A motley crew of brownish orange, burnished pink and bruised purple, like careless splatters of paint, color the sky canvas.

"Gray, ah...you have to let the cops do their job." His tone is careful and measured, and I wonder if a police officer stands over him.

"Of course. I want them to come and help, but I can't wait. He's already had them too long." My foot taps the brakes even though the car is already crawling. "Listen, I think I see the car. I gotta go."

"Gray, wait. Don't do anything." I end the call, and the car is nearly stopped.

Daisy's vehicle, or what looks like it could be hers, is parked a little way up the road in front of an A-frame wood cabin. I don't want to reveal my presence until the right moment, so I park my car off the road, making sure it's out of sight.

Quietly, despite still being many feet away from the building, I get out of the car and shut the door.

A shiver skitters down my spine like a colony of ants. It could be the chill in the air or the anticipation of finally seeing Daisy and Henry.

The twilight atmosphere is cooler, almost cold, and easily dropping thirty degrees or more from Los Angeles. My exhalation leaves a wispy white mist, and the air is scented with fresh pine and sweet cedar.

Carefully, I trek up the road toward the cabin, sticking to the trees and brush, taking every precaution not to be spotted. Beyond the parked car, there's a thigh-high picket fence skirting a small wooden patio across the front of the home.

A bright turquoise front door is in the center at the base

of the triangle, and there are two windows, one on either side of the door. Toward the apex of the triangular home is a second-floor window and a balcony running across the top.

I approach the house from the side and send Silas a text with coordinates of the cabin's exact location, as well as a picture of the house. The police most probably have all of this, but I want to make sure they don't waste any more time trying to find the place.

Once more, I double check my phone is on silent and begin scouting the area surrounding the cabin. Both sides of the A-frame have no windows, so I can move about freely.

One side has a hot tub and backs onto a forest. The other side is narrower with a small storage area for firewood, and only a few feet from the house is the edge of a cliff. The back of the house has another patio, a few windows, and the forest beyond.

Running back to the front of the house, I crouch so as not to be spotted near the fence where I brace my hands on the railing and leap over onto the patio. Then I sink down to a crouch and crawl several feet to the nearest window.

None of the windows are covered, and I have an unobstructed view inside. It's small, the walls, floors, and ceiling are cedar, and it's sparsely furnished.

Jerome's back is to me, and both Daisy and Henry are tied up on a small sofa. Henry is screaming. Even from this distance, I can see his face is as red as a tomato and his lungs are getting a workout.

The gun is in Jerome's hand, and he's waving it around. My heart splinters at the sight, and the dull pain stabbing at my lungs doubles in size, so crushing that I'm no longer able to ignore it. I want to kill Jerome.

30

DAISY
THE SLIP OF A FINGER

*M*y heart bashes around inside my chest, and it's hard to hear anything else, even Henry's crying. He's inconsolable.

We lost Jellycat somewhere along the way, and we're tied up, hungry, and cold. The only good thing is that Henry is next to me, not in Jerome's hands.

"Shut him up," Jerome yells for what feels like the hundredth time, hands going to his ears.

The gun is still firmly in his grasp, and I'm no closer to figuring out what he wants. The drive here was excruciating, but I didn't have any time to freak out or lose my shit.

Given I was behind the wheel and my son was hysterical for more than half the journey, I was preoccupied.

Eventually, Henry passed out for nearly the last hour. He tuckered himself out with all the crying, and Jerome finally relaxed a bit, lowering the gun to his lap instead of wedged in my ribs.

I tried to get him to talk, and at first he did, confessing to texting the picture and article from my first date with Gray. If only I'd looked into it some more. At the time, I'd thought it was some Trojan fan.

After that, he went on about his disappointment in me for falling into bed with Gray before switching gears to how it was my fault he kidnapped us. If only I'd done the photo shoot, since I wasn't busy with other ones.

That's when the last-minute photo shoot cancellations made sense. Jerome had been behind all of that in an attempt to free up my schedule. He figured if I wasn't busy, I'd have jumped at the chance to do his shoot.

When I set him straight of that crazy notion, he shut up, only speaking to give me directions. When we got here, he shared that this cabin is a rental and that he booked it under a fake name. No one knows how to find him.

My only hope is in my car. My phone. While driving, with the foot that wasn't on the gas, I tried to locate my phone. I didn't want Jerome to find it. It fell from my hands when I was talking to Costa before I went into the house.

And to further confirm this, the buzzing could be heard, albeit faintly, when someone tried to reach me once or twice while I drove to this place.

Both times, I rambled, raising my voice and shifting in my seat. I tried anything without looking like a lunatic or drawing suspicion so as to mask the vibrations of the phone.

It's still somewhere in the car, my guess is under one of the front seats, and I can only hope Gray or someone else has tapped into the app to locate us.

Once we got here, Jerome tied us up, and through all that,

I berated myself for not probing more about why Jerome left Europe when he had shown up at my door nearly a year ago.

The sad truth was, I didn't care enough. Maybe a part of me was glad to see someone else from that world, to think the great Jerome had also been relegated to another career path like me.

His presence was confirmation there was life after the glitz and glam of runway modeling. And now, what did it matter anymore? Even if I'd gotten him to tell me some of it, I doubt it would have changed the shock Costa brought with his news.

And would I have put two and two together and landed at Jerome as my rapist? It's hard to say. There's so much I just didn't see, and I can't tell if it's because I was too trusting or foolish enough to ignore the cues.

The blatant truth that festers inside of me, even now as I'm bound and helpless, is that Jerome is a madman and we're going to die here if I don't figure a way out of here.

Scowling, Jerome seizes Henry and tears him from my side. Both my son and I howl, Henry harder than before, as he puts the gun to my son's head.

"If he doesn't stop crying, I'll take care of it myself." He fires a killing look my way and I shiver, and it has nothing to do with how cold it is inside this little cabin.

"He's scared. Just bring him to me. If you untie me"—I hold up my hands, secured at my wrists—"I can hold him, and if you had some food. Water. He's most probably hungry too."

"No. Not a chance. I'll feed him." He storms over to the small kitchen, holding Henry like a football under his arm.

He places the gun on the counter, and as if someone has turned up the volume, my heartbeat and breathing are deafening. If only I could get the gun.

Henry whimpers at his side, and Jerome mutters to himself as he rummages through a bag that was already here when we arrived. He pulls out a bottle of water, unscrews the cap, and brings it to Henry's mouth.

My son sputters and coughs, choking on the water.

"Hey, you can't do that." I straighten, coming to my knees on the couch and glaring at him. "You're pouring too fast. He'll choke!"

Henry's cries intensify. Jerome slams the bottle onto the counter, spilling almost half the water everywhere. Then he picks up the gun, and once more, the muzzle is pressed against my son's head.

"God, no!" I plea, voice breaking, and quickly scour the past for any sign that Jerome may know Henry is his son. I doubt it. He never could tolerate my son or any child.

"Make him stop." Hand shaking, he glowers at the crying boy.

All it would take is the slip of a finger and Henry would be dead. "Stop! Put the gun away! Please." Tears come in torrents, and I hardly recognize my voice.

I have to stop him from killing my son. I have to do something to make him care, rethink this madness.

Without true thought, acting purely on instinct and an innate desire to survive and to save Henry, I blurt out, "He's your son!"

Jerome lowers the gun, eyes widening as he glares at me. "What did you say?"

As if Henry senses the shift in the air, his cries weaken to small whimpers. I don't know if speaking the truth has sentenced my son's death or saved his life. Jerome hasn't confessed anything about what happened to me. Am I wrong, and maybe Jerome isn't the man I think he is?

"Paris, just a little under three years ago..." I clear my throat, fighting the bile scratching its way up my throat.

"Go on." Jerome's tone is somber and serious.

He steps from the counter, bringing my son to me. Henry rests his head on my shoulder, his little body curling into my side once more. Suddenly, something loosens in my lungs, and air starts to move more freely.

"The flat Sasha and I lived in. We had a party one night during the week that followed Fashion week. You were there."

He nods, folding his arms over his chest. His dark gaze rakes over my body from head to toe.

"You drugged me and came into my room..." Silent tears rain down my cheeks, and I don't need to say any more when a lascivious grin slashes across his face.

There's a sick feeling in the pit of my stomach. It's been there since I spoke to Costa about what likely happened that night. But now it's a monster of disgust, filth, and loathing. Hungry and merciless, it writhes and seethes within me, seeking its due.

Now, more than ever, I want to give in to the malicious drive. I never dreamed I could hate another person so much that I'd wish them dead. But now I know it's possible and that I do.

"You remember." His tone isn't flat or matter-of-fact.

No, he says those two words about something I have been so desperately seeking—to remember—like he's flirting with me. I want to gouge his eyes out.

"So Henry is mine. From that night?" He stares at the small slumbering form of my son, burrowed in between me and the cushions of the sofa.

Henry's so exhausted that each exhale is a shuddering sigh, and more of my heart cracks at what he has endured. The horrible things done to him in just one day of his life.

I only hope he's too young to remember this. I won't let myself consider any other outcome than getting away from this man. Henry will have a good and long life without Jerome.

"Daisy, answer me." His tone is razor sharp.

"Yes. That night."

"What about Costa? The boy could be his. I thought it was his." He talks as if he's speaking about an object, not a human being.

"No. Costa can't father children." Those words are still so acrid on my tongue, and I'm quick to add, as if I need to say it even to this barbarian, "And there was no one else."

I won't repeat the words I said not too long ago. It pained me to tell him Henry was his son.

No. Even at that, he isn't a father, and Henry will never be his son.

Like Gray said, DNA, biology, call it what you want, it's only one part of who we are. And in many cases, it's the least important factor of them all.

Jerome laughs, and it's cold, evil, and far too delighted with this news. My fingers curl into my palms and teeth gnash together. A growl passes through that enamel barrier, and my nostrils flare.

"I had never intended on coming to LA, to this godforsaken place. I wanted to live out my days in Europe. Retire and live in Paris was always the plan." He uses the end of the gun to scratch at his jaw and how I wish the thing would go off. Blow off his face.

"What changed?" I know the answer, but if I can keep him talking, maybe he'll relax, slip up, and the opportunity for escape will come to me.

"Shit happened." He sighs, shaking his head. "I won't bore you with the details, but I had to leave, and you were the first person I thought of. You'd always been nice to me, and you were oh so sweet...in every way." He licks his lips and waggles his eyebrows suggestively as if I'd find any of this anything but repulsive.

"What are you going to do with us?"

It's the one question I've asked numerous times on the way to this cabin, and each time he froze me out with his silence, refusing to give me any indication as to what his plan was.

This time is different, and he opens his mouth, hopefully to answer the question, and then pauses. He glances over his shoulder toward the windows and front door. I study them, too, searching for any indication as to what caught his attention.

There's nothing.

"My beautiful, I want a life with you." He inches closer, grinning like a wolf, teeth bared. "And now, with a son, this is perfect. We'll be a family." His hand caresses my bound ankles, and quickly, I draw my legs up to my chest.

He laughs again, a wicked pleasure that rattles my insides, and I shiver. Not learning from retreat nor caring, he reaches a hand toward me to touch my shoulder this time, maybe even to warm me.

I flinch, trying to move away from his grasp. "Don't touch me."

"My beautiful, don't be like that." He doesn't push though, dropping his hand to his side. "You must be cold. I'll get some wood for the stove."

31

GRAY
SMILES LIKE A LUNATIC

I scurry to get off the patio and climb over the fence as Jerome makes his way to the door. He's coming outside. This might be my chance to ambush and incapacitate him.

The door opens, and I dive for the bushes at one side of the house, making it just before he steps out of the cabin.

Jerome shoves the gun into the back of his pants as he passes through the gate. Despite the faint rustling of the leaves, an aftershock of my landing, he isn't wary or even alert.

He saunters in the opposite direction to where I am hidden and I hold my breath, willing my body still until he's out of sight, around the side of the house.

I dash in his direction, sticking close to the trees and other foliage for cover. Firewood lines a small penned in area, rows upon rows of neatly chopped wood. Jerome gathers as much as he can carry.

Now is my chance. Hands full, unarmed and unaware, the opportunity to jump him isn't going to get much better than this.

The wood is stacked against his chest all the way up to his chin, and he meanders back the way he came, more gingerly this time since his view is somewhat obscured. When he is almost to the front of the cabin, closer to where I am, I lunge for him as if I'm sliding into home plate.

He's knocked to the dirt, and I go with him. Firewood sails through the air in every direction, and a log hits me in the shin, another grazing a forearm.

"What the—" Jerome yells.

At first, his arms bend over his face, covering himself in protection, but the motion is only for a beat or two. He must then realize his fall wasn't a result of his own clumsiness, but someone caused it. A threat is here, and he can't lie around on the ground.

He rolls to one side, trying to scramble to his feet with one hand while grabbing for his gun with the other. His movements are inept and awkward, and I'm on him.

My fingers curl into the front of his shirt, and I haul him to standing. His eyes widen in shock at the sight of me, and I can't stop the smug, sure to be arrogant, grin that crosses my face.

"You ass—"

I drive my fist into his face, killing any of his words. And over and over again, my hand pounds into his face, the repetition of my punches bringing a sweet satisfaction, all control or reason gone.

It's the crack of bone when my fist connects with his nose,

thwack, that snaps me out of my bloodlust trance. Even broken and bloodied, the man smiles like a lunatic, staggering on his feet.

"Ah, the little drummer boy finally shows up." His body sways, and one eye swells, unable to open. "I'd hoped to never see you again, little fucker."

He sneers, pulling his gun out from his back. Anticipating the move, my arm slams into his in the fading light, and I knock the weapon from his grip.

Jerome lunges for the gun, now several feet away from us. I do, too, as my body jabs into his side and I hit the ground. The force of contact jostles him, and his fingertips knock the gun, sending it gliding across the now rocky terrain.

I can just make out the gun, stopping a mere foot from the edge of the cliff. Bodies entangled, we grapple.

His fingers rip at my hair, and his other hand tries to punch at my back, but he's never quite able to get in a solid blow. The hits graze, some cause a wince or grimace, but nothing I can't withstand.

My thumb presses into the corner of his eye socket, and the flesh sinks and gives way to the pressure. And my other hand grips part of his throat, trying to get a solid grasp, a strong enough hold to choke him, but he's wriggling too much and my hand is slick with his blood, maybe mine, or both.

At some point, he manages to put a little distance between our bodies as we still roll on the ground. I don't see the strike because of how we are lying on the ground and because of the now dark night. Only excruciating pain slams into me when his knee rams into my balls.

Air is knocked right out of me and I'm blind for seconds, curling in on myself. Agony consumes me, and in those moments, Jerome gets to his feet and rushes in the direction of the gun.

If not for the grunts and groans of Jerome, the flash of movement, I might be dead. But all those things remind me that this isn't over and I'm forced to bury my misery. If Jerome kills me, Daisy and Henry are done for.

The cops still aren't here, and I've given up on them. No, this is up to me. Their chance of getting out alive is on me.

I have to save them, and with that thought, I leap to my feet, and my eyes have adjusted to the pitch black. The dim glow of the lights from the cabin provides some illumination, and Jerome whirls around at the sound of my approaching.

The gun is in his outstretched hand, aiming at me. "I had her before you did, sucker." A slimy smile inches onto his crimson mouth.

Oh, he wants to talk, does he? I'll play this game. It'll give me what I so badly need. Time. Time to figure out a way to get the gun from him.

"Doesn't matter what you had. What you fucking stole from her. You raped her!"

I'm feral and fearless, and we're close enough now that Jerome must see some of this. Even though he has the gun, he inches back a step, away from me. But he must remember the drop-off is somewhere close at his back—at least I think it is if I have my bearings straight—and he stops.

He holds his ground but doesn't try to inch me back, closer to the cabin. "You're a dead man. She'll forget you in time."

I spit blood at his feet, wiping at my mouth with the back of my hand. We're maybe a foot or less apart. Lunging at him is tempting, but the risk is great. We could both go over or the gun could go off.

"That's where you're wrong, bastard. You're a dead man, and you've never been on her mind or in her heart."

He cackles, tilting his head back, then winces, now gripping at the side of his body with a hand. "She'll never forget me. I'll always be with her. Henry's mine."

Fighting with a dead man is futile. But even still, the animal inside me, that loosened beast, scratches at the surface, having never retreated too far. It snarls, and something in his words, the way he claims ownership even if he's delusional, snaps at the little sanity I have left.

My sole purpose is to keep him from ever getting to Daisy and Henry, my family, again.

"He'll never be yours and neither will Daisy." I attack him without a care for the weapon in his hand, or the drop-off right behind him, or even my death.

It happens so fast, there's no time to process anything or even stop and think. Jerome scampers backward, away from me. His cry is haunting in the pitch-black night.

A loud, sharp *pop* cracks the air, and the tips of my boots falter, grappling to find purchase on the earth. I glance down into a vast dark nothingness, the valley below. Before it's too late, I thrust my body backward onto solid ground.

Jerome falls off the cliff.

Forever.

It feels like forever as I lie there on the ground, panting, heart hammering in my chest at the near-death experience.

I stare up at the starry night sky, listening to the silence and the choppy in and out of my breathing as it slowly grasps its natural rhythm.

On my feet, I step to the edge, this time far more careful to stay where I am and look into utter darkness. I can't see if Jerome is dead or hurt or anything.

Black. Night. That's all there is.

Daisy and Henry's voices cut through the dark and I turn toward the cabin, shouting her name and running, not able to get to her fast enough. Her head snaps up as I rush through the door.

"Gray." Her lips tremble, curling at the corners into a watery smile, and I gift her one of my own. "Are you all right? How did you find us?"

I'm at her side, kneeling before the couch and working at her bound legs. "I tracked you through your phone."

She lets out an almost relieved sigh, closing her eyes for a blink. "But you're hurt." She lifts her hands, clasped together to my face, fingers brushing over the swell of a blooming bruise.

"I'm fine." My hand slides up her leg, squeezing her calf now that her lower limbs are free of the rope.

"Jer...Jerome...it was him." She looks to the door, scared. "Where is he?"

"He went over a cliff. I jumped him when he came outside, and we fought." I straighten, wincing at the stabbing sensation in my side.

"Oh my God." Daisy's hand shoots out to where the side of my torso burns, but she stops short of touching me. "You're bleeding."

Confused, I look down, and sure enough, blood seeps through my shirt. "The gun went off. I'm shot?" It comes out as a question, but it's clear I am.

And now, for the first time since the loud, unforgettable noise of the gun, the pain hits me.

"We need to call the police. You need a doctor." Her voice shakes and the sight of her still tied hands gives me something to focus on other than how much a gunshot wound hurts.

"They're on their way. I'll be fine." I undo the knot on the rope around her wrists, and Henry lies listless at her side, sleeping. "How is he?"

"Traumatized. Exhausted." She shudders and shakes out her hands and fingers once free.

Together, we untie Henry's hands and feet, and she cradles him to her chest, weeping into his soft brown hair.

My arm bands around her as I drop to the couch, gritting my teeth at the impact, and then I nestle them to my uninjured side. With my other hand, I pull out my phone, readying to call Silas.

That's when I hear the sirens, growing louder and louder. Not long after, police cruisers and SUVs, including an ambulance, come to a screeching halt outside the cabin.

Flashing lights, like strobes in a nightclub, streak across the dimly lit room, and two officers enter the house, weapons drawn.

The next several minutes, maybe even hours, are both long and arduous and over in a flash. The police talk to Daisy, take notes, and ask her countless questions as well as to reenact a few instances that took place in the cabin.

A rescue crew sets out to locate Jerome, and while Daisy's questioned and Henry is changed and fed, a paramedic treats me in the ambulance.

I'm lucky. The bullet grazed my side, tearing the skin just below my ribs, but it's only as deep as a flesh wound. The EMT cleans my cuts and scrapes from the fight, and I'm stitched right there, on the spot.

The hospital is out of the question even as he stresses its importance. Finally, the poor medic relents, giving strict instructions to see my doctor as soon as possible for pain killers and a prescription for a course of antibiotics.

Henry is tired and a bit cranky, but he's calm in either his mother's or my arms, and he's more than thrilled to have Jellycat. He nuzzles his face into the plush fabric, wrapping its tentacles around his neck, and I'm grateful for throwing the toy into my car when I took off from Daisy's house.

In addition to the food and water found in the bags in the kitchen, they also find an arsenal of guns and knives in a large duffel bag in the bedroom. The police speculate Jerome planned to hole up in the cabin with them for perhaps days, or longer if they'd remained undiscovered.

At some point, one of the officers returns from searching for Jerome. They found him dead, likely on impact, and I can't say I'm upset. Daisy is conflicted, relieved he can no longer threaten or hurt her, but also shocked.

Eventually, well into the night or more like the start of a new day, we are released and given the nod to go home. The lead detective offers a police escort, and I gladly accept.

The traffic is most probably light at this time, but the

faster we can get home and safely, the better. The police cruiser follows us home, and we don't talk much on the drive.

I'm in the front alone, and Daisy sits in the back with Henry. While he sleeps for the entire ride, she wants to be close in case he wakes and is afraid.

Once home, she puts him to bed, and I linger in the doorway to his room, watching him drift off to sleep.

Our eyes lock as Daisy tiptoes from the room, turning the doorknob on the way out. Voice lowered, she takes my hand. "Can we just sit here for a bit?" Her gaze dips to the floor of the hallway, and her cheeks flush. "I don't want him to cry out and not find me, and truth be told, I'm not ready to let him out of my sight."

"Of course."

Side by side, our backs to the wall, we slide down onto the hardwood floor in the hallway. The stitches stretch and pull, and I try to hide my wince and any discomfort.

"Gray, thank you for coming. For saving us." She angles her body to face me and interlaces one of her hands with one of mine. "I love you so much. I know we need to talk, but—"

"Hey, that can wait." My fingers squeeze hers. "I just want to be here with you. I'm so happy that little boy is asleep in his bed, not a hair on his head touched. And you."

I draw her to me, and she carefully slides into my lap, mindful of my bandaged side, and loops her arms around my neck. "I love you."

The house is quiet save for our breaths, and most of the lights are out, with just the glow coming from her bedroom at the end of the hall. Her gaze shifts to mine, and her soft, gentle fingers trace the outlines of my face, the curve of my jaw.

She brushes the hair out of my face, and her thumb strokes my mouth before her lips seek mine for a kiss.

"I don't know how I got so lucky to have a man like you in my life." She kisses my neck.

My heart strains, almost too big for the confined space of my chest, and I stroke her hair behind her ear, whispering, "I'm the lucky one."

She shudders, and I burrow my face into her shoulder, inhaling the warm vanilla scent of her. Sliding from my lap, she stands and leads me to the bedroom.

And that night, I make love to her, showing her just how lucky and blessed I am to be with her and Henry.

My home.

My family.

32

DAISY

HIS KISS SHATTERS ME

One month later

"Henry, come on," Jocelyn croons from the third floor of our beach house, one floor below where I am. "Where are you?"

Familiar giggles and the pitter-patter of tiny feet make me grin as Henry calls, also from below, "Find me."

I laugh, bending and placing a hand on our new bed, so perfect for our rooftop bedroom. The sound of the surf is just past the open glass doorway, and I can taste the salt on my tongue.

After the cabin, Gray moved into the beach house, or he moved his things in but stayed at my house until I was ready to leave. There was no question I wanted to be with him in every sense. I needed a little time to come to terms with the news of Jerome and what he'd done.

About a week later, the police informed us they had

searched Jerome's home and found GHB and Rohypnol, both date rape drugs, among other things. He was a predator, an evil excuse for a human, and had likely assaulted many more women than we'd ever know.

Despite all the evidence, I requested a DNA test, and it was confirmed that Jerome was in fact the monster who raped me. And as for Henry, the entire nightmare didn't leave too much of an impression on him.

He was clingier than usual for a few days following the cabin, but now he's himself again. And if one day he asks about his father, I'll tell him the truth. Jerome may have shared his DNA with Henry, but he isn't his father in the truest sense.

My feet slide into my high heels, and I twirl around to face Gray, watching me. "You look fantastic."

"This old thing." I shrug, spinning once more in my slinky black dress, now facing the mirror.

Raw silk and spaghetti straps, the dress is cut to kiss my curves then flare out at mid-thigh to where it ends just above my knees. It isn't new. Gray has seen me in it before, but I might as well be naked for the way he feasts on me.

He grabs me from behind, and one strong arm wraps around my waist, crushing my back against him. His other hand slides upward from my stomach, up to my chest, where the tips of his fingers linger, sensually grazing the underside of my breast.

His touch and the soft caress of silk against my skin is nearly my undoing. My nipples pebble, twin peaks, and my insides liquefy. Just the sight of the two of us, our reflection in the mirror, turns me on.

I tilt my head back against his shoulder, raising my arms to thread them around his neck, opening my body to him. He lowers his mouth below my head, and his stubble scrapes along my skin as his teeth nip at my neck.

"I could eat you." His lips brush against my ear, tongue darting out to lick the sensitive flesh.

The hard length of him presses into my backside, and my legs rub together to ease the growing ache between them. My sex clenches, greedy to have him inside me.

His hand, at my stomach, glides downward below my belly button until his fingers press into me. I'm so wet, my panties are of no use and my arousal may just seep onto the dress, where his hand holds me.

"Gray," I moan, trying to turn around to face him, and he murmurs approval but his hand on my middle stops me.

He's everywhere, bringing my body to life, and my breasts grow heavy, needy for him to stop teasing and give me what I need.

Any thoughts of dinner with Pansy, Silas, Jared, Eva, and Sasha vanish. Forget going out, all I want is for him to fuck me.

"Daisy," Jocelyn calls, and my name is a bucket of ice water, dousing the fire and bringing me to my senses.

"Yes?" I wrench away from Gray, and a rich chuckle floats over my head.

Gray's shaking his head, thoroughly amused with how I'm acting like a teenager almost caught making out with her boyfriend. I glare at him and straighten my dress and hair.

Jocelyn's approaching steps sound louder, and he turns

his back to the room entrance, adjusting himself and likely willing his hard as steel erection to go away.

"Henry has something for you." The nanny's cheeks are flushed, and I wonder if she saw us or knows what she interrupted.

"Oh, okay." From my peripheral vision, Gray comes to stand beside me, fingers combing his hair from his face.

"Hey, Lovebug." I smile as Henry moves past his nanny on the staircase and then into our room.

Jocelyn slips back downstairs, and I marvel at how we also got lucky with her. She isn't a live-in nanny—that was our choice—but even when she's here, she makes herself discreet and yet she's fast becoming part of the family.

Henry walks to Gray's side, placing his little hand in Gray's big one, and the two of them share a look. It's so much more than a passing glance, and I wonder what's going on. This isn't just about Henry coming to say goodnight.

"Daisy, I wanted to do this right and I wondered about the timing." He glances to Henry who's giddy and grinning from ear to ear. "I thought I'd had the timing all figured out when I first showed you this place." Gray mashes his lips together, not needing to remind me how that ended.

I want to protest and tell him, once again, that timing wasn't the issue, and none of how I reacted was his fault. That was on me. But I don't want to interrupt whatever this is.

"Anyway, I realized timing doesn't matter but how I do it does. So, with Henry's permission, as the most important man in your life..." Gray pauses, getting down on one knee, and my son giggles, covering his mouth with a hand. "Daisy and Henry,"—he looks to the little boy still holding his hand —"will you marry me?"

Henry pulls a box from his pocket, and my heart thuds as his chubby fingers pry open the lid. A pink-hued diamond halo engagement ring gleams up at me, and I gasp.

"Gray." Now it's my turn to cover my mouth, blinking back the prickle of tears gathering in my eyes.

"Say yes, Mommy!" Henry almost shouts, jumping up and down. "You're supposed to say yes."

"Yes. Yes." I laugh and cry as Gray gets to his feet and slides the ring onto my finger.

He scoops me into his arms and covers my mouth with his. Henry makes a "yuck" sound and runs for the stairs. I laugh and kiss at Gray's neck, brimming with happiness.

Slowly, he places me back on my feet and wraps his arms around me. "Are you sure about this?"

His warm gaze studies me, looking for any sign of something I haven't said or could be hiding. It isn't that he doesn't trust me or even thinks I'd be dishonest, but more he's so attuned to what I've gone through.

Gray stood by me and gave me the space and support while I worked through everything. While I continue to work through it all.

"I've never been so sure of anything in my life." I kiss him once more. "We're going to have a lot to celebrate tonight."

Gray's hand slides down to grab my bottom and he squeezes, grinning. "That we are. I wish we could stay here, and I thought about doing it another night, when we'd be at home but—"

Two fingers press to his mouth. "It's perfect, and I want to share our engagement with our friends and family. We'll have plenty of time for just us."

"The car's here," Jocelyn says from down below.

"Oh, thanks. We'll be right down." He takes my hand, and I grab my coat from the bed, staring down at the ring on my left hand and grinning.

We make our way downstairs, saying our goodnights and sharing with Jocelyn our good news. She hugs us both with tears of joy, and the two of them wave to us as we drive away.

Silas spared no expense for tonight. We are celebrating so many things. India's album is finished and set to release any day now. Both Silas and Gray are thrilled with the end result and already have several other high caliber artists clamoring to work with them.

We're also toasting that Sasha is now an Angelino. She just came back from Paris where she spent almost two weeks packing up her things, and she's moved into the place I rented. While it's smaller than she'd like, she's also scaling back her work schedule, and this affords her the time and space to find a neighborhood she loves and to settle in.

Then there's the end to the Jerome ordeal and our moving into our Malibu beach house. I truly love it and half the time never want to leave. I'd be content to stay there day and night and have people come to me.

"You happy?" Gray grabs my hand and brings it to his lap, shifting a bit as he wrinkles his brow.

"Never been happier. Are you okay?"

While his stitches have been out for a while from where he was shot, it's still tender. And the gunshot wrecked his tattoos, which gave Gray another reason, like he needed one, to curse Jerome. His side is sore because he just had two new tattoos done to cover the scar.

One is of a daisy and the other, an octopus for Henry.

"Yeah, just a little tender. No big deal."

Releasing my hand, he raises his to cup my face, crashing his mouth on mine. The full force of his kiss shatters me. But I don't care. I'm in good hands. The best hands.

Gray will never let any harm come to me or our son. Yes, *our* son. We have started talking about Gray adopting Henry, and now more than ever, I want to make that happen as soon as possible.

He breaks our kiss but doesn't go far, his lips a breath from mine. "When we get back tonight, I promise you, I'm going to take my time with you, wife-to-be."

EPILOGUE
ALL THE CALE

GRAY

Four months later

"Anyone home?" Daisy's voice carries to the floor above her where Henry and I are in his room, rummaging through his clothes looking for something for him to wear swimming.

"Hey, Daze." I stand at the top of the staircase, awaiting her gorgeousness to come into view.

Her smile is the first thing to blind me and then her overall glowing appearance. Her happiness washes over me, flooding my senses. I never tire of laying eyes on her, especially when she hasn't a care in the world like now.

Even though it's Saturday, Daisy had an early photo shoot and then an appointment with her therapist.

Things haven't been easy for her since Jerome kidnapped

them. At first, after the cabin and his death, she tried to pretend everything was okay since she had a name and face to put to that horrific night in Paris.

But she was lying to herself, and sadly, for a while I was too, wanting to believe her. Unlike his mother, so far Henry seems to have forgotten or been unaffected by what Jerome did to them.

I wanted to believe Daisy would be okay, but in the days after Jerome's death, she withdrew. Thankfully, Eva was able to reach her in her gentle, unassuming way.

Jared's now wife—they got married over Christmas—is an old soul and sees more than most. She has a manner about her, offering insight and sage advice without you even realizing it.

Eva introduced Daisy to her therapist, Connie. The woman uses an untraditional approach, having sessions outside of an office, and sometimes, their appointments consist of activities where they don't even talk about how Daisy is feeling or Jerome or any of that.

But no matter her method, it works for Daisy, and she's doing so much better, even talking about moments in the past, whether in LA or in Paris, where she now sees Jerome in a different light.

And most of all, for the most part, she bears very little blame for not seeing how nefarious and sick the man was. He had everyone fooled, for many years.

"Hey, what are you guys doing?" She takes a few steps up the stairs toward us and stops when Henry slides in beside me, vibrating with frustration. "What's wrong?"

"Mommy, where my swim tunks?" He holds up a pair of trunks that no longer fit him. "The red and blue ones."

"We're going for a swim." I tilt my head in the direction of the Pacific Ocean, only feet from our back door. "Did you eat? There's some leftover salmon in the fridge. I put it on the grill with the cedar plank how you like it, and there's rice and green beans."

"Yum, it sounds good, but I had lunch with Eva after my appointment."

"That's go—"

Henry interjects, "Mommy," and waves the offending shorts at us, quite upset with nothing to wear.

"Easy, Lovebug. They're in the laundry room. Remember, they had sand in them and I washed them? They're on your hook."

He scampers past me, running down the stairs, or as best as he can with his short legs.

"Hey, slow down." Her fingers ruffle his thick head of hair as he flies past her.

"As you can see, he's excited." I saunter down to the main floor and wrap an arm around her waist, bringing her with me into the kitchen. "Did you have a good session?"

"Yeah. It was amazing. Eva joined us."

"Really?"

"Yes. Connie mentioned flotation therapy a few weeks ago, and I talked to Eva about it. Remember, that's what she does for her headaches and pain?"

I nod, recalling something about it. If my memory serves me right, Eva mentioned getting into a private pool-like pod where you float for a period of time in a mix of saline solution, or something like that.

It's supposed to be a zero-gravity environment, and somehow it lets your body reduce pain and stress. Eva swears by it.

"Gray, it was fantastic. You have to try it!" She grabs at my hand, and that's when I notice her tied-back hair is damp. "It was so relaxing and soothing with absolutely no distractions. Nothing. It totally gave me clarity, and I feel so centered."

She's beaming, and I can't help but smile too. I don't care what she does so long as it helps her deal with everything in a healthy way.

"Sounds cool. Maybe I could try it sometime."

She's nodding her head up and down when Henry clomps awkwardly into the kitchen with black rubber flippers on his feet. One leg at a time, he lifts them high into the air and takes a giant, wobbly leap forward, and I can't help but laugh.

"Daddy, I'm ready. Let's go." He's got his snorkel in one hand and goggles in the other.

"Okay. We need to put your sunscreen on, and I've got to get changed."

He groans, dropping his equipment onto the tiled floor. "Why aren't you changed?" His gaze flits to his mother. "Mommy, stop talking to him. We're going swimming."

Daisy feigns offense, clutching at her chest, and her mouth gapes open. "Ouch, Lovebug."

"Hey, little man, that isn't nice. We're happy Mommy's home." I curl one hand around Daisy's neck and squeeze. "You up for a swim?"

"Yes. I just need to take my equipment out of the car and then I'll join you." She pecks a light kiss on my cheek and heads back to the front door.

Her business is going well, no thanks to Jerome. It turns out he was behind the canceled bookings, which at the time had made no sense in light of her award. She wasn't in the right frame of mind to care or follow up with those clients, not until much later.

The bastard spread rumors about her lack of dedication and said she was difficult to work with. Fortunately, Daisy was able to smooth things over, and her work is now more than booming. So much so, she's expanded to larger office space and hired a few more staff to assist with scouting locations and photo shoots.

And through the growth of her business and meeting new clients, she stumbled upon Minka, a small not-for-profit program for victims and survivors of sexual assault and domestic violence.

She quickly bonded with Marta, the founder and mother of Minka, the woman who died at the hands of her attacker, and has been a huge supporter ever since. For free, Daisy put together a media campaign to help raise awareness and funds for the program. It launched only weeks ago, and they've already doubled their fundraising goal.

Daisy's giving a lot to this small program but also getting an immeasurable amount of purpose and joy from the work she's doing. And Marta is talking of expansion, which Daisy is all too happy to support in any way she can.

Jerome took something from her, something she still

struggles to name or understand, but she's healing and stronger than ever.

"Don't forget we have the cake tasting this afternoon." She saunters into her home office, just off the kitchen, with a bag in hand.

"I know, and we're still taking Henry? I've got Joc on standby."

Our wedding is a month away, and choosing the cake is the last thing to do. Both of us want small and intimate so there wasn't a lot of planning involved, although Daisy might disagree. She's done most of it with Pansy's help, of course.

We're getting married on the beach, just outside our back door with a small gathering of friends and family.

"Yeah, let's take him. He can help us decide, and I haven't seen a lot of him this week."

She comes from the room, shutting the door, and hooks her arm around my waist from behind. The front of her slender body presses into my back, and her chest rests on my shoulder blade.

"He'll love it." I twist my neck, only able to glimpse the golden crown of her head. "You know, he might not be able to choose. He's going to want all the cake."

She laughs and the vibrations echo in my own chest. "I don't care. We'll figure it out."

Her lips lightly press at the nape of my neck, sending a tingling shiver down my spine, and at the same time, Henry bounds into the room. His face is covered in white gooey sunscreen.

"I'm ready!" He comes to a screeching halt, and his smile falls with one look at me. "Daddy, you aren't dressed."

"Relax, Henry. It'll take me only a minute to change."

"You better go before he has a meltdown. I'll meet you outside," she whispers to me so he can't hear and releases her comforting hold around my middle. "Let me rub that into your face, Lovebug."

She crouches, motioning Henry to her, and begins to sweep her hand over his creamy white cheek. All the while, she murmurs silly, soothing words about his patience and how much fun we're going to have on the beach.

He giggles, offering goofy suggestions of games we'll play, and Daisy goes along with it, providing some of her own outlandish ideas. And I watch, my chest expanding and squeezing in an all too full but euphoric way.

Henry's adored toy, Jellycat, lies on the tiled floor not too far from them, and Daisy's photography gear crowds the front entrance. Our home is lived in although Daze might say it's a little messy, but I love it.

This is all I've ever wanted. A place to call home, a family of my own.

EPILOGUE 2

ELI
On the hunt

This is insane. I'm a grown man for crying out loud, and I've had my fair share of dating and hookups. Heck, I've even had a couple of serious relationships, but here I am uploading my dating profile.

What? How did I get here? Desperately seeking someone interested in a long-term commitment. I'm a father and too old for casual flings and dead-end relationships.

Hitch is an exclusive dating app, currently in beta testing and only available to an elite group of individuals. Prominent public figures who could never post their profile on any of the many dating apps out there for fear of bringing out the crazies and stalkers.

I foolishly agreed to participate in the beta test because the more conventional way of meeting people was proving to be a nightmare. Hitch is different in many ways, and unlike the swipe, where you're relegated to the dumpster with the flick of a finger, the person on the hunt can like or comment on a profile to show interest.

Then it's up to me to decide if I want to start a conversation. And instead of sweating over what to write for your measly profile, the app prompts you to answer things like "I may not be...but I'm...", or "At a party, I'm the one...", or "The secret to a lasting relationship is..."

I stare at the casual shot of me in a T-shirt, shorts, and running shoes. Consciously, I'd picked an image that in no way related to my career, past or present, even though eventually they'll figure out who I am.

In reality, I feel like a loser. My profile should read "Retired rock star and rising actor, in a critically acclaimed drama television series, unable to find woman to spend his life with."

Sure, I don't have a problem *getting* dates, it's finding a woman who isn't after me for my fame that's the problem. Or more importantly, finding a woman who likes kids and will be a great mother to Crystal, my daughter.

But no, more times than not, the women I've dated have no interest in being a mother to someone else's kid. And the only thing they want to focus on is how my stardom can serve them.

Ping.

My phone vibrates and my stomach clenches. I've got my first like.

If you need help:
Canada: Ending Violence Canada
UK: National Domestic Abuse Helpline
US: National Domestic Violence
1-800-799-SAFE (7233)

Thank you for reading Smash! Eli's story is next in Rush, available at major retailers or grab it here: www.smwestauthor.com.

Thank you for reading and please leave a review on your favorite book site, including tell a friend. Reviews help readers find books!

. . .

For exclusive content, a free book and to find out when I have new releases, please sign up for my newsletter at www.smwestauthor.com.

ABOUT THE AUTHOR

S.M. West is a USA TODAY bestselling and award-winning author of sexy, angsty romances about brave hearts, wild love with a few heart-pounding twists along the way.

For new releases, exclusive excerpts, giveaways and more, sign up for her newsletter.

For other books by S.M. West, visit: *www.smwestauthor.com*

www.ingramcontent.com/pod-product-compliance
Lightning Source LLC
Chambersburg PA
CBHW051959240626
47153CB00005B/1817